CHEF'S KISS

A GIA, SAN FRANCISCO ROMANCE

STEPHANIE SHEA

Copyright © 2021 by STEPHANIE SHEA

All rights reserved. No part of this publication may be reproduced, distributed, or transmitted in any form or by any means, or stored in a database or retrieval system, without written permission from the author, except in the case of brief quotations embodied in critical articles and reviews. To request permission and for all other inquiries, contact stephaniesheawrites@gmail.com.

This is a work of fiction. Names, characters, businesses, places, events and incidents are either the products of the author's imagination or used in a fictitious manner. Any resemblance to actual persons, living or dead, business establishments, events, or locales is purely coincidental.

Edited by Amanda Elle Edits

WARNING:

This book contains brief mentions of cancer and the death of a parent prior to the story.

SYNOPSIS

*V*alentina Rosas has always known what she wants. Mostly. Sort of. At least, she does now. And what she wants is the coveted staging role at Gia, San Francisco. With four years at the top of her class in culinary school and enough tenacity to fuel the entire Mission, no one doubts she is about to land the job of her dreams—including the three-person cheer squad made up of her best friend and adorably overbearing parents.

Renowned chef Jenn Coleman is not a people person. Her rise to the top of the culinary industry stems from a cultivated blend of top-tier schooling—from her nonna—and bouts of carefully managed misanthropy. Owning and operating two Michelin starred restaurants doesn't leave time for much else anyway. Just ask her ex.

When the new stage at her restaurant trips into her with all the grace of a baby giraffe, it's a sure recipe for disaster. But for all of Jenn's reserve, Valentina has twice the allure, and the chemistry between them is just…chef's kiss.

If only Jenn wasn't Valentina's boss with nearly ten years between them.

Oh, Mexico

CHAPTER 1

Richmond, San Francisco, was a gorgeous place to die.

Valentina's heart raced, her lungs burning, feet quick against the paved trail as she upped her sprint through Golden Gate Park. The sun beamed across the sparsely cloudy sky, casting a glow over the evergreen shrubs and goldfields, and faint traces of lavender wafted in the air—always lavender, despite the medley of wildflowers scattered about the park. J Balvin echoed from her earphones at a reckless volume, drowning out the burble of the lake and chirp of birds she'd failed at identifying.

A pair of men darted by her in a blur of leopard print shorts. *Seriously?* The taller glanced back, shooting her a wink and a crooked smirk. If Val wasn't on her final mile and seconds from passing out, her competitive streak might've won out. But the Tai Chi group on the north lawn seemed that much more tempting.

Why had she decided to take up running again?

The words "stress relief" ricocheted in her mind in a voice that sounded suspiciously like Zoe's. Zoe, who was undoubtedly still asleep back at the apartment. A lifetime of friendship and Val still hadn't tapped into Zoe's level of Zen. Then again, it had been Val's idea to move an entire time zone and burn through her savings in one of the most expensive cities in the country, with its beautiful weather and varied terrain and art, and culture—*her* culture. And food. God, the food. Maybe moving was completely worth it even if she was verging on broke, and her dream was dead. She could almost hear her father's voice now, accent twice as heavy as the lilt in his tone. "You're a great chef, cariño, but your true calling is drama." Her lips curled up at the thought as she slowed her pace beneath the shade of a large oak tree and doubled over to grip her knees, catching her breath.

The beat of her music cut off, replaced by the insistent chime and buzzing of her phone. She cast a glance where it had been strapped to her left bicep, the screen lit up with an unidentified number. With as many job applications as she and Zoe had filled out lately, she did not have the luxury of letting her phone ring unanswered. Even if she would pick up sounding like a pack a day smoker. Then again, she couldn't remember ever getting a job offer on the weekend. "Hello?"

"Valentina Rosas de Leon?" The woman's tone carried the buoyancy of someone who spoke to people for a living, or at the very least, enjoyed it.

Val could relate—sort of—but the use of her full name meant one of two things. Offer or rejection. She forced down a gulp, trying to keep her tone even. "This is Valentina."

"Hi. I'm Avery, calling from Gia, San Francisco."

The pace of Val's heart picked up.

"Congratulations! You are this year's recipient of our

coveted staging post hosted by our very own Jenn Coleman."

Val blinked, her brows drawing closer, chest tightening. She mulled over the words in her mind, actually trying to pick out traces of Zoe's voice in the woman's tone. The staging spot for Gia had been announced. Three weeks ago. If ranting about it as recently as last night was any indication, Val had not made peace with losing something she'd dreamed of all through culinary school. But she wasn't delusional. And this was a prank too far. Even for Zoe. "Zo, if this is you—"

"This is Avery," the woman cut in gently, an audible smile in her voice.

Val paused, mumbling, "Avery," as if saying the name herself would somehow erase her confusion.

"Yes. From Gia. San Fran-cisco." She separated the syllables the way one did for a small child, and Val crossed her arms over her chest.

If this person was actually calling from Gia, she had very nearly ruined any prospect of making a positive first impression. But Avery was still on the phone, reiterating how Val had been picked for the staging position, and this made about as much sense as one ply toilet paper. She slid a hand across her sweat-dampened forehead, into her hair and down her ponytail. "I'm sorry. How is this happening?"

"What do you mean?"

"I mean, didn't the spot already go to that guy from Auguste Escoffier?" Tall, blonde, skipped too many leg days, looked like he could barely tell when oil was hot. Okay. Definitely not over it.

"Right," Avery chirped. "Unfortunately, he's no longer able to participate. Unforeseen circumstances and all that. But you, Valentina, come highly recommended by all your instructors at the Institute, and we would be so happy to have you if you're still open to joining us."

"Uh—Um. Yes. Of course." Was that even a real question?

Avery chuckled. "We understand this is unexpected and your plans for the summer may have changed. Would you be able to give us your answer in a day or two?"

How could she gracefully tell this woman that working at Gia was the plan of her life? "Yes." She shook her head. "I mean, thank you. I...don't need to think it over."

"Okay. I'm seeing here that you're in New York, but just so we're clear, you do know the summer staging role is for San Francisco, not Manhattan?"

"Yes. That won't be a problem. I actually moved recently."

"To San Francisco?" The question resounded with a skepticism that made Val balk.

"Yes?" Her answer was more than a little bashful.

"Wow. You are impressively prepared for this call."

Val could think of a few other ways to phrase moving to another state for a job she hadn't been offered, but there was nothing tying her to New York anymore. Besides, after a perfectly acceptable period of sulking, she'd convinced herself it was still possible. Okay, her parents and Zoe had convinced her. And sure, she'd have to do it the hard way— by waiting for an opening that met her qualifications, hoping her application caught their attention, then somehow impressing Jenn Coleman enough to be offered a spot in her kitchen. But here she was, running through a gorgeous park in San Francisco on the hinges of an audacious if ambitious plan, with Avery from Gia offering her the equivalent of an internship. Her favor with the universe was fickle as fuck, but days like this definitely made up for it.

"Well, we were slated to begin on the 6th, and while we are prepared to allow you an extra week, something tells me you're ready for that, too."

A laugh bubbled up in Val's chest, her breathing finally back to some semblance of normal. "The 6th works just fine."

"Be here at 10 a.m. I'll get you settled with some paperwork and give you a tour."

"Sounds perfect. Thank you, Avery."

"Looking forward to meeting you, Valentina."

The call ended with a beep and her thumb moved to cut off the booming resumption of "Loco Contigo" over her earphones. Her lips stretched in a smile as she replayed the conversation in her mind, wondering, *did that really just happen?* Across the lawn, the Tai Chi instructor had begun an awkward combination of bent knees and slow flailing arms that left him looking constipated, and Val's smile turned to a full-on laugh. When at least one participant in the front row—an older woman with striking silvery hair—shot her a disapproving glare, she turned toward the burbling lake and readied herself for a run back home. Zoe was never going to believe this.

VAL JOGGED up to the door of their building and keyed in the entrance code. It still amazed her that they'd managed to land an apartment in a recently constructed building that had all the new wave amenities of Virtual Doorman and Google Fiber Webpass, but no parking for her charmingly aged Prius. It made for its fair share of wrangling for nearby spots on the street, and each night, a routine glance out the window of their second-floor apartment before she could sleep, but what was the alternative? Trading the first meaningful thing she'd actually been able to buy herself for a bicycle she'd definitely wind up pushing up more hills than she cared to count?

Not. Fun.

Inside, she crossed the empty lobby, taking the stairs up to their apartment. Her body buzzed with excitement, and for the first time in the week since she'd started running again, she didn't feel on the verge of passing out at the door. As she unclasped her necklace to get to the key she wore as a pendant, she tried to remember if the lump beneath the blanket on Zoe's bed had looked big enough for two people to have been underneath when she'd left earlier this morning. Perks of sharing a place that had been advertised as a two bedroom, but actually turned out to be one with a second bed off to the far end of the living room. If Val had anticipated getting an eye full of some guy's remarkably manscaped junk a week into moving in, she would've thrown the deciding round of Rock, Paper, Scissors that had landed her the actual bedroom. It was her fault, really. She knew Zoe. Loved Zoe.

Zoe loved sex.

Sex with strangers? Even better.

Val pushed open the door with measured caution, one hand clasped tightly over her eyes. "I have news I'd prefer to share with everyone's clothes on."

Zoe's soft, infectious laugh filled the room. "Don't we have a standing promise to at least text if we have someone over?"

"Like you've never forgotten that promise." Val dropped her hand, grateful to find Zoe alone in a tank top and shorts as she straightened the corners of her comforter. She stood to her full height—a dignified five feet three with curves for days—and swept ruffled blonde curls out of her face.

"Okay, Val. Be a snarky bitch." She rolled her eyes—greyish blue orbs that always shone a little too brightly against her pale ivory skin. "So, I forgot once. Twice."

Val shot her a look.

"Maybe three times, but you're the one who brought home a screamer last week."

One of Val's brows inched up and she cocked her head to the right. "Fair." Of course, she had no way of knowing the woman would turn out to be so... expressive, but she did feel bad Zoe hadn't been able to sleep half the night. Especially since she'd had her first shift as a junior pastry chef at Cakes and Stuff the next day. A grin spread across Val's face at the memory of her call earlier, and she bent to start undoing her laces.

"Tell me you're not having flashbacks right now."

"What? No." She laughed, crossing their modest open floor plan to Zoe's "bedroom". "I got a staging offer."

"Really?" Zoe's eyes widened. "Where?"

"Gia."

Lines drew in her forehead. "How?"

"I don't even know, Zo." Val fell into the loveseat with no grace and too much drama, her smile never leaving her face. Could a person feel high on good news? Her memory's comparison to the few times she'd had pot brownies said yes. Absolutely. "The woman who called said the guy from Auguste had to drop out. I actually thought it was you for a second."

Zoe tsked, frowning. "I know my prank skills at the institute were A1, but I also know how badly you wanted that spot. I would never."

"I know." Val nodded. "I guess it just seemed so unbelievable." Somewhere, deep in her subconscious, there was a part of her that was disappointed to not have been the first pick—to have been offered the spot only because someone else could no longer take advantage—but she couldn't bring herself to dwell on it. It's not like she'd pass on the opportunity out of pride. She was a lot of things. Stupid wasn't one of them.

She gave Zoe a quick rundown of the details, knowing she'd have to go over them again when she called her parents. The look on their faces would be worth it though. Maybe they'd returned to Mexico having never quite attained the American dream, but she knew how much it meant to them to see her succeed. Even if it had taken an MBA she'd barely used and leaving a job with a comfortable salary to start all over at culinary school, then become essentially an intern at twenty-eight years old.

Zoe chuckled, shaking her head as she plopped down next to Val on the sofa. "Leave it to you to land exactly the job you wanted. I swear, I don't know if it's magic or sheer willpower."

"Probably both. Besides, it's not *exactly* the job I want."

"Right. Because your real plan is to walk into Gia, learn everything you can from Jenn Coleman and mutiny your way to head chef."

Val tossed her head back in a laugh. "I can't believe I'm two days away from standing in a kitchen with a living, breathing legend."

"A *gorgeous* living, breathing legend," Zoe enhanced.

Val shrugged, her gaze fixed on the lines of the ceiling. "Minor detail."

"Minor detail?"

"Mhm."

"I don't know, V." Amusement laced Zoe's exhale. "You

may swing both ways, but women like her are definitely your kryptonite."

Val sat upright and narrowed her eyes at Zoe's baby blues. "You have zero evidence to back that up."

Zoe's brows rose. "Our Intro to Gastronomy instructor?"

"Healthy admiration."

"You were ten minutes early everyday all semester."

"*And* an enthusiastic interest in my education."

"Sure."

"Even if you were right," Val acquiesced. Barely. "She was my instructor. I wouldn't have actually done anything about it. You know how badly I wanted Gia. Trust me." She stood to head to the bathroom for a shower. "I am not jeopardizing my chances of actually working there someday just because Jenn Coleman happens to have a nice face. Besides..." She glanced over her shoulder, actually thinking back to the screamer this time. Stevie, was it? "This city is full of beautiful people. I'm sure I'll do just fine."

CHAPTER 2

*G*ia, San Francisco, sat on the corner of Harrison Street, marked by a polished hanging wooden sign with the name in glorious swooping font. In the beaming glow of midmorning, it stood out like a beacon of hope—an aspiration come to fruition, built on blood, sweat, tears, and Jenn Coleman's genius take on Italian meets Mexican cuisine.

Val tightened her grip on the steering wheel of her third-hand Prius, angling her head to peer out the window at the building. Not that she had time for it. In fact, the digital clock on her dashboard screamed that she *really* didn't have time for it, but there was something enthralling if not intimidating about seeing the building up close; it's taupe horizontal siding and casement windows were the picture of simplistic. Maybe it was physically being there—this wasn't a rabbit hole Google search brought on by another fit of daydreaming. This was her opportunity to prove that finishing top of her class at the Culinary Institute of America was not a fluke, to charm these people with her talent and grace—okay, probably not grace per se, she was kind of clumsy sometimes—

Shit. Ten minutes before your first shift is not the time to be working through your imposter syndrome, Val.

A scarier thought entered her mind and she glanced down at her white button down. Had she put on deodorant? She tilted her head and chanced a sniff, almost immediately met by a subtle whiff of shea. Of course, she had.

Her phone buzzed in the holder fixed to her dashboard and the screen lit up with a text from her mom. Then another.

Mami (9:53 a.m.)
Buena suerte, mi vida.
Your father is planning a celebration for your first day.
Any reason to throw a party.

Val's grin exploded to a hearty laugh at the eye roll tacked onto the end of the message. When had her mom gotten so versed in emojis? Still, the presence of her, through a simple series of text, filled Val like the calmest of deep breaths, reminding her that belief in herself stemmed from an infallible support system, even with thousands of miles between them now. She gave herself a steadying look in the rearview mirror and made a mental note to reply to her mother later, when she had more time for the string of questions that would certainly ensue.

She grabbed her bag and exited her car onto the inclined sidewalk—not the steepest she'd encountered in the city so far—and crossed the few feet to Gia's main entrance. The scent of cheese and garlic hit the second she opened the door, and her eyes roamed the modest entryway. Ashwood floors, exposed beams and hanging lights. A simple layout of polished tables and chairs that read as modern rustic through daylight, but at night could easily pass as more elegant. Romantic, even. Although, the image her mind had recalled of the dim lighting and candle-lined wall ledges probably had everything to do with that. Unlike the well-stocked bar, the bread rack stood bare, and she found herself wondering if bakers were kneading away in the dough room right that second.

"Valentina?"

Her head snapped up at the sound of her name, the tap of heels more apparent at the sight of the woman approaching. She led with a smile that graced every inch of her delicate Asian features, dark hair caught in a ponytail that swung in her wake. "Avery?"

"Yes. Right on time." Her perfectly arched brows shifted in a way Val took to be approval.

"I'm just happy to be here."

"We're happy to have you." She gestured toward a four top then moved to slide one of the chairs back. "Sit, please."

Val took a settling gulp, sitting in the opposite chair. A sit down in the dining room two minutes after walking in wasn't what she'd been expecting. Nerves crept through her like tendrils on a vine. Interviews were a necessary evil. But were they? Wasn't the point of a stage that she wouldn't have to go through the nightmare of a personality test that usually went with a resume?

"Relax." Avery chuckled. "This isn't an interview. The stage is already yours. You're still required to do all your best work in the kitchen."

Val breathed a hopefully casual laugh. "HR and a mind reader."

"No. My brother just happens to be a chef, too. Aren't you all a bit anti-interview by default?"

"I feel like that's a trick question and I need to find a more diplomatic answer than yes."

Avery raised both hands. "No tricks here, I promise. But —" She glanced down at the gold classification folder in front of her and skipped over page one of, well, a lot. "There are a few things we need to go over before getting you into your whites. As you probably know, our staging process is more intricate and longer than most in the States, rounding out at four to six weeks. By the fourth, you'll know where you stand, if there's a chance of joining us on a more permanent basis, or trying elsewhere. Either way, a brief stint at a Michelin starred restaurant is usually enough to at least get our former stages in the door almost anywhere."

Didn't Val know it. But she didn't want just any starred restaurant. She wanted this one. She tempered the urge to blurt out as much, reaching for the small notepad and pen in her bag, listening intently as Avery went over salary, which, legal or not, didn't always come with a stage. Not that she minded either way. She'd budgeted this move down to the penny, and she had a six-sheet Excel doc to show for it. Pie charts included. Besides, she was confident that with enough drive and charisma—neither of which she'd ever been lacking—she could land a twelve-hour stage anywhere. Six weeks of hard work—zero delusions about that—for a chance at her dream seemed like a no brainer.

When Avery stood, announcing it was time for a tour, Val grabbed her notepad and followed with restrained zeal. At least, she hoped she'd managed a little restraint. Coming off as the eager, young intern was not the game plan. More of a seasoned newbie, one who'd seen enough of the world to know what she was about now. And, well, she'd seen New York, and Mexico City, which was close enough.

"I *will* let one of the kitchen staff take you through the actual tour of the kitchen since they are so much better at knowing where everything is, but in addition to the main dining room, we do have two private dining areas and a dough room. Guest bathrooms are on the first floor—we'll get to those in a bit—and the staff restroom is just off the break room in the back. There are two offices. One I share with Mel, our head chef, and Jenn's. Those are last on the trip. Questions?"

"How much time does she spend in there?" Val bobbed her head toward the kitchen. "Ms. Coleman, I mean."

Avery laughed, starting up a brief but winding flight of stairs, the spikes of her point toe pumps taunting in a way that made Val appreciate the pair of Chelsea boots on her own feet. "Code for how much opportunity will you have to learn from her?" Avery maintained her pace up the stairs without a glance back. "The answer to your question is a lot. We can't get her out of the kitchen, really. And don't call her Ms. Coleman. She hates it."

"Gossiping about me to our newest, Ave?"

Something tightened in Val's chest—exhilaration and panic bursting at its grip—and she paused a few steps beneath where Avery had gotten to the landing. Was that who she thought it was? Of course, it was. She could pick out the husk in Jenn Coleman's voice in a fifty-person choir. All those interviews. The one Iron Chef appearance Val had watched a questionable number of times. It was inspirational, engrossing. It was...

Jenn. Coleman.

She stepped into view, her hair swept up in a loose bun, skin soft and brown in the glow of morning light all around them, and Val was grateful she'd had the good sense to not utter Jenn's name out loud like a starstruck fan. *Jenn.* Something about it bounced around Val's mind with a distinct newness, which was weird because Val had probably mentioned her by name a few too many times in the last year alone. Had freckles always dusted her nose and cheeks like that?

"Is it even gossip if it's true?" Avery's retort punched a bit of sober into Val.

"I suppose not." Jenn leaned into the wrought iron of the small upstairs balcony, dazzling hazel eyes fixed on Val. "Welcome, Valentina."

Val's stomach flipped. Jenn Coleman knew her name, and she was officially what Zoe would lovingly term a basic bitch. "Hi, Miss—I mean, Jenn." She managed a smile. Barely. "I can't thank you enough for offering me this opportunity."

The closed lip smile Jenn returned seemed forced, awkward at best, though it gave away faint signs of a pair of dimples in her cheeks. She started toward the landing of the stairs, and Val resumed her ascent, bracing herself for a terse handshake and minimal eye contact. This didn't seem like part of the plan—running into their boss midtour. She anticipated quick and painless. She anticipated Jenn disappearing after, finishing her tour with Avery then changing into her whites and getting set up in the kitchen. Twelve hours on her feet would be hard, but she'd anticipated that too, even splurged on a pair of dreadful Birkenstock Londons. She did *not* anticipate tripping on the final step, or the embarrassing squeal that had wrenched its way from the back of her throat.

The pair of hands on her—one on her arm, the other firm on her waist—registered before the fact that she'd closed her eyes. She opened them to a delicate three chain necklace nestled against warm brown skin, gold circular pendant between the open top buttons of a simple black button down. *Shit*. Her gaze snapped up to Jenn's—a kaleidoscope of forests and fire staring back at her—and every rationale said her chest would give under the violent race of her heart. But she *had* almost crashed to the floor in front of her boss on day one. Would the fall have killed her? Unlikely. The embarrassment? Jury's still out.

"Oh my gosh. Are you okay?"

Val shrunk back at the alarm in Avery's voice. "Jesus. I'm so sorry. I'm clumsy on my feet, but great with my hands, I swear."

Jenn's brows crept up and her eyes widened ever so slightly.

"I mean—" Val cleared her throat. This was what she'd brought to the table—terrible coordination and a ruthless case of foot in mouth. *Nice, Valentina.*

"We understand." Jenn straightened, posture nearly as rigid as the lines of her lips. Clearly, Val was not making a good impression. And yet, she couldn't help thinking from her vantage point—close enough for the scent of shea and chamomile to dominate the permanence of spices and cheese in the air—pictures, videos... They really didn't do Jenn justice. She took a step back then moved to walk around where Val now stood safely on the landing. "I'll let you get back to your tour, Ave. Valentina."

Val didn't know what to make of the way Jenn had said her name. All politely dismissive. She willed her head not to turn when Jenn's shoulder brushed hers, to follow with her eyes as Jenn disappeared down the stairs.

Avery's eyes lit up with mischief and a grin spread on her face. "Way to make an impression."

Maybe it was the teasing quality of her tone, or her earlier assertion that nothing leading up to Val's duties in the kitchen had any bearing on her staging at Gia, but she felt comfortable enough to shut her eyes and breathe a laugh. Even having just experienced the third most embarrassing moment in her life. "She hates me."

"No." Avery chuckled. "She can come off as being a little stoic, but Jenn doesn't hate anyone. Once you get in the kitchen and get to know her a little better, you'll see."

Suddenly, the concept of facing Jenn in the kitchen seemed more daunting than anything. How would Val erase the ineptitude of what had just happened? Had Jenn noticed that Val, however briefly and completely unconsciously, had stared at her chest? Did she now think Val was some kind of sleaze? *Ugh*. And the hands. Why the fuck would she say the thing about the hands?

"Come on," Avery beckoned. "I'll take you through private dining and I can't give you names, but I can tell you stories about worse first encounters with our other stages. Starting with the guy who mumbled 'I love you,' on his first handshake with Jenn then proceeded to fake a fainting spell."

Val's jaw dropped, disbelief and amusement all twisted into her expression. The tension in her body began to lift. The last five minutes were still stuck on loop in her head, but she appreciated what Avery was trying to do. When the time came, she'd just have to leave it all in the kitchen—let her skill and the talent she'd spent the last four years honing speak for themselves—and hope that it was enough.

CHAPTER 3

Another chit popped out on the rail, followed by a cry for "Four enchilada raviolis on the fly!"

"Four enchilada raviolis? Heard that!"

Jenn lived for the weekend rush. The bustle of waiters in and out of the kitchen, bellowed instructions and acknowledgements between exchanges about partners, kids and how the 49ers or Giants were doing. She wasn't much for sports and neither of her haute cuisine instructors would approve, but she welcomed the chatter, even if her participation tended to be minimal. Everyone from the escueleries—she'd always found that somehow more imposing than dishwashers—to her head chef, Mel, had been with her long enough to be accustomed to the culture at Gia.

Everyone except the new stagiaire.

Maybe it had to do with Valentina's day-one outburst—something about being good with her hands that Jenn had had to excavate from her own brain the second she realized it was, thankfully, not a double entendre—but Valentina didn't strike Jenn as someone withdrawn. And yet, she'd been remarkably quiet all week, only speaking when spoken to, watching with unparalleled intensity from some out-of-the-way corner whenever she'd found her hands free. Then, she'd seemed quite attached to her pen and notepad. Tonight, having been tasked with dicing, coring and seeding tomatoes almost since the rush had begun around 7 p.m., she'd had no such luck. A strand of dark brown hair drifted free of her white skull cap and one of her arms rose, hands tinged red, in a failed attempt to brush her hair out of her face with her bicep. Her brows drew closer, lips pursed as she reached for her chef's knife and gripped the tip between her thumb and forefinger to core another tomato.

"Hot behind!"

Jenn refocused at the warning over her shoulder, checking the Mexican chicken parmesan that had been slid in front of her to ensure the layer of avocado and roasted peppers had been met with the right ratio of cheese, the chicken a crusted golden brown, fettuccine al dente. As much as she loved cooking and creating, on nights like these —with the restaurant brimming with bookings—she'd taken on the role of expo more times than she could remember. Making sure each dish was perfect before traying it up for a server required a level of experience and precision she was certain her ex would label as controlling—in fact, controlling was exactly the word Rachel had used on multiple occasions. For Jenn, some things were simply necessary.

A waiter burst through the kitchen's swing doors with a gust of chill air from the dining room in her wake. "Is this table 12's?" The garnet bowtie she wore seamlessly matched the calligraphed "Gia" etched into the pocket of her button up. But red bowties weren't a part of the uniform. This was the problem with hiring out of high school, or even college —their constant need for self-expression.

Something nagging, compulsive, probed at Jenn's mind. She half-considered whether it would be worse to ask the waiter to get rid of the bowtie and finish her shift without it. Better yet, surely, they had spares of the proper ties stashed in the admin office. It wasn't as if they had time for all that either way. Not tonight. She trayed up the fajitas next to the chicken parmesan, making a mental note to mention the uniform breach later. "Table 12."

"Thanks, Chef." The waiter spun for the door with a blinding smile and exaggerated flash of her ponytail.

An order of two dozen spaghetti tacos boomed out, something about having more covers this Friday than last mumbled on the tails of it.

"Okay, let's pick it up, people!" Mel yelled above the flurry in the kitchen, her voice shrill yet commanding. Jenn could always count on her to give the staff that extra kick—one of many aspects of being head chef she seemed to enjoy almost as much as all her other managerial duties. Unlike Jenn, purchases and cost control, liaisons with suppliers were approached with enthusiasm rather than a sense of duty. Even if only one of them had devoted their life to the place.

"I think Rosas is in the weeds over here!"

Jenn's head snapped up from the dish she was traying, just in time to see Valentina scramble to pull something from the undercounter refrigerator at her station.

"How are you doing over there, Rosas?" Mel called.

"Good, Chef!"

If not for the way Valentina's reply had begun with the slightest tremor in her voice, Jenn might have been convinced. She clenched her jaw, stepping back from the expo stand. "Mel, can you take over here?"

"Sure, Jenn."

Jenn weaved her way toward the back of the kitchen where Valentina appeared to be starting on a batch of roma tomatoes. The strand of hair still dangled from her hat, and she raised her arm in another fruitless attempt to push it back with minimal interruption to her dicing. Jenn's gaze followed the tight grip on her chef's knife, the way the fingers of her guide hand were more extended than she would've ever been taught. She knew better—Jenn had been observing her all week, her technique, precision, attention to detail. "Valentina."

The knife slipped with a clatter against the cutting board and Valentina stilled it with her palm. "Sorry, Chef." Her hands shook, probably from the sudden lack of use, and she curled her fingers into fists before bringing them to her side.

Jenn followed the motion of a single drip of tomato juice to the tiled floor.

"I'll get that cleaned up right away." Her eyes, nearly the same shade of brown as her hair, somewhere between hickory and chocolate, shifted everywhere but Jenn's.

Jenn struggled with how to lessen the blow of what Valentina had clearly read as a reprimand. "Take a breath," she said softly. Her hand moved to tuck the rogue strands of hair back into Valentina's hat. It wasn't anything she'd never done before—she'd redone countless top buttons on the coats of some chef or another, adjusted their hats, straightened the ties of waiters—but as Valentina lifted her head to slowly meet Jenn's gaze, something about the moment felt strangely illicit.

Valentina's lips parted, almost as if she'd taken the instruction to heart. Had made a deliberate effort to breathe.

A tightness grew in Jenn's chest, the feeling akin to one she only ever got whenever she felt exposed, uncomfortable, unnerved. Things she never felt in her kitchen on the busiest or most significant of nights. "Take ten. I'll cover your station."

"I—" Valentina frowned, shaking her head slightly. "Have I done something wrong?"

"No, but from what I just saw you were about three knife rotations from losing a finger. Listen, Valentina..." Jenn tried to keep the sharpness out of her tone. She wasn't in the business of chewing up eager young chefs, only to spit them out less all the enthusiasm they'd walked in with. But she couldn't help being annoyed at the fact that she was being made to have this conversation in the middle of dinner service. "You don't do yourself any favors by not asking for help. You don't do anyone any favors. This kitchen"—her gaze rounded the room in a split second—"any kitchen, for that matter, only works as well as it does because of a team."

"Chef, I—"

"Next time, ask for help." Jenn bobbed her head toward the door of the break room as she moved to the nearby handwashing station. "See you in ten."

"Yes, Chef."

Jenn ignored the way Valentina swiped the hat from her own head, letting that strand of hair dangle against her cheek again and she didn't watch her go. And she didn't think about why the whole encounter had left her feeling so...strange. Or why this supposed strangeness undoubtedly had everything to do with the new stagiaire.

LONG SHIFTS always came with a burst of adrenaline that wore off just around closing. Jenn, though in love with her career and entirely devoted to giving everything to Gia since the moment she'd conceived the idea of the Manhattan locale, was no exception. The melody of Semisonic's Closing Time streamed from a cellphone speaker, while most of the remaining staff completed their nightly checklist in relative silence—too tired for much else. Except for Landon, a station chef and Avery's younger brother, and Warren, a recent addition to the commis chefs, who Landon had apparently taken under his wing.

"Tell you what, War..." Landon's volume, as always, was anything but discreet.

Jenn kept her gaze trained on the laminated checklist in her hand, her dry-erase marker set to confirm the walk-ins had been organized and shut tight.

"We'll go out after shift tomorrow. Try to get your mind off her."

How many times had Jenn heard that advice?

Faint humming drew her head up from her list to Valentina, back turned as she bobbed her head along with the music, hands occupied with restocking a line station. She'd been cleared to leave half an hour ago. Jenn had never been one to assign too many closing tasks to new staff. Too much room for error. But Valentina's gentle humming and swaying projected an air of contentment that felt too pure to be disturbed, compelling Jenn to look on with envy, perhaps even mild adoration.

"Chef Coleman?"

Jenn blinked, turning to find Warren next to her. Her eyes burned with telltale signs of exhaustion, which she blamed for the fact that she hadn't heard Warren approach, and not because she'd obviously been distracted. She never got distracted. As always, his face—with skin a rich blend of reddish-brown undertones—free of blemish or scruff made him look much too young and bright-eyed. He seemed sweet? Impressionable, especially under the unyielding confidence of someone like Landon Dimaano. But he was her employee, not her child, and who he spent his free time with was none of her business. "Yes, Warren?"

"I wanted to confirm if we're still on for the food drive tomorrow."

"Oh. Right." Jenn's brows inched up and she spared a glance at her checklist again, already knowing it had nothing to do with Warren's question. Half the staff had already left for the night, and the names of people who'd volunteered was on another list. On her phone. Left on the desk in her office. She cleared her throat, readying herself to address the remaining staff in the kitchen. "Food drive!"

Valentina turned at the sound of her voice, eyes alert and fixed Jenn's way despite the red tinge to them.

Jenn really hated having to address any form of group setting—another one of the 64 reasons she needed Mel as head chef and Avery as admin. "We're still on. I'll be in for 7 to start prep, and we leave for Dolores and the shelters at 8:30."

Valentina's brows drew together. She glanced across the kitchen as if in search of answers, before pursing her lips. "Sorry—uh—food drive?"

"Yeah." Warren bobbed his head. "Twice a month we come in early and make food for the homeless, or shelters. You can cook or drive them over. Or both. It's kind of cool."

"But not mandatory," Jenn clarified.

"Can I come? I mean—" Valentina pushed a strand of hair behind her ear, shifting as if to take a step forward before seemingly deciding against it. "Are last minute volunteers allowed?"

"Of course." Jenn didn't know what to make of Valentina's lack of hesitance. Not many of her employees were jumping out of their skin to come in at 7 after leaving at almost 2 in the morning. Then again, stages were easily among the most enthusiastic in every regard, constantly tripping over themselves to make a good impression. Quite literally, in some cases. An image of their first encounter flashed in Jenn's mind—the way Valentina had held on to Jenn when she'd tripped, the slow realization in her deep brown eyes when she'd lifted her head after an eternity of forcing Jenn to just hold her too close for comfort, close enough for the soft smell of her hair and skin to have laid roots in Jenn's mind and resurface a full five days later. A headache pulsed at Jenn's temples. She tried not to wince. "Any more volunteers? Last minute cancelations?"

"Count me in, too, Chef."

Jenn's head jerked in the direction of Landon's voice.

Customary for this time of night, his chef's coat was unbuttoned displaying a white undershirt that looked a size too small, though he'd obviously taken great care to keep his slicked back pompadour in place. He grinned, jutting his chin out and Jenn followed his gaze to where Valentina and Warren stood by the line station. Maybe she'd always been too occupied observing his knife skills and recipe execution, but she couldn't remember ever seeing him smile at Warren like that.

Valentina's gaze shifted skyward as she bit down on a smile.

Oh. The realization hit with flustering force, unearthing something buried in the pit of Jenn's stomach. She shifted on her spot, clearing her throat again.

"You okay, Chef Coleman?" Warren frowned at her. "Seems like you might be coming down with something."

"I'm fine, Warren. Thank you." She glanced up at Landon. "And you, Chef Dimaano." She didn't need perfect memory to recall that he had shown up to exactly one food drive in his three years of being employed at Gia—right after he'd gotten the job and Avery, as his older sister, had probably encouraged him. Jenn had heard enough of his talk in the kitchen to know he'd much rather turn up at a club after a twelve-hour shift and wake up next to a stranger well into the morning. She didn't think less of him for it. He was a gifted, young chef. Never shut up but worked hard.

And she didn't look at her as she left the kitchen for the last time that night, but she sure hoped Valentina knew what she was doing.

CHAPTER 4

Jenn had never failed to see the practicality in living this close to Gia, especially on food drive mornings. As she parked along the curb—a mere five-minute drive between the restaurant and the contemporary Edwardian she called home—echoes of Rachel's voice stirred in her mind. Echoes of long buried arguments over how living too close to Gia exacerbated Jenn's "workaholic ways", fights about it even after they'd moved nearly half an hour further to the Financial District. Because contrary to what Rachel believed, proximity didn't make Jenn work more, it simply made work more accessible. Of course someone who worked remotely had trouble understanding that, but Jenn couldn't wrap her head around why—nearly two years after their breakup—she had woken with *this* on her mind.

As she exited her car and started toward Gia's side door, she longed for the walk over from her flat. It would've taken three times as long, but this time of morning—just after sunrise with the fog barely passed, the air crisp and streets quiet—was the best remedy for unwanted thoughts.

Not unwanted, exactly. She couldn't bring herself to think of someone she loved as unwanted. And she did love Rachel. After more than a decade, it was impossible not to. She just wasn't *in love* with Rachel anymore. The distinction had been hazy for a while, and yet—

Her gaze caught on a figure leaned against the wall of the restaurant, dark hair in loose waves down to her chest, one hand clutching a bag to her shoulder in a way that tugged a bit too much on her French terry top. The sliver of smooth, olive skin left exposed drove Jenn's scrutiny to a screeching halt, although she hadn't missed the hug of jeans and curve of hips that followed.

Valentina turned and her face lit up with a smile that left Jenn wondering how she could look this... *radiant* after less than five hours of sleep. "Morning."

Jenn's temples throbbed—last night's headache as obstinate as it was inconvenient. Cold crept through her despite the morning being a manageable 60 degrees and the sweater she'd picked out this morning being more than adequate. Maybe Warren was right. Maybe she was coming down with something. She passed Valentina with a grumbled, "Hello," and riffled through her pockets for her keys.

Silence hung between them as Jenn shuffled the keys in her hand in search of the right one. It wasn't meant to be difficult—she'd labeled them with neatly drawn letters precisely so it would never have to be difficult—but she really didn't like to be examined, and she could *feel* Valentina's eyes on her. Was this why she'd shown up before everyone else? To disturb Jenn's peace of mind with her watchful stare and unnerving silence and—

Jenn startled at the honk of a truck horn and the keys fell against the pavement with a rhythmic jangle. "Damn it."

She bent to retrieve them, only for Valentina's hand to beat her to it.

"Sorry." Valentina chuckled, raking her hair out of her face. A pair of beauty marks sat on her right cheek, one just beneath her eye, the other closer to her chin.

Warmth embraced the cold spreading through Jenn. She had the strangest urge to snatch the keys from Valentina's grip and ask that she take a step back. But her eyes shifted to the movement of Valentina's delicate hands—her nails painted the rich hue of blueberries—and then Valentina held up a key between her thumb and forefinger. "Is this the one?"

Jenn's jaw clenched as she took the offered key, "Thank you," and slipped it into the lock. She stepped into the building, flipping on switches as she went deeper into the kitchen.

The door shut behind her with a thud, and Valentina followed in silence.

For someone who'd never minded quiet, who even preferred it outside of her kitchen, Valentina's reluctance to say more than a few words at a time unsettled Jenn. Her very presence was unsettling. And it wasn't as if Jenn could change it, but she found herself needing to make sure Valentina knew, "You don't get extra points for turning up early." Not that stages at Gia had ever been held to a points system. Jenn's only interest lay in their knife skills, culinary knowledge, attention to details, execution of instructions. "Volunteering has no sway in whether you'll get the job at the end of all this."

"I know," Valentina answered softly.

"Then what are you trying to accomplish by being here this early?" Jenn paused at a line station and faced Valentina again. "You can't have gotten much sleep."

Valentina shrugged. "No less than you. What are *you* trying to accomplish?"

Jenn mulled over the words in her mind, searching for a hint of snark or irony, only to come up empty. Valentina stared at her with measured sincerity, her eyes unwaveringly brown, something like rejuvenated confidence in them. No sign of the overwhelmed, skittish girl Jenn had had to ask to step out of her kitchen last night. And even knowing very little of her, this version emanated authenticity, if not audacity. Was a good night of sleep all she'd needed, or did it have something to do with whatever exchange Jenn had caught between Valentina and Landon toward the end of shift?

Valentina took a step back, perhaps assuming Jenn wouldn't be answering her question, as she said, "Joey."

Jenn's brows drew together.

"He hangs out around Dolores Park sometimes. Pretty sure he's homeless. It took me a week of weaving around tourists to realize it's practically unrunnable, but I did see him a few times. I try to have an extra sandwich or something whenever I happen by there."

Lines drew in Jenn's forehead, the beauty marks on Valentina's face beckoning her gaze again. Valentina's skin glowed beneath the fluorescent beams, the kind of natural tan made richer by summer afternoons spent on the beach, or maybe in the parks. How old was she? It'd been on her application, and Jenn's mind drawing a blank on a number made her wish she paid more attention to things like that. Then again, what did it matter? "That's nice," she answered. Interesting, but nice. "You can have the Dolores route, if you'd like. Maybe you'll see him."

Valentina placed the bag on her shoulder on a prep station. "Is that how this works? We make the food then take routes?"

"Yes. In pairs, if we can help it."

"Okay."

Jenn watched her a moment longer, waiting for another question or comment. For the life of her, she couldn't seem to not watch her. Valentina rummaged through her rucksack. The minutes stretched without another word—the tick tock of the nearby clock the only sound between them. Jenn pulled her gaze away and started for the handwashing station.

"So—"

Jenn halted her steps, gritting her teeth.

"What do we make?"

These were all valid questions, expected questions, and yet, Jenn wanted nothing more than for Valentina to either come out with them all at once or for them both to get on with their cooking. Preferably in silence. She completed the last few steps to the sink and pushed the sleeves of her sweater up to her elbows. "You make whatever you'd like. Preferably something not from the Gia menu. Something...personal."

"I was hoping you'd say that."

Jenn glanced over her shoulder in time to see Valentina pull a yellow package out of her bag and hold it up with both hands, cheeks bunched in a grin that did bizarre things to Jenn's chest and stomach, things her mind almost, almost recognized as—

"Chocolate Abuelita!" The words rolled off Valentina's tongue with an accent not heard seconds earlier. Made sense though with a last name like Rosas de Leon.

A smile tugged at Jenn's lips. Her body tensed at the impulse, but she narrowed her gaze to the bag in Valentina's hands, and a warmth flooded her senses. The memory floated to the forefront of her mind. 2009. Mid December, standing beneath El Ángel in Reforma, Mexico City, with her mom next to her and steaming cups of hot chocolate clutched in their grips. Chocolate Abuelita. The second to last trip they'd taken together.

Valentina stepped forward. "Chef, are you—I mean, Je—" She stopped, lips snapped shut. For the first time all morning, she seemed unsure of herself, unsure even of what to call Jenn. "Did I say something?"

"No." Jenn shook her head, lips curled in a wistful smile. "That's a good one. Perfect with a little cinnamon and just a hint of—"

"Vanilla." Valentina's features softened. "You've had it?"

"Once or twice."

"Ugh. Tell me you tried it with Rosca."

Despite herself, Jenn chuckled, and maybe it was the memory of her mom—sad but fond—but Valentina's excitement was infectious, irresistible. The kind that wore someone down with an innocuous charm they never saw coming until it was too late. Too late for what? To be decided. "I did. But unless you have a loaf of it in that bag of yours, we don't bake that here."

"You totally should."

"A week on the job and you're already trying to change my menu?"

Valentina's shoulders rose in a shrug and she raked her fingers through her hair. "I was raised to aim high." She breathed a laugh. "And by that I mean, your menu is flawless and I'm absolutely kidding."

"About your ambition or the menu?"

She chewed on her bottom lip.

Jenn's eyes fell to the motion.

"Neither, I guess," Valentina murmured.

The moment dragged. Something shifted in the air. The temperature. Pull of gravity.

A door clanked open—Jenn's heart lurching at the sound—and she looked up to find Warren stepping into the kitchen. "Chef Coleman." He beamed. "Hey, Val."

"Hi, Warren."

Jenn took a steadying breath in an attempt to slow the race of her pulse. *So damn jumpy this morning.* "Good morning, Warren." Unlike Valentina, she was familiar with his prompt arrival—usually no more than twenty minutes after her own—and even being his boss, even standing in the restaurant she'd all but built with her own two hands, guilt spread through her at her lack of preparation. She glanced up at the clock on the opposite wall. 7:17 a.m. Seventeen whole minutes and all she'd done was…talk? Her brain hit a wall in processing it. All at once, her carefully managed misanthropy set back in. Along with her headache. She could feel Valentina's eyes on her again.

"So, you're an early bird too, Val?" asked Warren. "No one ever beats me here. I mean"—he laughed, and there was that naivety again—"besides Chef Coleman."

"Uh, yeah. I guess you could say that."

Jenn wondered at her hesitance then mumbled a curse under her breath, willing herself to snap out of it. Whatever *it* was.

"What was that, Chef?" Warren looked at her, his eyes expectant.

"I said you know the drill," she fabricated. "Take whatever you need for your recipes and get cooking. The others should be on their wa—"

The door opened with another obnoxious clank. "Good morning, beautiful people!" Landon burst into the kitchen —hair and smile equally pristine. His eyes locked on

Valentina as he started toward her and Warren. "A special good morning to Gia's newest and brightest, and to you"—he looked up at Jenn—"Chef Coleman."

Jenn met his greeting with a terse nod. "Hello, Landon." She requested Warren refresh Landon on the basics if necessary and announced that she needed to grab some ingredients from the walk-in. As she started out of the room, she tried not to be bothered by the fact that none of them seemed to care.

CHAPTER 5

*V*alentina's phone vibrated with a muffled buzz as she tugged on her favorite black bomber jacket. She paused, one arm caught midway, and turned toward her bed for a glimpse at her screen. Her lips curled in a smile as the phone buzzed again and another text popped up.

Landon (8:13 p.m.)
We're downstairs.
Are you guys almost ready, or do I need to dig into my dad lines repertoire to give War a pep talk about how this will be nothing like those middle school double dates he went on?
I mean, I'm no therapist, but I think there's some trauma there.

Val laughed, rolling her eyes as she tapped out a quick message in return.

Val (8:14 p.m.)
I don't see why you'd need to give Warren a talk about dates for a hang out among friends.

She'd been clear in her agreement to go to dinner

tonight—this was *not* a date. Ignoring the minor detail of Zoe being anti blind dates since the "I just want to watch you eat" incident their first year at the Institute, there were a few things about going on a date with Landon that screamed bad idea, despite his blatant interest. Not that Val wasn't known for her fair share of bad decisions, especially when they were six-feet-tall and Darren Criss hot. Post-Glee —*no shade, Blaine*—and twice as rugged. Then again, how rugged could a character from Glee even be?

"Val, I swear to God, if this is a set up…"

Val breathed a laugh, turning as Zoe unceremoniously marched into her room, finally settled in a burnt orange pocket crewneck, curve-hugging high-rise jeans and a pair of strappy heels. Her shoulder-length blonde hair glowed with signs of a fresh blowout and a purposefully wielded curling iron, her makeup no less flawless. Val's brows inched up. "Well, damn, Z. Should we want it to be a date?"

"Ha ha. You don't get to talk when your shirt is basically a bra."

Val frowned, glancing down at herself. "It's a crop top." And okay, maybe she owned too many, but she'd gone through a phase after she'd finally gotten drunk enough one night to get her belly button pierced. Neither of her abuelas were to ever find out about it, but damn if she wasn't going to wear her skimpy, budget Forever 21 buys wherever else she damn well pleased.

"And you're showing that much skin because you're not interested in Hot Chef?"

Val dropped her jaw in mock shock. "And those are the words of a feminist?" She grabbed her purse, sparing a glance at herself in the mirror mounted over her dresser. A hand went up to comb through the long, dark strands of her hair. She'd barely passed a brush through it, because despite her best friend's teasing, this was not a seduction mission, and Landon Dimaano would not be crawling into her bed tonight, nor her in his. "Speaking of, they're downstairs. Are you ready?"

"Pretty much." Zoe glanced over her shoulder as if in search of something she'd suddenly missed.

Val started toward the door, hand moving to the key around her neck just to make sure she had it, although Zoe never forgot hers.

"Tell me about Warren again."

The puff of air Val released came out laced with equal parts humor and exasperation. "There's not much to tell, Zo. I've been working with the guy for a week. He's sweet—always says his pleases and thank yous, which might not be the kind of sexy you're looking for, but he also saved me from a major vacuum sealer blow up my first shift. Pun intended. And just in case there's some tiny part of you that *is* hoping this is a date, he's totally easy on the eyes."

"If you would've gotten his Insta, I would have a lot more to go on."

"I'll be sure to get on that."

"And this restaurant, Alioto's... It's at Fisherman's Wharf?"

Val nodded, hitting the button to the elevator. "Yes, Zo."

"Isn't that a tourist trap?"

"It is." Val smiled. "But in Landon's words, until we've lived here more than a month, we pretty much *are* tourists. Besides, it's a great restaurant from what I've heard. I'm sure plenty of locals go there."

"Did Hot Chef tell you that, too?"

"Okay." Val shot Zoe a look. "How long is Hot Chef going to be a thing you keep saying?"

The elevator dinged and Zoe stepped in, offering Val an

exaggerated shrug. "Hard to say. Probably until it's so annoying you don't even see it when you look at him anymore."

"Oh, I think we're heading there fast," Val deadpanned.

"Good."

"Why is it so important anyway? Usually, you're all 'I would climb him like a tree.'"

"Jason Mamoa. *Only* Jason Mamoa. And Landon is your coworker, V." The doors to the elevator opened on the first floor and they both exited, only for Zoe to tug on Val's arm, putting them face-to-face. "At your dream job, which you *just* started."

"I think I'm intimate with my own hopes and dreams, Zo."

Zoe huffed. "You know what I mean. You said it's been a rough first week."

"Because Jenn Coleman hates me," Val mumbled under her breath. Jenn had barely spoken to her all week, but for a passing comment once or twice a day, and not counting Friday when she'd practically thrown Val out of her kitchen. Val *could* have asked for help, but she had it under control. Really. Even if she'd lost count of how many tomatoes she'd been made to seed, core and dice, and her fingers were so cramped, she could barely feel them anymore. Takeaway from her first Friday night shift: an Italian-Mexican fusion restaurant uses a ridiculous amount of tomatoes, and if she was going to be stuck on prep next week, she'd need to up her game.

And then there was yesterday, before the food drive. She'd overheard talk of Jenn's awkwardness and stoicism, but Val was sure she'd worn her down even for a moment. They'd connected over the Chocolate Abuelita, and right before Warren had stepped in. What had *that* been? Banter? Something else?

"V, I know you." Zoe's eyes glimmered with sincerity. "I know you latch onto the first bit of escape whenever things aren't going according to your carefully laid out plans."

Val glanced down at her Chelsea boots. "What's your point, Zo?"

"My point is, don't shit where you eat. It's bad form."

A laugh bubbled up in Val's chest and she reached out to link her arm with Zoe's. "Don't worry. Chefs know that better than anyone."

They exited the building to the image of a black sedan, Warren's back turned, Landon leaned against the hood of the car, hands in wild gestures as he relayed something too exciting. His signals came to a halt and he slowly straightened to his full height, lips curling into a grin the second he noticed Val and Zoe. Val's gaze swept over him in a swift appraisal—his slicked back hair and crooked smirk, plain red V-neck, dark jeans and sneakers. The kind of understated attractive he was probably going for, had calculated, but Warren wore more naturally.

"Um…" Warren took a hesitant step forward, both arms tucked behind his back. The emerald button-down and tiny studs in his ears signalled 21st century, but something about his approach struck as weirdly Victorian. For a second, Val thought he was actually about to bow, which wouldn't have been too out there with him having at least half a foot on Zoe. "I'm Warren." His smile lit up against his sepia complexion and he extended a hand to her.

Zoe accepted, staring up at him, her lips slightly parted as she murmured, "Zoe."

Val shook her head, bending to whisper, "Just Jason Mamoa, huh?"

"Landon!" Landon raised a hand, yelling his own name in introduction, "If anyone cares!"

Val started toward the car. "Don't think anyone does, Lan."

VAL LEANED into the wooden bench, her lips drawn in a permanent grin as her gaze flitted about Pier 39. An empty stage stood before her, but people milled around every inch of the pier—in and out of the sports grill and arcade off to her left, the crab cakes stand just to her right, the rotating carousel filling the air with music from the calliope. It was the kind of communal energy that always left her buzzing with excitement, contentment rather, and sent her twenty years into the past all in one go. To summer afternoons at Luna Park with her parents.

A light breeze stirred up, salty and chilled with the proximity of the ocean. Val stuffed her hands into the pockets of her jacket, hugging them against her midriff as Landon shifted closer and stretched one arm along the back of the bench. "I know we said this wasn't a date, but War and Zoe seemed to have hit it off."

Val smiled, reluctantly pulling her gaze from two women standing nearby, Ben and Jerry's ice cream tubs in their hands, both caught in a fit of laughter as one leaned in to brush her thumb against the corner of the other's lips. "Serendipity, I guess."

Landon's eyes gleamed with unwavering confidence as he leaned closer. "I don't believe in things like that. Chance or luck. I'm more of a master of my own destiny kind of guy, you know? I go after the things I want." He smirked, casting a fleeting glance toward Val's lips. Cologne wafted off him in waves, his dark, long-enough-for-a-man-bun hair perfectly slicked back. He was the kind of guy who drove a Honda but would fork out $400 for the next Tom Ford fragrance. All about the short game. The first impression. Wasn't that why she'd agreed to come out with him in the first place? Because she knew *serious* wasn't what he was after—there was no whirlwind romance gone bad to be had here. She wouldn't have to wonder how they'd ever work together if it ended badly. But Zoe was right, if all Val wanted was a hookup, there were a hundred better places to start than her place of employment. Besides, something told her Jenn wouldn't like it so much.

Which reminded her... "Does Gia have a fraternization policy?" Somehow, she couldn't remember Avery mentioning it on her first day.

Landon's grin went to Cheshire cat heights. "Does that mean you're considering it?"

"You have a one-track mind."

"Okay, okay." He laughed, raising both palms in surrender. "We don't. I mean, there's nothing in writing that says so anyway. My sister would've mentioned."

"Avery's your sister?"

"Did you think there were two unrelated Filipinos named Dimaano running around the restaurant?"

Val cocked her head to one side. "This is actually the first time I'm even hearing Avery's last name. Besides, I couldn't exactly tell by looking at the pair of you."

"You mean I don't look Filipino. You can say it." Landon shrugged. "I take after our mom, I guess. But, my point is, Avery is the quintessential big sister, even if it's only by two minutes. If there was any chance dating could get either of us in trouble with Chef OCD, she'd be on me like a scratched record."

"Um..." Val ran a hand through her hair, brows drawn together. She wasn't sure if she was more bothered by the fact that Landon had apparently discussed her with his sister, or that he seemed to be referring to Jenn with less than flattering intentions. And sure, plenty of people spoke poorly of their boss—two years working logistics in a distribution company that prioritized numbers over people, she'd done her fair share of talking about her bosses too—but something about Landon's comment didn't sit right, especially since OCD could be so debilitating for people who lived with it. "Does Jenn suffer from OCD?"

"Oh, no." Landon waved away the possibility as if it was completely ridiculous. "I mean, I don't think so. It's just... she's so uptight, you know? You see her. Hovering over every dish, making sure everything down to the sauce is drizzled right. We can't even take out the trash at close without her overseeing it."

Val shifted in her seat. "You're exaggerating."

"Am I? Didn't she kick you out on Friday for not dicing the tomatoes evenly or something?"

"That's not what happened. I needed a break. She could see that, even if I couldn't."

"Oh, come on, Val. Don't tell me you're one of them."

"One of what?"

"Those fresh out of culinary school, bright-eyed interns who think Jenn Coleman walks on water."

Val flinched back, narrowing her eyes to his. She waited for his smile to fade, for him to take it back, but his expression never wavered. There was even something in his widened eyes and raised brows that suggested he was waiting for her to laugh? Val bit down on her bottom lip, nodding as she stood. "Yeah, I think...I'm going to go find Zoe and Warren."

He reached for her hand. "Val—"

"Nope." She untangled her hand from his. "We're not going to do this. We had a nice meal and our friends seem to really like each other. Sounds like a successful night to me. Now I'm telling you I'd like to go. It *can* be that simple, Landon. Let it be that simple."

"At least let me drive you home."

"Don't worry about it." She dug into her pocket and came up with her phone, twisting it from left to right so the screen was visible to him. "Uber."

"You're seriously leaving?"

"Yeah." She took a few steps forward before stopping. "And I may not think Jenn Coleman walks on water, but I do think she's pretty fucking incredible."

CHAPTER 6

"Val, hang on a sec!"

Jenn glanced up as Valentina rushed into the kitchen, her attention piqued at the mention of Val's name. Her eyes scanned Valentina in a brief once over—silky, dark strands of hair clinging to the back of her neck though the rest had been swept into a messy bun, the line of her jaw, impatient purse of her lips. A hand reached out and grabbed her arm, bringing her steps to a halt, and Landon entered Jenn's line of vision.

Valentina breathed an exasperated sigh.

Given the way they'd left for the food drive on Saturday —teaming up for the Dolores route with an enthusiasm of nauseating high fives then stumbling back into the kitchen an hour later, rambling about having dinner the next day— Jenn would never have foreseen that there'd be trouble in paradise. This soon? And, usually, she didn't make it her business to get involved in her staff's personal affairs. There were no rules preventing them from dating. She'd decided early on that was the kind of rigidness she never wanted to enforce—dictating who people were allowed to see, allowed to love. As long as they could be adults about it, and their jobs weren't affected, she'd never have to be bothered with it all—something both she and California law seemed to be on the same page about. And yet, here she was, concerned about the scowl on Valentina's face and delicate slope of her brows.

The weight of the iPad in her hands served as a palpable reminder there were other things to which she needed to attend. Starting with the pre-shift meeting that was to begin in—she cast a glimpse at the time—six minutes. Whatever was happening between Valentina and Landon was exactly that. Between Valentina and Landon. But surely, Valentina didn't think it would reflect favorably for her to get involved with a colleague and bring drama into their place of work only her second week in. Somehow, she seemed smarter than that. Or maybe that had only been wishful thinking on Jenn's part—this niggling sentiment that constantly kept Valentina at the forefront of her mind whenever she was close, that had drawn Jenn's thoughts to the memory of her waiting outside the restaurant Saturday morning; the way her eyes gleamed a little brighter when she talked about Chocolate Abuelita and Rosca, the way she chewed her bottom lip—

"Hey, Jenn. Did you still want to go over next month's shift before I post?"

Jenn snapped out of her daze at the sound of Avery's voice.

Avery stopped within inches of her, impeccably garbed in a white silk blouse, pinstripe ankle pants and a pair of navy stilettos. Typically, her hair had been caught in a neat ponytail, her make up pristine. If there was one thing about the Dimaano twins, they knew how to present themselves—not that they had to try very hard. Jenn eyed Valentina and

Landon again. Maybe she couldn't blame Valentina for being... a little distracted, even if she herself had never found men appealing in that way. Even if it had been a while since she'd taken a romantic interest in anyone.

"Jenn?"

"Yes, sorry." Jenn blinked, hesitantly pulling her gaze from Valentina's slowly shifting expression, from the ghost of a smile crossing her features.

"Guess those two are making up, then."

Jenn faced Avery, frowning slightly. Did she know something about what had happened on Sunday? Why Landon seemed to be apologizing?

As if she'd reached in and plucked the thought straight out of Jenn's mind, she shook her head, offering, "I don't know what happened. He wouldn't say. But if I know my brother, he said something stupid, and Val doesn't seem like the kind of woman to put up with it."

"Hmm."

"He mentioned they'd be hanging out, along with Warren and Val's best friend, Zoe, I think. I made it clear they shouldn't rush into anything that might be..." She bobbed her head from one side to the next, gaze wandering. "Problematic."

"Right." Questions ping-ponged around Jenn's brain. Questions she had no business asking. So, she didn't. *Let's hope they're smart enough to heed that advice.* "Send me the shift. I'll look it over and have it back to you after the meeting."

"Perfect." She took a retreating step then stopped, clicking a pen Jenn only then realized she'd been holding. "And Jenn..."

Jenn compulsively surveyed the spot where Valentina had been standing, sighing at the now empty space. "Yes?"

Avery's forehead creased as she tilted her head, studying Jenn. "Are you okay?"

"Of course." The intonation in Jenn's tone probably didn't help her case, but she straightened her posture that much more, attempting to look more like herself. Even if she didn't feel like it. "Is that it?"

"No. Uh…" Avery hadn't bought it, but she shook her head as if deciding not to probe further. For now, at least. "So, I've been here since you opened. I know our lunch and dinner service crowds like the back of my hand, go over the POS reports, help Mel with predicting covers…You haven't had changes to the shifts I've made in a year."

Jenn furrowed her brows. Where was this going? Did Avery want a promotion? A raise? They could discuss a raise, but this wasn't exactly the time.

"I'm just saying, you have enough on your plate without needing to go over a roster."

"Right." Jenn mulled over the thought. "I don't mind checking." She liked checking. Checking gave her peace of mind.

Avery's lips stretched in a closed smile. "Got it." She waved her hand in no particular direction. "I guess I'll see you in there then."

For a moment, Jenn watched her walk away, pondering their exchange. If there was one person in her employ at Gia who could claim to know her better than anyone, who she could classify as a friend, it was Avery. Avery knew all about Jenn's mom, her grandmother, her relationship with Rachel —the ups, downs and in betweens. They'd commiserated over difficult relationships with their fathers, sat across each other in restaurants all over the West Coast. Avery had managed to coax Jenn into going to a club. Twice. Which was exactly how Jenn knew there was something she'd missed just now, how she knew Avery's acquiescence was reluctant at best, and at most a consequence of her disappointment. *Because of a roster?*

Her watch beeped with a reminder she need not check, and she started toward main dining for their daily pre-shift meeting. She exited the kitchen to find most chefs and servers already seated and waiting with Mel by the bar, ready to begin. Making her way toward a four-top near the back, her eyes roamed the floor, casually taking note of each face, though all staff on shift were required to attend. Valentina and Landon sat together closer to the entrance, both settled on bar stools as Landon whispered something that resulted in Valentina shoving him playfully.

"Before we hop into the daily grind," Mel announced, waiting for the individual chatter to dissolve. "Did we all have a good weekend? Does anyone have anything big they want to share? Engagements, birthdays, you found a way to expand your castle on Minecraft?"

"My birthday's on Friday," offered Gavin, one of the more seasoned servers, though he only ever worked part time. "But to accommodate you all, I'll start accepting gifts now."

"There are no birthdays this week," Avery popped in. "I don't know why you even try when you know we have them all on file."

"Seems like we got an engagement though." Gavin jerked his head toward Valentina and Landon.

Landon grinned. "Be my best man, bro?"

"You two are hilarious," Valentina put in. "I'm sure we all know Landon is already pretty married to himself."

A roar of laughter stirred up—Avery nodding as if she couldn't help but agree with Valentina's words, even if they'd been said in jest.

"All right. That's enough of that," Mel arbitrated. "We do have one menu update for lunch service. No nopales. Our usual supplier is out, but we did manage to get a last-minute delivery from Fresh Farms, which should be here in time for dinner. I'll update you once that's settled. Now..." She reached for her own tablet, swiping across the screen before peering up at the group. "Side work assignments."

Jenn's gaze drifted to the window next to her, the constant flow of cars rushing up and down the hill as she half-heartedly paid attention to Mel's run through of the agenda. A strange hollowness lingered in her chest, and not for the first time, she questioned her inability to connect with her staff on a deeper level. She didn't set out to be strict or unapproachable. It just never came as easily to her. Maybe it had something to do with so many of them being younger, by as many as twenty years in some cases. Then again, Mel and Avery didn't seem to have that problem, and Mel was even older than her. But it wasn't only staff either. It had been two years since she and Rachel had called it quits, and while they were still in each other's lives for Tommy's sake as well as their own, she knew they'd never be romantic again. Not that she wanted to be. Sometimes she just couldn't help feeling like—

"Valentina!"

Jenn tuned back in to the sound of Mel's voice. Her watch signaled three minutes to the end of their meeting, and it occurred to her with disquieting clarity that she must have checked out for well over ten minutes. She needed rest. Proper rest.

"So, we didn't want to spring this on you your first week in." Mel shot Avery a conspiratorial glare.

Avery stepped forward, gesturing vaguely with her

hands. "We wanted to give you a chance to realize we're nice people first. That you maybe even like some of us."

"Why do I feel a deep, aching sense of dread right now?" Valentina asked, hints of a smile in her voice.

"Come over here for a minute? Two, tops."

The air hummed with something sprightly, positive—the kind of energy Jenn wanted from them at the start of every shift; it was why she had, with Avery's guidance, incorporated pep talks and praise into these meetings, as well as the newbie initiation.

Jenn's entire being warmed at the smile Valentina wore, questions as much as mirth in her eyes.

"Here's the thing. We all had to do it," Avery told her. "Even the big boss back there."

Eyes shifted to Jenn briefly, but somehow, she couldn't bring herself to meet any but the pair trained on her from the front of the room. Valentina's lips parted to release a breath and her stare took on a singular intensity—one second, two—before she scoffed and glanced at her feet. "Okay. Lay it on me."

"In twenty seconds, a song will come on over the restaurant speakers," Avery explained. "All you have to do is one dance. Your choice. And since we all know what it's like, we have a standing rule. No cameras. It's just us."

Valentina tossed her head back in a laugh—the melody full-bodied and contagious.

"Oh. It's probably worth mentioning that if you don't do this, you lose your stage," Mel added.

Valentina's eyes widened, her mouth falling open, and Jenn actually found herself wanting to laugh too, despite Mel's comment being a terrible joke.

A Chubby Checker song blared through the speakers.

For a moment, Valentina hesitated, gears seemingly turning in her mind before she beamed and spurred into the *Twist*.

A laugh bubbled up in Jenn's chest as she shook her head. She had the strangest feeling that only Valentina could make this ridiculous tradition look downright adorable. Their eyes locked again, Valentina's glowing with the absurdity of it all, and Jenn's smile gradually began to fade, replaced by a barely conscious dulling of her senses. The hooting and laughter, lively beat of a 1960s song they were all too young to truly appreciate—Jenn included—the cool of the air conditioning against her skin...

The music cut off as abruptly as it had begun, met by the standard round of applause after moments like this. Avery and Mel wrapped their arms around Valentina good-naturedly, before Mel mumbled something about having a good shift, and it being time to get the doors open.

Jenn couldn't shake the feeling creeping through her, but she knew better than to try and identify it. The drag of chairs across the floor signaled the beginning of shift—kitchen and floor staff alike moving to their respective places. Before she could stop herself, before she could quantify all the reasons why she probably shouldn't, she stepped forward and said, "Valentina, can I see you for a minute?"

Valentina halted her strides toward the kitchen, laughing as she promised one of the servers to catch up later.

How had she even settled in with *everyone* so quickly?

She came to a stop in front of Jenn, fingers of one hand gently brushing the shorter strands of hair clinging to her neck, eyes still glinting.

"You handled that better than most," Jenn commended.

Valentina shrugged, shaking her head. "I come from a

big Mexican family where everyone loves to dance, and everyone gets laughed at. I learned to be a good sport early."

"I thought they had you with the song for a bit."

She tilted her head, her full, dark brows inching closer. "What do you mean?"

"Well, aren't you a little young to know what to do when a 60's hit comes on?"

"Maybe." There was something in her pause, the intensity of their eye contact, or perhaps how her voice had pitched slightly lower when she said, "But I'd hazard a guess I'm older than you think."

Jenn became acutely aware of the beat of her own heart —not racing exactly, but something other than normal— and she tightened her grip on the tablet in her hands. "Well, I uh...I actually just wanted to make sure everything is okay."

"Okay?"

"With Landon," she clarified. "You two seemed to be arguing earlier."

"Oh, yeah. Don't worry about that." Valentina's lips snapped shut before parting again. "Not that you *were* worried about it. We're fine. Everything's fine. Just two coworkers coworkering."

"Hmm." Jenn hummed, nodding slowly. "You should probably get to work then."

"Yes. Of course." Valentina took a step back, rubbing the nape of her neck again and then she turned on her heels, disappearing with a muttered, "See you there, Chef."

CHAPTER 7

"Three pizza quesadillas and an Italian fajita, extra guac!"

Saturday afternoons were nothing compared to the never-ending rush of Friday nights, but after last night's shift, a bit of calm had finally started to settle over Val about working at Gia. Dinner service later would be equally brutal. Still, she had every confidence she could handle it. Two weeks of relentlessly sharpening her knife skills, moments of being able to observe the different station chefs as well as a trip to the bakery had given her a bit more confidence. Landon still made it his duty to toss her a wink across the kitchen every now and then, even optioning another group outing within the last week... But as much as Val had been settling into her role as stagiaire, while garnering more attention from Jenn, this internship was kicking her ass. Between her morning runs, twelve hour shifts and trying to sync schedules with Zoe so they could do more than drone good mornings across the apartment before stumbling off to work again, she didn't have time to entertain the wooing of a guy who was definitely trying to get into her pants. Outside of work, anyway. At Gia, he had the perfect excuse to keep trying, though he claimed to understand Val was neither looking for a relationship nor a hook up, but that they could be friends.

A month ago, maybe even less, he would've been exactly the kind of distraction she would have welcomed. But some things were more important. Her dream, her—

"They're easier to chop if you keep them cold."

Val stilled her knife at the signature husk in Jenn's voice, her comment just audible amid the typical rumble of the kitchen. Cries for another order, steaming pans and grills, clinking utensils in the dish pit. Val nodded. "I try to, Chef. The lowboy helps, of course."

Jenn returned an amused hum as she eyed the under counter refrigerator, the slight movement of her lips enough to yield a glimpse of her dimples.

"Dead plate!"

Val glanced up, Jenn immediately turning as Gavin burst through the door with a single-serving beef enchilada ravioli in one hand.

"Guy claims he wanted his SOS."

Sauce on the side? Val scrunched up her face. *For ravioli?*

Jenn started toward Gavin. "Extend our apologies and let him know his meal is on the house. I need a beef enchilada ravioli, on the fly!"

"Heard that, Chef!"

It took a moment for Val to realize she'd been staring, maybe even vaguely entranced by the way Jenn commanded a room with her mere presence. Val narrowed her gaze to the parsley on her board and resumed chopping, but not for the first time, she found herself questioning Jenn's role at

Gia. It wasn't rare for owners to act as executive chefs in their restaurants, but Jenn seemed to insist on having a say in everything and assume a comparatively unimposing role all at once. She sat in the back of team meetings, but rarely ever spoke. Even in the kitchen, Mel was the one giving direction half the time. Still, they had a strange way of both being in charge and neither clashing with the other.

Val's mind flashed back to what Landon had said on Sunday by the pier. Chef OCD. Maybe if she let herself think long enough, she could understand why he'd said it. But in her two weeks at *Gia*, she'd found Jenn to be an equally enigmatic chef and person. The more glimpses she got of the latter—casually dressed on Saturday morning, with her hair pulled back in a messy ponytail, skin warm and freckled—

"Rosas!"

Val's head snapped up at the sound of Jenn's voice. Her knife slipped and a burst of pain shot through the tip of her forefinger straight to her toes. "Fuck." She clasped her free hand around it, clenching her teeth.

Jenn took a hurried step closer. "Let me see."

Valentina glanced skyward, freeing her grip slightly. Her stomach churned. She'd witnessed chef's slice into their own fingers before, but she really, really, really didn't like the blood.

Jenn's gaze narrowed to hers, her searching eyes alive with flecks of green and gold, and maybe the slightest hint of panic. Her lips parted then shut. She glanced over her shoulder. "Mel, get someone to cover Rosas! We need to take a look at this hand." She placed a hand over the one Val had clasping her injured finger, her other hand high on Val's back as she guided her toward the break room.

Landon ducked his head beneath a range, peering at

them as they rushed by, before returning watch on the smoking pan of ground beef in front of him.

Jenn pushed open the door to the break room and led Val toward the single faucet sink by the counters. "You don't need to look, but we need to get some water on it. Okay?"

Val closed her eyes, fixating on the pound of her heart, on the steadiness of Jenn's hand against her own trembling one. "Okay."

"Take a breath."

She winced at the stream of water against her finger, but admittedly it wasn't as bad as she'd expected. Her eyes fluttered open, Jenn's proximity setting in, drawing Val's gaze to the line of her neck, evenness of her complexion, Val's every breath laced with subtle hints of something floral. Herbal? Her mind had latched onto the scent of chamomile the day they'd met, when Val had tripped right into her. Now, Val wasn't so sure.

The water shut off, replaced by a towel wrapped tightly around Val's finger. Her skin prickled beneath her chef's coat, the room somehow twice as warm as when they'd entered. Jenn stepped away to pull out a chair from the nearby four-seater table. "Sit. I'll grab the first aid kit." She padded across the room in long strides and opened the leftmost top cupboard, stared inside then shut it with a grumble of, "That doesn't go there," before opening another.

Blood seeped into the towel, staining it a dark, unsettling red, but bizarre as it was, Jenn's hurried movement and slamming of cupboard doors were comforting, if not distracting. Just when Val thought she was getting the hang of this, she had to go and bleed all over the parsley and send her boss into a spiral about the tea bags being in the wrong fucking cupboard. Her mind doubled back for a second. *Shit. The parsley.*

"Here we are."

Val stood as Jenn faced her. "I need to—"

"What are you doing?"

"The parsley, I—"

"Valentina, please sit." Jenn drew out a chair in front of Val's. "I assure you, everyone out there was fully briefed on the dangers of using bloodied produce."

Val breathed a laugh, settling back into her chair. "That was funny."

Jenn grimaced. "Why would that be funny?"

"I mean—Um…Well, we all know we shouldn't—"

"Valentina, I'm kidding." A bemused smile graced her lips, her hazel eyes twinkling with just a hint of mischief.

And okay, maybe Zoe was right to be concerned when Val had told her about staging at Gia, because a not so tiny part of her would willingly lose another liter of blood if Jenn would keep looking at her like *that*.

Jenn popped open the first aid kit and pulled out what Val guessed to be a tube of antibacterial and a bandage. "Okay," she whispered, so softly Val wondered if she was meant to even hear it. Jenn gently reached for her hand, unwrapping the towel as she made eye contact with Val. "Have you always been afraid of blood?"

Val half-considered denying it. A phobia of blood in a career where people cut themselves fairly frequently was almost embarrassing, especially seated in front of someone who clearly had no qualms about it. Someone she admired. "No," she decided. "I mean, I don't think so."

Jenn examined the cut. "Keep talking."

"My best friend got hit by a car when we were eight. Could've been nine."

"Zoe?" She reached for the antibiotic.

Val tilted her head in confusion. "How do you know that?"

"I may have overheard something in the kitchen."

"Oh." She got the feeling Jenn knew a lot more than that. Was that the reason she'd asked Val about Landon on Tuesday? Did she think they were dating? Then again, half the staff thought they were dating. Val jerked at the drop of ointment on her finger. "Ouch."

"Sorry." Jenn frowned. "So, I'm assuming she got better. Zoe."

"Yeah. Just a broken leg. I guess, the image of her lying there, those minutes before the ambulance came, with her head and leg all bloody, kind of stuck with me." She didn't mention the gut-wrenching pierce of her mom's scream when she ran out and thought it had been Val who'd been hit, or the way she'd cried for an hour straight worried that her best friend would never open her eyes again, and how it would've been her fault because Zoe had never wanted to race bikes on that street in the first place.

"I'm sorry you had to see that," Jenn murmured. "I'm glad she's okay."

"Yeah. Me too."

A stillness fell over the room, steady eye-contact, Val's quickening pulse and their brushing knees between them. Val's fingers tingled with the urge to move closer, the same fingers that were—She glanced down to find her finger bandaged, her hand still cradled in Jenn's.

Jenn withdrew her hand, fingers clenching into a fist as she slid back her chair to stand. "It um—" She cleared her throat, her words only marginally less raspy as she went on. "It should be okay, but if the bleeding doesn't stop, you may need stitches."

Val's brows inched up, her heart pounding for entirely different reasons. "Stitches?"

"I'll go with you. I mean—*Someone* will go with you, if you'd like."

Val slowly got to her feet, the space between them unintentionally though pleasantly narrow enough for the tips of their Birkenstocks to touch.

Their gazes held.

Jenn took a step back. "How badly does it hurt?"

"Not too much, I guess." Val's finger throbbed, but her desire to make sense of Jenn's shift in demeanor demanded more attention. It was almost as if she was caught between standing her ground, and literally running away.

"If you're okay to finish your shift, double your gloves," Jenn instructed. "We can put you back on prep or you can spend the rest of the day observing."

"Okay."

"Come out when you're ready. I'll discuss it with Mel." She crossed the room in three long strides and disappeared behind the door.

Running away it was then.

VAL DRAGGED her feet out of the bathroom, one towel draped around her neck as she adjusted the other wrapped around her hair. The sound of Jane Fonda's voice drew her attention to *Grace and Frankie* being streamed on the TV a few paces away in the living room. Her head snapped to Zoe on the couch in readiness for her monologue on the sheer betrayal budding in her chest, before she realized it was an episode they'd already watched together. Twice. Instead, she turned toward the kitchen and made a beeline for the refrigerator, yelling, "Want anything, Zo?"

"No, I'll just have a spoon of yours."

"You don't even know what I'm getting."

Zoe picked up her phone, smirked then rapidly began tapping against the screen. "Greek yogurt topped with peaches."

Val rolled her eyes and grabbed the snack with her uninjured hand, only pausing for a spoon before crossing the living room to plop down on the sofa next to Zoe. "Whatever. You saw it prepped in the fridge."

"No." Zoe dropped her phone, shifting to grab the spoon midway to Val's mouth and slip it into her own. "You just happen to be the most spontaneous creature of habit I've ever had the good fortune of knowing. It's Saturday night—"

"2 a.m. technically makes it Sunday morning."

"And pointing that out technically makes you annoying."

Val laughed, reclaiming her spoon.

"You're wired from work, and ever since you read that article, you're convinced calcium helps you sleep better. You just happen to prefer your calcium fermented." Zoe's phone buzzed in her lap, drawing their attention to the notification on display.

New message from Warren.

Zoe palmed her phone and quickly scanned the text, her cheeks reddening by the second.

Val raised a brow at her. "Remember when you stormed into my room, insisting I better not be trying to set you up with Warren. Now, you basically have a boyfriend."

Zoe held up a hand. "We haven't had the labels talk, but speaking of Warren." She turned to Val again. "Why did I have to hear from him that you almost lost a hand today?"

Val scoffed around the perfect ratio of yogurt and peach.

Between her best friend and her parents, was she expected to be any less dramatic? "You heard before I told you because your boyfriend's a gossip."

"He's not—" Zoe's eyes narrowed to slits. "Just tell me how your hand is."

"It was only my finger, and it's fine. Barely even hurts anymore." Val stared into her bowl, aimlessly drawing shapes in the creamy white yogurt as her mind drifted back to the way Jenn had rushed toward her—all instinct and care, gentle in every touch and spoken word.

"He also told me Coleman took great care of you."

"She did." Val scooped up another bite. "I'm sure she would've done it for anyone."

"Why don't you try saying that with a little less disappointment in your tone?"

Val sighed, resisting the urge to actually pout. "Zo..."

"Jesus, Val."

"Okay, but nothing happened. I just—She looks at me so fucking softly sometimes."

"She looks at you softly?" Zoe echoed.

"Yes, Zo. Her eyes get all green and gold and glowy, and she barely even talks to us if it's not work related, but she made a joke for me today."

Zoe leaned into the backrest, glancing skyward as she shook her head. "Hot Chef was a red herring. I knew Coleman was the danger. The day you told me you got this stage. What was it you said?" She cleared her throat as if in preparation to mimic Val down to the tenor. "'*I am not jeopardizing my chances of actually working there someday just because Jenn Coleman happens to have a nice face.*'"

Val winced. "You're the worst. But okay. I hear you." She dragged in a deep breath. "Eyes on the prize."

"And the prize is?"

"Head chef of Gia in six years, by merit or mutiny."

Zoe grinned. "Welcome back, old friend."

Val chuckled, giving Zoe a playful shove. "Let's just watch some TV." Winding down after a long shift had always been hard, but one episode was usually enough for the exhaustion to set in, and for her to get some rest. They still had work later. Val still had a job to earn, no matter how distractingly beautiful, caring or enigmatic Jenn Coleman happened to be.

CHAPTER 8

Jenn gave the July budget a quick once-over on her laptop, checking for anything that immediately stood out.

"We do have the website domain fee coming up, so that's in there," Mel pointed out as she followed on her tablet. "There's also the order of new linens for private dining 2, and the service provider for the POS software notified us that the cost of the subscription would be increased from $390 to $400."

"Right." Jenn nodded. "They sent an email."

"Mhm."

"What about the microwave in the break room?"

Mel shook her head, her ginger curls bouncing with the motion. "Still doing that weird, flickering thing."

"It's already been repaired twice. Let's start looking at quotes for a new one." Jenn's phone began vibrating in her pocket, and she absentmindedly reached in to grab it.

"Sounds good to me."

A picture of Tommy stared up at her, the screen of her

phone lit up with an incoming FaceTime call. "Actually, Mel, can we finish this in a few? It's my son."

"Sure thing, boss. Lucky for you, yours is old enough to know he can't just call whenever the sitter won't let him play ten more minutes of video games."

Jenn laughed, "Yeah, I'm not so sure," sliding her thumb across the screen as Mel made her way out. "Hey, T."

"Mom, you've got to talk to Mama about her new girlfriend." His hair, which he'd been so kind to inform her was a high-top fade, had grown at least an inch since she'd last seen him, though his razor-sharp hairline and the wavy part curving toward the back of his head signaled a fresh haircut.

"Hello to you, too, Son." Jenn reclined in her chair, preparing for the rant she knew was coming. If Tommy was any indication, thirteen-year-olds were always singing the end of the world was near.

Tommy grinned, his gleaming honey-colored eyes a mirror of Rachel's. "Hey, Mom. How's your day going? You sleeping enough?"

"Yes, and I know you're used to your mom monitoring my waking hours, but that is not your job."

"Well, someone's got to do it." He shook his head, mumbling, "Especially since she's all distracted with Luna now. What kind of name is Luna anyway?"

"You better not be giving that woman a hard time. Your mom is allowed to date whoever she'd like."

"Can she date someone who doesn't want to convince me jackfruit can taste like chicken? Because I like jackfruit, I do, but it's not freaking chicken. And cheese! She's trying to take away cheese, Mom."

"Slow down. Veganism is a respectable lifestyle choice that you do not have to adopt."

"Who's going to tell her that?" His brows rose, his stare direct in a way that Jenn couldn't help but find amusing. "Because I just saw the grocery list and it's wild."

"Tommy, I love you. I will do absolutely anything for you, including buying your personal grocery list—"

He opened his mouth to speak.

Jenn cut him off with a raised finger. "If it's within reason. What I will not do is interfere in your mom's relationship unless…" She trailed off, eyes in search of an answer she already knew wouldn't emerge among the bare white walls of her office. "Unless Luna is a danger to you."

"That's what I'm saying, Mom. She *is* a danger to me."

"Boy, give me that phone." Rachel stepped into frame, skin ever a radiant umber, braided cornrows wrapped in a neat bun.

Tommy sucked his teeth, standing from a bar stool situated by the island counters Jenn recognized from their home in the Financial District.

Rachel slid onto the now unoccupied stool, holding the phone up to her face. "I think he takes after you with the drama."

"Sure." Jenn smiled. "We'll go with that."

Rachel glanced over her shoulder with feigned impatience—the twitch of her lips giving away how much she enjoyed poking at Tommy this way. "Can you excuse me? I need to talk to your mom in private."

"That's my phone," he argued.

"Yeah, well I paid for it."

Something like a grunt echoed out of frame, then a grumbled, "Man," before Rachel faced Jenn again, beaming with victory. Just like a big kid sometimes.

"Well," Jenn started. "Actually, *I* paid for that phone."

"Same difference."

Jenn breathed a laugh. "Sounds like things with Luna are going well. She's influencing your grocery list now? Must be serious."

"She's been spending more time here. It only makes sense for us to buy things she eats. Nobody is trying to take away the boy's damn cheese."

"Good. Because I'm not sure the Italian part of me is fully in agreement. Even if more and more studies argue a non-dairy lifestyle is better for us. Give me some time to evolve."

"I don't know," Rachel countered, still smiling. "You're pretty stuck in your ways."

Jenn knew she didn't mean it as a jab at her, but somehow her brain had processed it that way. Change didn't come easily. She took comfort in routine, structure, things she could rely on. How could she have any of that if things were ever changing?

"You have a doctor's appointment this week?" Rachel drew her back.

"Are you spying on me?"

"It's on the shared calendar."

"Right." Sometimes, Jenn wondered why they'd kept it all this time. They didn't need a shared calendar to co-parent a teenager. They communicated well enough, made sure they both attended the important events. Soccer and water polo games. Award ceremonies. Parent-teacher conferences. Yet, moments like these, Jenn *was* grateful they still had it, moments when Rachel, being Rachel, would mention something that had been on Jenn's mind but Jenn would never have brought up on her own. "My GP recommended a specialist. I found.... I don't know. *Something*. In my right breast."

Rachel's expression turned somber. "Do you want me to come?"

Jenn shook her head. "It's okay. I did some reading. It's probably nothing."

Rachel nodded, her eyes knowing, understanding Jenn was terrified because her mother had spent countless visits with specialists and surgeons and still hadn't lived to see her sixtieth birthday. "Well, you know where to find me if you change your mind. I'll be there, no questions asked."

"I know." A moment passed, Jenn desperately needing a change of subject. She was at work. There was no room for all the things she felt about this at work. She tried not to think about how maybe that's the reason she spent so much time there. "I could talk to Tommy about coming to stay with me for the summer. So you and Luna could probably have the house to yourself a bit more."

"Are you trying to manage our son so I can have more sex with my girlfriend?"

"Mom!" Tommy's voice rang out.

Rachel rolled her eyes. "That's what you get for listening."

Jenn laughed, shaking her head. "I bet he's gone now."

"Mhm."

"But really," she picked up. "If you want to, he can come. I miss him."

"You miss the theatrics?" Rachel goaded. "Of course, you can take him for the summer."

"Perfect. I'll talk to him."

"But, Jenn…" Rachel paused, gaze direct in the only way she knew how, especially when she had something meaningful to say. "I don't want him alone all the time."

A knock on Jenn's door drew her attention, and she looked

up to see Valentina stick her head in. Her brows furrowed, her focus momentarily caught between reverting to the conversation on her phone, or staying with her unexpected visitor. But her body led on instinct, pushing out of the chair as her lips parted to ask, "What can I do for you, Valentina?"

"Sorry, I can come back."

"Um." Jenn swallowed, glancing down at her phone. At Rachel.

"It's okay." Rachel waved a hand. "I have a team meeting in five anyway. Call me later."

"Of course," Jenn confirmed, eyes drifting back to Valentina's.

"Love you."

"Love you, too." The words tumbled from her lips with the same reflex as always—a bizarre sort of declaration between exes, but one that wasn't even remotely romantic anymore. She brought her thumb to the power button and slipped the phone back into her pocket, waving Valentina in. "Is everything okay?"

"Yeah, no—I um—" Valentina raked a hand through her hair, the settle of the waves across her shoulders only mildly distracting. "I'm sorry. I really can come back."

"Valentina." Jenn smiled. "Please. You're already here. How can I help?"

"I was just..." She took a few steps forward, but stopped within reasonable distance, giving Jenn adequate personal space.

Jenn tried not to think about why she found that somewhat disappointing.

"I wanted to ask if there was any way I could probably come in earlier for a few days. Practice a bit. I know you wouldn't have time to oversee something like that, and I'll take my own supplies. I won't damage anything, I swear. I just—"

Jenn frowned, moving closer, but stopping within reasonable distance herself. Albeit, less reasonable. "Valentina, what's wrong?"

"I don't feel like I've lived up to my true potential here. And I hear how that sounds. I'd just hate to screw up my chance at being offered my dream job in two weeks because I keep doing things like trying to serve my finger in the garnish."

Jenn's expression softened. *Dream job?*

"What I'm trying to say is, I'll work harder. Faster. Better. I'm only asking for a chance to do it."

"You're too hard on yourself." Jenn breathed in, ignoring the delicate traces of shea in the air as she leaned against the edge of her desk. "You wouldn't still be here if I didn't think you were cut out for this. That being said, if you do want to come in earlier, I'll allow it. See you at nine on Tuesday."

"Wait, um…" Valentina shook her head, her lips pursed before parting. "Like, you'll be here?"

"The summer stage at Gia, San Francisco, is a chance to work with Jenn Coleman." Jenn grinned, raising a forefinger to point at her own face. "Jenn Coleman."

Valentina's chuckle warmed Jenn from her chest to the tips of her fingers in the most captivating though treacherous way.

"Thank you, Chef." She started in backward steps toward the door, her eyes locked on Jenn until she added, "I won't let you down."

"I know you won't. And Valentina…"

She paused, one hand on the door as she glanced over her shoulder.

"You *can* call me Jenn. This isn't the Institute."

Her expression turned considering, and something indecipherable glittered in her darkened gaze. "Got it." She chewed on her bottom lip. "Jenn."

CHAPTER 9

*V*al grounded herself in the beat of her own heart as Jenn stepped closer, clouding Val's thoughts with her proximity, the fragrance of her skin, aromatic and heady and distracting in ways that were beginning to make Val think coming into Gia a full three hours early was a very bad idea. Not intrinsically, of course. Extra practice in the foremost impressive kitchen Val had ever had the pleasure of standing in, let alone working in, was meant to help her—her confidence, her skill, at the very least make her feel even marginally more comfortable about where she'd stand next week once they'd reviewed her progress as a stage.

But *this*...This was beginning to feel dangerously similar to just letting Sophie Sanders sit in her lap at sophomore spring fling, even though there had been a perfectly empty chair right next to them, "because girls do it all the time". Never mind that Sophie—pre lip fillers—looked like the girl of Val's dreams, and Val had only narrowly escaped becoming a teenage heart attack statistic.

Jenn tapped the knuckles of Val's knife hand with the tips of her fingers. "See? The way you're holding the knife now is perfect," she rasped out in a tenor that seemed to be meant only for Val.

Val kept her gaze trained on the leaf of the green onion lying in front of her. At this rate, they'd never get done with the damn taco lasagna, and she'd only barely survived the Sophie Sanders incident to have a do-over more than ten years later. Was mooning over a beautiful, kind, woman of color who'd found iconic success in an industry dominated by white men any more respectable?

She closed her eyes, willing the words "healthy admiration" into her subconscious.

"You know why you cut yourself on Sunday?"

Her eyes snapped open, her hand tingling where Jenn's fingers still touched—long, delicate fingers, ending in manicured, clear polished nails. "You yelled at me and my mind flashed back to teachers in middle school?"

A breathy chuckle resonated close to Val's ear. "So you were *that* student?"

"Some days."

"So you'll need a firm hand then."

A gulp slid down Val's throat. That was a joke. She'd spent enough one-on-one time with Jenn to know, despite what the likes of Landon thought, Jenn was perfectly capable of making them. Which was nice. Really. She liked being able to see a part of Jenn not everyone had. But Jenn wasn't just some unsociable coworker. She was her boss—she signed Val's paychecks in every sense of the term. How could she politely ask her *boss* not to say anything her brain might misconstrue as being remotely sexual?

"You've been doing a good job," Jenn spoke again. "That's what I yelled to say on Sunday. Good job. But this…" She took Val's forefinger and extended it to rest atop the blade of the knife then reached for the hand Val had on the green onions, gently untucking her fingers from the typical claw shape she employed for chopping. "You can't do that. You get sloppy when you're fatigued, but you can't afford to. And you can't get jumpy in a place where people are constantly yelling. That's why you hurt yourself."

The words hit like a log in Val's stomach. She knew better. She just wasn't used to twelve-hour shifts spent slicing, dicing, chopping hundreds of pounds of produce. And it had taken probably the one person she wanted to impress to notice a flaw in her technique. But the easy, perhaps even tender, way Jenn had said it left very little sting to the admonishment, left it hardly feeling like an admonishment at all.

Jenn retreated, putting some space between them. "Keep going."

Val made quick work of the onion before reaching for a red jalapeño and casting a furtive glance toward Jenn. "So, why Italian and Mexican?"

Jenn's brows crept up, her glowing hazel eyes following the motion. "Well, my mom never cooked much, but my father was Italian. *Is* Italian. Due to circumstances out of my control, I didn't meet my nonna—his mother—until I was fourteen, but she insisted I come spend the summer with her in Florence and I just kept going back every year after. My formal instructors will beg to differ, but she taught me everything I know. It's why I named this place after her."

Val put the garnishes aside, reaching for the nearby glass bowl and tub of ricotta.

"Add the sour cream and eggs too," Jenn instructed.

"Mhm." Val peered up at her. "And the Mexican?"

"After I finished culinary school and came back to the states, my mom and I started traveling together. It was something she always wanted to do when I was younger. She never really got to, though. Single, black mom working a mid-level job. As soon as I could, I took her wherever she wanted to go."

Val stared, captivated by everything from the wistful tone of Jenn's voice to the faraway look in her eyes. So distractingly beautiful simply standing there, with her hair messily caught in a bun, nose dusted with freckles, dressed in a simple button down with the sleeves neatly rolled up to her forearms.

A soft, humorless laugh resonated from her. "Mexico." Then, she turned and looked at Val, lips tugged in a frown, brows furrowed almost as if she wasn't sure why she'd told Val any of that. "You mentioned you were from a big Mexican family."

An expert redirect, if Val had ever heard one. She nodded anyway. "I am. The kind where a 'small gathering'" —she poised her fingers for air quotations—"includes aunts, uncles, all the cousins and abuela's friends from church."

"So, you know all about the food?" Jenn asked, her dimples a welcomed sight. "Have you been secretly analyzing my recipes for inauthenticities?"

Val tossed her head back in a laugh. "You got me. I'm actually planning an exposé as we speak. How renowned fusion restaurant Gia is the Taco Bell of fine dining."

"I knew it." Jenn sighed dramatically. "And all this about practice. It's just to get in my good graces and make me spill all my deepest secrets."

"Only the ones you're willing to share." It came out with a sincerity that had caught Val herself off guard. But because she was Valentina, because she literally couldn't help herself, she doubled down with, "I'm actually pretty good at keeping secrets."

Was it in her mind, or did Jenn's eyes seem glossier somehow? Jenn's lips parted almost imperceptibly, but Val's gaze caught the motion and latched on. Soft, full lips that left Val wondering about the steady rise and fall of Jenn's chest, left her wondering what would happen if she leaned in, brought her hand to the back of Jenn's neck and just—

"Valentina..."

Especially when Jenn said her name like a warning—all breathy and raspy.

"Valentina, your phone," Jenn whispered.

Val blinked, eyes meeting Jenn's decidedly darkened gaze. "Sorry, what?"

"I think your phone is ringing."

Val glanced across the room, frowning at the table where she'd left her bag upon entering the kitchen and finding Jenn already there. Heat flooded her blood stream. Had she actually thought that Jenn saw her as anything more than an ogling weirdo, that Jenn *felt*... God, anything? *Qué fucking oso*. She started across the kitchen toward her bag. "Sorry. Let me just turn it off."

"Sure."

The buzzing stopped then started up again. Val dug through her rucksack and came up with her phone, the screen lit up with a FaceTime call from *Mami*. *Shit*.

"You should take it," Jenn offered.

Val quickly shook her head. "It's just my—I can call back."

"They called twice. It's probably important." Jenn moved toward the door. "I'll give you some privacy."

"No. Please. Stay." Val sighed. "It's my mom."

"Then you should definitely take it. Don't worry. You're not on shift, and I really don't mind."

"Really?"

Jenn nodded, both her brows raised. "Yes, Valentina."

"Thank you," Val breathed out. "I'll make it quick, I promise." Dropping her gaze to her phone, she swiped her thumb across the screen in answer. The image of her mom and dad seated shoulder to shoulder, almost smushed together to fit in the frame, instantly tugged a smile from her, especially when her mom smiled and said, "Hola, cariño."

Val warmed at the sight of them, the heavy lilt of accents they'd never lost even after years of living in Brooklyn before returning to Mexico. "Hola hola."

"It's been three days," her dad started. "You haven't called to let us know you're alive, or if you've been kidnapped."

Val's eyes rolled. "And you say I'm the dramatic one."

"You are, but where do you think it comes from?" her mom chimed in.

"Right." Val nodded, instinctively casting a furtive look at Jenn—her back now turned to Val as she paid keen attention to the spread of ingredients on the counter, the same ingredients which had excited Val the minute Jenn mentioned they'd be making something from the Gia menu. That had left her with a buzz still coursing through her veins in an entirely different way than being alone with Jenn hours before anyone would likely show up. *If only...*

"That doesn't look like your apartment."

Val fixed her eyes on her parents again, her mother frowning, lines drawn along her faintly wrinkled forehead.

"Are you at the restaurant already? At this hour."

"Mami—"

"¿Cómo vas a darnos nietos si siempre estás trabajando?"

"Mami, ahora no es el momento," Val argued. Seriously?

Now was when her mom wanted to do this? She hit the volume down button three times, gaze flitting across the room again, though Jenn gave no indication she'd understood her mother's words.

"At least, give us a tour of your fancy kitchen," her dad put in. "Is it everything you dreamed?"

"Yes, Papa, but later."

"Ay, cariño. How will we see? You never call when you're working."

A clink of utensils drew her attention toward Jenn, who turned to mouth an earnest, "Sorry," before facing the counter. Val tugged her bottom lip between her teeth, biting down on a smile. There was something oddly assuaging about the moment—something that didn't spell mentor and apprentice, almost as if they'd done this before and would do it again.

"Are people there with you? Let us meet your coworkers."

Val sighed. "There's no one here."

"Then who do you keep looking at?" her mom insisted.

Relentless, the pair of them. "It's not a good time, okay?"

"Vale—"

"Es mi jefa, okay!"

"Tu jefa?" Their eyes widened, lighting up like a pair of cartoon characters.

"We must say hello to the woman who has made our only daughter's dream come true. It's only right."

"Papa, no."

"Valentina—"

Her head snapped up at the sound of Jenn's voice, her heart racing all over again, especially when Jenn's eyes glinted—all fiery hazel—and she pursed her lips, simultaneously hinting at a smile and burying one. "It's okay. I'll say hello."

"No, Jenn, you really don't have to."

Jenn started toward her, gait fully resolute. Val waited for her steps to slow within inches of her, for Jenn to stop and wait to be offered Val's phone. She didn't count on Jenn sidling up next to her instead—close enough for the tips of loose strands of her hair to brush Val's shoulders, for her smell to creep into Val's every breath and leave an imprint on her mind, especially when she leaned closer and said, "Hi, Mr. and Mrs. Rosas."

"Que bonita!"

Val snapped back to the screen, scolding, "Mama!"

Jenn beamed, muttered a gentle, "It's okay," to Val then redirected to her parents. "Gracias. Ha sido un placer tener a Valentina con nosotros en Gia. Tiene un futuro brillante en el mundo culinario."

Val's eyes widened at the slew of words rolling off Jenn's tongue and she tried not to scoff. Of course Jenn spoke Spanish, because why the hell not? Val didn't know whether to be amazed by it, or completely embarrassed that not five minutes ago Jenn had been in the same room to witness Val's parents ask when they'd be getting grandchildren. As the moment passed, though, her parents and Jenn engaged in full dialogue about where she'd learned to speak the language so well and how grateful they were Val had been selected for the internship, pure amazement took over. And all she could do was stare—the kind of lost, helpless staring that confirmed everything she already knew.

This was so, so fucking bad.

CHAPTER 10

Jenn rested her head against the steering wheel of her car, her nine and three grips excruciatingly tight. The wave of nausea rising in her stomach had lingered the whole twenty-minute drive from the doctor's office back to Gia—cresting and crashing in an emetic cycle. Somehow, she felt numb with the dread of coming weeks, and inexplicably, regrettably, like she could burst into tears at the most inconsequential news. The recollection of the last time she'd cried—her mother's funeral—loitered in the back of her mind. But she was determined to keep it there. Safe, cherished, agonizing.

"Fibrocystic breast disease." A memory of Doctor O'Connell's pale, wizened face flashed behind her eyes, his voice a taunting echo. Low. Steady. "We'll have to do some tests to make sure the fluid isn't cancerous. Once we have your results, we'll decide next steps."

Logically, Doctor O'Connell's diagnosis had been a good, if common, one. It meant more frequent testing, more caution. But hadn't she known this was coming? Someone with her family history. Then again, wasn't that precisely why her chest had caved in, mind clouded with fear, the second the lump had materialized beneath her fingers.

Cyst, she reminded herself. She closed her eyes, grounding herself in the facts. Multiple microcysts in both breasts. One larger in the right—the one she'd felt. Four centimeters. None of this meant anything. Not without the test results. And even so, they'd caught it early. She'd caught it early.

Doctor O'Connell's voice reverberated in her head. *"Cancerous..."*

"Not cancerous," she mumbled. Her breaths grew shorter, the imaginary vise on her chest barbed and insistent. Why hadn't she let Rachel go with her? Rachel had been there for her with her mom. Rachel would know what to do now. Her hand shot out for the phone on the passenger seat, her grip tight despite her sweat dampened palm. The screen lit up. She paused. *12:13 p.m.* Middle of the day. Rachel would be stuck in a meeting, or elbows-deep in one of those process developments. Jenn couldn't pull her away. For what? The *possibility* of cancer? Not even the disease itself.

She closed her eyes, making a conscious effort to deepen her breaths and put her thoughts somewhere else. Lunch service had just about started. She needed to go in, coordinate with the staff. She shook her head. Mel would've taken care of it. They'd discussed that she'd take care of it when Jenn told her and Avery she might be in late.

A knock jerked her out of her fruitless take on meditating, and Valentina's face emerged on the outside of the passenger side window. "Jenn?"

A shallow, ragged exhale left Jenn's lips, and she looked away, forcing a gulp against the tension in her throat. Staff couldn't see her like this. Valentina was her staff—a stage at that, who was at Gia because she looked up to Jenn as a pinnacle in the culinary world, not someone who sat zoned out in her car after a bit of not-so-bad news, shirking her responsibilities. Valentina, who frightened and fascinated Jenn in the most unexpected ways, who she'd spent the last two mornings mentoring, getting to know and showing parts of herself she'd never been driven to expose to any other staff. But not this. She didn't get to see Jenn like *this*.

"Jenn?" Her voice resonated softer, barely audible over the zoom of cars on their street.

Jenn closed her eyes. "Not now—I can't—You can't."

A soft pop caught her attention, and her eyes flew open to find Valentina cautiously slipping into the passenger seat. "I'm just going to sit."

"Vale—" The rest died in her throat.

"It's okay." Valentina shook her head. "Just breathe." She dragged in a deliberate breath, nodding encouragingly, willing Jenn to take one, too.

Jenn's eyes followed the rise and fall of her chest, the motion placating, though Jenn's body remained tense with resistance.

"Can I take this?" Her hand crept toward Jenn's, Jenn's phone still fisted in her grip. "Do you need to call someone?"

An ardent head shake was all Jenn could manage.

"What if you just hold my hand instead? Squeeze as tight as you need to."

Jenn looked her in the eyes, anchoring herself in the touch of their fingers, in her gradually evening pulse. "Okay." In ten minutes or so, she would regret every second of how vulnerable she must look to Valentina like this, how it would alter Valentina's...*respect* for her? She'd trained herself very early on to not obsess too much over people's opinions of her—it had done wonders for her through high school, being a bookish misanthrope, who spent her Friday nights in the kitchen rather than out with friends. It did wonders for her even now. She had a good rapport with her staff, but she'd heard at least one mention of the words "Chef OCD" to know their image of her was hardly flawless. She just couldn't afford to care. Then, an intern trips into her with faltering grace, patient eyes and a zeal for everything, especially a future in the kitchen, and God help her, she cared too much.

"Are you okay doesn't seem appropriate right now," whispered Valentina.

"I *am* okay," Jenn muttered perhaps a little too firmly. Valentina's hand still clutched in hers suggested otherwise, but... minor details.

"You were having a panic attack."

Jenn gritted her teeth. She'd never liked that term, what it implied, especially after, when her thoughts had settled enough for her to reason that her reaction had been completely unreasonable. Unwarranted. Dramatic.

"Hey." Valentina gently tugged on her hand, waiting for their eyes to meet. "There is nothing wrong with that. You know that, right?"

"I know." Jenn would certainly never judge anyone else for having one. But this was different.

Valentina's brows drew together, and she tilted her head to maintain eye contact. "Has it happened before?"

"Yes." Once or twice a year for almost twenty years seemed like too much information.

"Do you want to talk about it?"

"I don't."

"Do you want to talk about what brought it on?"

"I can't, Valentina."

"Okay." She paused, her mind seemingly at work with something else to say, some way to make it better. "Is there anything I can do? Would you like me to just stay here?"

The questions hung between them, Jenn absentmindedly brushing her thumb over Valentina's knuckles, memorizing the shade of brown Valentina's eyes attained in the glow of daylight. The word, *Yes* lingered on the tip of her tongue. *Yes, please, stay. Yes.* But she withdrew her hand with aching reluctance, and she sat upright. "No. Thank you, but no. You should go in. You're late anyway."

Valentina nodded slowly, pursing her lips as she reached for the handle of the door. "Just..." She glanced back at Jenn, one foot already out. "Talk to someone, okay? Mel or Avery or your girlfriend. Just...someone. It helps." The door slammed shut behind her.

Jenn watched her stride up the inclined sidewalk where she disappeared down the alley toward the staff entrance. *Girlfriend?* Where in the world had she gotten the idea that Jenn had a girlfriend? Had that been part of the grapevine she'd been exposed to by Landon? Someone else?

Jenn sighed, dropping her head against the headrest of her seat. It didn't matter where she'd heard it. Deep down, Jenn knew she was right. Sitting here in her car, ruminating over Doctor O'Connell's words wouldn't change anything. At worst, it would lead straight to another...spiral. But for the first time, working didn't seem like a suitable remedy, or distraction. She wasn't at her best like this—Gia deserved her best. Spending twelve hours with Valentina within reach —her hand which had just been in Jenn's, as soft and soothing as her tone and eyes—surely wouldn't help either. And it wasn't like Jenn would spontaneously pull her to the darkest corner of the restaurant so they could just *be* for a moment, but she didn't trust herself to not *want* to.

All she wanted was to just *be* for an hour. Maybe two.

Her phone chimed with an incoming notification, and she glanced down to see the screen aglow with a text.

Rachel (12:29 p.m.)
How'd it go?

Jenn contemplated her answer. There was no reason to worry Rachel until she knew definitively there was something to worry about, and even then... She knew Rachel. She would drop everything to obsess over caring for Jenn, just when she was moving on, just when she'd found someone who made her happy again.

Jenn tapped out a quick response.

Jenn (12:30 p.m.)
Good.
I'm actually on my way there to pick up Tommy for lunch.

A second chime alerted her to another text—indubitably Rachel's response—but she'd already started her engine, ready to make her way there.

IF THERE WAS one thing Jenn missed about the high-rise condo she used to share with Rachel, it was the view—being completely drawn in by the enormity of natural light and the skyline, never mind the striking span of the Golden Gate Bridge against a backdrop of the Pacific.

"I always knew those bay windows were why you caved on buying this place," Rachel murmured.

Jenn shifted further into the corner of their all-white sectional—*Rachel's* all-white sectional—and squeezed a throw pillow tighter to her chest. "That, and the rain showerhead had surprisingly good water pressure."

A full-bodied, hearty laugh filled the air as Rachel tossed her head back. "You and that damn showerhead. How you grilled the poor realtor."

"Good water pressure is important," Jenn deadpanned, her lips twitching with a smile.

"Sure, Jenn." Rachel hummed contentedly, staring off as if the memory lurked beyond the chaise across the living room. When she faced Jenn again, her expression had grown slightly more solemn. "Are you going to tell me how the appointment really went?"

"Well." Jenn nodded. "It went well."

"So well that you're here for an impromptu lunch date with our son, instead of back at Gia?"

"I've been a little distracted at work lately." The sensations came back with visceral force—the security of Valentina's hands in hers earlier in the car, even a few days ago when Valentina cut herself, the intensity in her deep brown eyes when she looked at Jenn sometimes, as if she knew Jenn was more than a little taken by her. Helplessly, uncomfortably taken by her. "Besides"—Jenn cleared her throat—"like I told you, I miss him."

"I know you do, but that's never stopped you from working yourself to the bone before."

This was the thing about having had Rachel in her life for almost fourteen years. For better or worse, she knew Jenn like no one else, except maybe Nonna. No. Not even Nonna. And yet, for reasons she couldn't explain, Jenn found herself saying, "People change."

"But not you, Jenn. It's one of the wonderful things about you. How amazingly consistent you are. Dutiful, diligent, loyal, but also incredibly stubborn."

"What's your point, Rach?"

"Being here in the middle of the day isn't like you, especially when you think you're the only person who can keep that place together after you basically hand-held all your staff through training."

"Rachel..."

"Hey, Moms."

Jenn's head snapped up at Tommy's greeting. Was it her, or had his voice deepened just a bit since they'd last talked three days ago? He crossed the living room—garbed in a navy, floral shirt, buttons done all the way to his collar, and a pair of shorts. Jenn smiled down at his bare feet as he plopped down on the sofa between them. Never could get him into the habit of wearing house slippers. "Are you coming out for lunch without your shoes?"

He raised a thick brow at her. "*Are we* going for lunch? You and Mama have been whispering in here for like fifteen minutes."

Rachel rolled her eyes. "One day you're going to eavesdrop something so traumatic to that tiny adolescent brain of yours."

"My brain isn't tiny, and I already overheard the..." He scrunched up his face, wiggling his torso as if hit by an actual chill down his spine. "*Plans* you have with Luna once I've gone to Mom's."

Jenn sputtered a laugh, reaching to slap him lightly on the back of his head. "Watch it."

"Okay, okay," he drawled. "Really, though, Mom..." He narrowed his eyes to Jenn's, brows drawn together. "Did your doctor thing go okay? I know you want to protect Mama, but I can take it, I swear."

Jenn's eyes flitted to Rachel's briefly and they shared a knowing smile. Their wonderfully sensitive, growing-up-too-fast, thirteen-year-old. Always convinced he needed to care for them in one way or another, that he was the 'man of the house'. She met his gaze, never capable of lying to him. "I have to take a precautionary test to be sure, but Doctor O'Connell doesn't think there's anything to be concerned about. And if there ever is, you two will be the first to know, yes?"

"Cool." He bobbed his head in earnest then looked away almost to suggest he was never worried in the first place.

Teenagers.

"I just have one more question."

Jenn's mouth twitched with amusement. "Yes?"

"When I'm staying with you...Mav can still come over, right?"

"Of course. Maverick can come over whenever you'd like so long as you two don't try to light the firepit on your own again."

Tommy tsked. "Yeah. Sorry, Mom."

"It's okay," she reassured. The glare she'd shot the pair of them that faithful January night probably had Maverick convinced he was never welcome back, but she'd never try to stand between Tommy and his best friend over a single act of stupidity.

Rachel nudged him on the arm. "Go put on your shoes."

They both watched him out of the living room and up the stairs. Jenn squeezed her cushion, bracing for Rachel's resumption of their earlier conversation. "He's really looking forward to spending more time with you this summer, Jenn. Don't show up, randomly dragging him off to lunch because you had a bad day, then go back to working fourteen-hour days when everything's good again."

Jenn clenched her jaw, letting the words set in. She understood. Really. And yet, "You act like I was never there for him. For you. And you may have carried him inside you, Rach, but I love him just as much. I'm not someone you need to protect him from."

"I'm not—" She shook her head, shuffling closer before grabbing Jenn's hand. "I know you would die for that boy, Jenn. I'm saying this because you *were* there for him. Always. But you work—"

"Rach—"

"Look at me. Your mom died and you threw yourself into Gia, and I know why you needed to do that. I know why you still do. I just don't want him alone all the time."

Like I was, Jenn thought. Her mom worked a lot—more circumstance than choice—and Jenn had grown into a socially-awkward control freak. Did Rachel really think a few nights alone would doom their son to the same fate? Did she think Jenn *wanted* that?

Jenn closed her eyes, dragging in a slow breath, never really one to act on impulse and spill all her feelings because they'd gotten hurt. When she opened her eyes to the familiar warmth and judgement of Rachel's, she tried to remind herself for the hundredth time that Rachel wasn't saying any of this from a place of malice. If anything, she'd always been fiercely protective and Jenn always a bit too difficult to understand. "I know, Rach. Today, it's just tacos from the food truck he likes down by the beach, gelato and a talk. See if he'll tell me any more about soccer camp, or Maverick, or that girl you say he's been texting. But...I *will* drop by the restaurant later to take care of a few things then take the weekend off. Okay?"

"Okay," Rachel answered softly.

Jenn placed the pillow at the center of the sofa and got to her feet. It couldn't have been more than twenty minutes since she'd been seated there, but she'd had her fill of heavy discussions with Rachel—sometimes it was as if they'd never broken up. *'Talk to someone, okay?'* Valentina's voice echoed in her mind. Was Rachel who she'd meant when she mentioned Jenn having a girlfriend? How would she have even known about Rachel? Jenn didn't mind the kitchen staff describing every detail of their personal life on shift—it kept them going through rushes and fatigue—but she liked to keep her personal life, well, personal. And somehow, she minded that wherever Valentina had been getting her information wasn't from her, that Valentina hadn't just come to her directly to…to what? Ask if she had a girlfriend.

Jesus, Jenn. You really are spiraling.

"Jenn?"

Jenn blinked. "You sure you're okay?"

"Yes. Of course." She waved off the implication.

"Let's go, Mom." Tommy punctuated his entrance by jumping the last two steps and finding the landing with an overstated thud, now dressed in a pair of sneakers he had talked one or the other of them into buying at a ridiculous price. "El Gallo's tacos wait for no man. Or woman. Or enby."

Just like that, her lips had tugged into another smile. "Come on, Mr. Philosophical." She shook her head, wrapping one arm around his shoulders only for him to flinch away, patting the back of his hair.

"Watch the fade, Mom."

CHAPTER 11

Val tapped her fingers against the ceramic counters in the main women's room at Gia. Her eyes burned, despite having closed them two minutes ago. Could've been five—she always developed an abysmal conception of time halfway through dinner service on Friday nights, though she was utterly in love with the rush of it. Sometime next week, she'd get word on whether she'd gotten the job, if she'd be allowed to stay at Gia on a more permanent basis. Yet, the fate of her future had only marginally occupied her thoughts all shift.

Jenn hadn't come in. Val had all but talked her through a panic attack earlier—seen her more scared, vulnerable, *human* than she'd ever imagined—and Jenn hadn't walked in twenty minutes, or even three hours later. She hadn't spent the shift organizing and traying up dishes at the expo window, making sure things were in perfect order, or dropping by prep just to correct, or compliment Val's knife skills, or simply make sure everything was okay. Although, very few things were *okay* when Jenn stood as close as she'd taken to doing, held eye contact a bit too long before hurriedly looking away. But just when Val had given up that Jenn would come in at all today, she'd strolled through the kitchen, mumbling good nights followed by a terse request of, "Mel, can I see you for a minute?" without a single glance in Val's direction. She hadn't come out with her checklist for closing either, but the navy X6 parked in the side alley when Val had taken the trash out confirmed she was probably still locked in her office. Had Val done or said something wrong earlier in the car? Was Jenn not okay? Both?

"Val!"

She startled, her eyes springing open at the bang on the door that followed.

"You good in there?" Landon called.

"Uh, yeah. I just…" she trailed off, narrowing her gaze to her own reflection, ruminating for the tenth time on the reason she'd been in the bathroom for well over the five minutes it had taken to change out of her whites. "You guys go ahead. I'm not—I don't feel well."

Did jonesing for a quick one on one with her boss classify as not feeling well?

Yes.

Absolutely.

"Do you need me to take you home?"

"No. I drove my car. I'm good. Just…" She shook her head, brows furrowed as she wracked her brain for something to say. "Have an extra shot for me!"

"Uh, you sure? I could just take you home if you're feeling sick."

"I think it's my period."

A beat of silence passed.

"Oh," Landon uttered.

Val exchanged an amused eye roll with her reflection.

Men. "It's really not a big deal. Go have fun. I'll catch up with you guys tomorrow."

"Yeah. Yeah, okay." The soft shuffle of feet sounded beyond the door, then, "Feel better, okay?"

"Thanks, Lan."

Val listened until his footsteps disappeared down the quiet hallway, a sliver of guilt cropping up in the back of her mind for blowing off not just Landon, but Warren and Zoe, too. She reached for her phone and shot Zoe a quick text that she wasn't coming out, but she'd explain at home. It wasn't like they didn't both know Landon kept devising these group outings because Val had refused to go out with him just the two of them. Besides, getting drunk at nearly 2 a.m. when they all had work the next morning was a decidedly terrible idea. One that would leave Val walking back into Gia later feeling like her abuela's shabby, five-year-old chanclas.

Her phone buzzed with an incoming text.

Zoe (1:03 a.m.)
Ugh. Thank God.
I feel like shit. I'll call War and tell him I can't come out either.
See you at home.
PS. I have leftover gelato paninis.

Val typed out a quick reply.

Val (1:03 a.m.)
You're a goddess.
Be home soon.

She slipped the phone back into her pocket and glanced up at the mirror. Should she be concerned that her hair looked like a child had swept it into a ponytail? Or maybe the bags under her eyes warranted more attention.

Jesus, Val. It's just a check-in.

She swept a few loose strands of hair behind both ears in one swift motion and started toward the door. At this rate, Jenn had probably left already, and Val had wasted all her time in the bathroom obsessing over nothing. Not that that would be the worst thing when her plan pretty much consisted of knocking on Jenn's door and being like, *Hey, just wondering if you're okay? Crisis averted and all that?* If she knew herself—and she only had twenty-eight years of experience to go on—that was exactly the kind of mortifying word vomit that would come out of her mouth once Jenn was in sight.

She crossed the rear of the main dining room, eyes roaming the chairs set atop tables, the dimly lit bar. She'd never really allowed herself to see Gia this way—in all her imaginings, the restaurant had been buzzing with chatter, waiters and hostesses weaving between the tables to the melody of soft instrumentals and clinking utensils. But there was a charm to this version too, something that made her want to have it all to herself, if only for one night. No. Not all to herself. Herself and someone to share it with. Nothing but low lights, open conversation and a delectable meal between them.

The sight of Jenn's door sent a flutter to her stomach, and okay, she should just turn around and go home to enjoy gelato paninis and shit talk with Zo until they couldn't keep their eyes open anymore. Surely, she didn't need anyone to tell her this wasn't a good idea. She could see how Jenn was doing tomorrow, or better yet, she could let it go. Jenn totally seemed like the type of woman to have a meltdown and just never mention it again. Which was fine.

Yes.

That's what Val would do. Turn around and never ever mention it, because the track she was on—the one where she cared about how Jenn was doing, and randomly thought about the flecks of green in her eyes, and how maybe, just one time, she'd like to count the freckles on Jenn's skin—was a surefire way of making sure she would never get this job. Or any job.

The door opened with a click and Val went completely immobile.

Shit.

Jenn paused, hand on the knob of her door, brows furrowed in question. "Valentina?" She glanced at the watch on her wrist.

Yup, Val thought. *Stalker hour.*

"What are you still doing here?"

"Um..." She licked her lips, raising one hand to scratch lightly at her forehead. "I don't know."

Jenn tilted her head.

Val took a step forward. "I mean, I wanted to talk to you. Check on you. Because of—" She shook her head. "Are you okay?"

"Oh." Jenn pursed her lips, peering down at the keys in her hand as she shifted them between her fingers.

The memory crashed to the forefront of Val's mind like a derailed metro. Three weeks ago, she and Jenn both early for the food drive and Jenn fumbling with her keys under Val's watchful stare. Her skin a golden, freckled brown in the first glow of morning, her movements flustered by Val's presence, or perhaps her observation. And Val hadn't planned any of it—hadn't dared to imagine she could unnerve a woman like Jenn Coleman—but she didn't hate it either. At least then, it wasn't just her who felt on edge every time they were within inches of each other. Although, she had to admit that everything she knew about Jenn said she was bothered by Val's presence for reasons that had more to do with her reservedness than anything else.

Jenn lifted a hand, thumb hooked toward her office. "Would you like to come in for a moment?"

"Uh, sure." Val followed Jenn's lead into the room, watched her flip the lights back on and take a seat at the edge of her desk.

"About earlier," Jenn started. "I *am* okay. What you saw… I'm not—I'm very rarely like that and *never* for anyone to see, especially one of my employees."

The word "employees" hit like a sucker punch. A matter of fact. Something Val would have been grateful for nearly a month ago, something she was grateful for *now*. And yet, she found herself more focused on the way Jenn's eyes didn't shine as brightly in the beam of the hanging pendant light, the tight grip she had on the edge of her desk, reproach in her tone. All Val wanted was to get closer and just—

"I'm sorry you had to see me like that."

"I'm not." Val shrugged. "Maybe that's not what you wanted to hear, or even what I'm supposed to say, but I'm not sorry, Jenn." Because, for a moment, back in Jenn's car, with their hands and eyes locked, Val felt like more than Jenn Coleman's summer intern, and it was a treacherous if dangerously misguided thought, but it wasn't as if she could help herself.

"This probably goes without saying, but I'd like it to just stay between us."

"I would never." Val tried to communicate her sincerity with a single look. "Besides, I'm good at keeping secrets, remember?"

Jenn breathed a laugh that went straight to Val's lungs. "I

do." Something passed in her eyes, something soft but penetrating.

Was she thinking about it too? How closely they'd been standing when Val had said the words two days ago during their private practice session, the smell of Jenn's skin and permanent husk in her tone, the burn of her fingers against the back of Val's hand.

A visible gulp moved down the line of Jenn's neck, drawing Val's attention to the collar of her button down, the undone first and second buttons, her gold necklace.

The hair on the back of Val's neck rose. Signals went off in her brain, tingly nerve endings and little voices telling her this was the moment to say good night then leave. Instead, she dropped her bag into one of the armchairs facing Jenn's desk and moved to sit next to her. At least this way, she told herself, she wouldn't have to look at Jenn head on, and the space between them was still respectable, as long as they didn't touch.

"I took your advice," Jenn rasped. "Talked to someone," she tacked on with a chuckle.

"I get the impression you don't do that very often."

"Your impression would be correct."

"Why not?" Val dared a glance at her, knowing how hard it would be to look away. "Why not talk? Isn't that what your people are for? To be there when you need them."

"I don't have many people. I have Avery, Rachel and my nonna." She paused. "By choice, I suppose."

Val nodded, processing the information. "Rachel is your girlfriend?"

"I don't have a girlfriend, Valentina."

Val frowned. "Wife?"

"Is that what Landon has told you?" For a second, her eyes sparked with more fire than forests and then she relaxed, looking away. "I don't like to be the object of workplace gossip, even if it is unavoidable."

"Gossip? You think I've been gossiping about you?"

"I can't imagine where else you would have gotten this ridiculous idea."

"From the woman you told you love her on the phone last week. Sounded a little young to be your grandmother." This was definitely the moment to reel it in, because Val didn't like the irrational hint of jealousy in her tone, or the pressure on her chest. "I know it's none of my business. I was just making conversation, I guess." She stood upright and started toward the chairs.

Jenn grabbed her hand. "Valentina."

Her heartbeat hammered in her ears. She faced Jenn with zero reluctance.

"I'm sorry." The words hung between them, their eyes locked, the slow rise and fall of their chests in sync. "I—" Jenn peered down at their linked hands, her thumb stroking Val's knuckles with something like encouragement, willing Val to take an unconscious step closer.

"Do you want to tell me?" Val asked. "What happened today."

Jenn shook her head, whispering, "Not really." Her free hand moved to tuck a strand of hair behind Val's ear.

Val struggled to keep her eyes open. *Do not shiver. Do not sigh.* "Jenn..." *Definitely do not breathe her fucking name like that.*

"You didn't have to stay. It's my job to make sure you're doing okay. Not the reverse."

"I don't do things because I have to."

"You don't understand." Jenn's gaze shifted lower before meeting Val's eyes again, and she leaned in with the slowness of an eternity—building the anticipation in Val's chest, stomach, tips of her fingers. Their lips brushed. "You really shouldn't have stayed."

The touch of their lips remained tentative in a test of restraint Val had already failed. But she held on that much longer, breathing Jenn in, fingers of her free hand trailing Jenn's forearm to the folded sleeves of her shirt, all the way up to her neck, curling into the soft tendrils of hair at her nape. "I think you're right." Her eyes fell shut, their kiss faint as a fading dream, leaving her lightheaded and restless.

A hand landed on her waist, gripping her tightly, and she stumbled forward, pushing Jenn back against the desk. A sound ricocheted between them—half sigh, half moan. She raked her fingers deeper into Jenn's hair, kissing her harder, pressing their hips flush together, making that thing coil in the pit of her stomach, that thing she recognized all too well.

She should stop.

They should stop.

Jenn cradled her jaw, parting Val's lips with her tongue. Maybe they didn't *need* to stop. Maybe they never, ever needed to stop. Maybe Val didn't need air if it didn't smell of chamomile, or to ever exist beyond the confines of this office, or to have Gia all to herself. All she needed was—

Jenn tugged on her shirt, pulling her closer, and she dropped her hands to Jenn's hips and lifted her onto the desk, breaking the kiss to press her lips just beneath the lobe of Jenn's ear.

"Valentina—"

She drew a trail down the column of Jenn's neck, roughly untucking her shirt from her jeans before going to work on the buttons. Then, she pulled away a fraction, enough to make sure she never forgot the look of sheer want in Jenn's darkened eyes, the unsteady rise and fall of her chest, full breasts hugged in a simple charcoal bra. Her hair fell against her shoulders in a tousled, gorgeous mess as she sat with her lips parted, swollen, red...as if Val had even *really* kissed her yet. And Val had had her fair share of women laid out exactly like this in front of her—pliant and ready for her to do her worst. But *fuck*. She was so unprepared for this in every possible way.

Jenn swallowed.

Val trailed the motion all the way down to her exposed stomach. Taut and soft with curves Val was desperate to explore. Not that she could even decide where to start. She leaned in for another kiss—that was always a good starting point.

Jenn flattened a palm against Val's stomach, breathing the word onto her lips. "Wait."

A chill ran down her spine. She gave in to the urge to trace Jenn's lips with her thumb.

"Valentina."

Val closed her eyes, in love with the way Jenn said her name—four little syllables bearing the weight of enormous emotions.

"You should go."

Val furrowed her brows, her eyes sluggishly opening as she pulled away. "What?"

The shift in Jenn's demeanor had struck in an instant—the way one hand deliberately held both sides of her shirt together with an inefficiency that left the swells of her breasts on display, the way her eyes grew wider by the millisecond as if she was horrified by the position she'd found herself in, that Valentina had *put* her in. But wasn't it Jenn who'd started this?

Jenn pushed against Val's stomach, buttoning her shirt

as she crossed the room, muttering, "You shouldn't have stayed."

"Jenn—"

"Fuck," she swore, dragging a hand through her hair. Somehow, the word sounded foreign leaving her lips. Val felt compelled to admit that there were sides to Jenn she had been lucky to see these past weeks, but she didn't really know her, did she?

"Jenn, it's okay."

"No, it's not." She shook her head. "It really isn't."

Val took a step forward.

Jenn took one back. "I would like you to leave."

"Jenn…" Val's pulse raced, her body burning with the intensity of *literal* seconds ago, her head spinning as she tried to make sense of Jenn's response. If anything, the way Jenn had kissed her, had held onto her, validated every emotion Val had been trying to suppress over the last two weeks. Probably since the moment they'd met. Every beat in her chest said Jenn felt it too. So why was she pushing Val away? "Please talk to me."

Jenn's eyes fell shut, her words barely audible when she reiterated, "I'm asking you to leave, Valentina."

Val pursed her lips, nodding as she grabbed her bag and started for the door. "I didn't mean to—" She cut herself off. She couldn't finish the sentence. She *did* mean to. She meant every word and every kiss they'd just shared, even if Jenn seemed to want to take them back. "Don't worry. I'll keep this a secret too."

CHAPTER 12

*O*ut of body experience. A sensation of being outside of one's body.

Jenn mulled over the words in her mind. She'd pondered them for hours already—stretched out on her king bed, staring at the ceiling, afraid to close her eyes and relive last night at Gia. The taste of Valentina's lips. The hint of apples on her tongue. Scent of shea on her skin. The way her hands and lips caressed like velvet but singed like the bluest of flames. Her every impulse had radiated confidence, and Jenn didn't want to—God knows she knew what had happened in her office last night was *not* okay—but everything about Valentina's lack of hesitation drew her in. Even now. The force of her body when she pushed Jenn onto the desk and lifted her onto it, unbuttoned her shirt, gawked at her like something to possess. To worship.

How could Jenn have let this happen?

It was her job to make sure it didn't. *She* was the one in a position of power, no matter how things had unfolded between them. And just when she'd come to her senses—overwhelmed by the look in Valentina's eyes and the feeling in her chest that if she let things go any further, it could never be only a one-time thing, she just what? Dismissed Valentina like an employee who'd earned themselves a reprimand. God, what she must be thinking now.

Her last words echoed in Jenn's mind. *"Don't worry. I'll keep this a secret too."*

Did she think she *had* to keep it a secret? The last thing Jenn wanted was for her to have felt forced into anything—before, during or after.

Jenn's stomach churned. Every *Me Too* headline of the last year flashed behind her eyes. Reasonably, she knew what had happened between her and Valentina wasn't the same. She wasn't some grabby chauvinist who had threatened or coerced a scared employee into her bed. And yet, bile rose in her throat at the completely illicit nature of it all. The owner slash executive chef and a recent culinary school graduate who hadn't even made it a month into her staging role. How would that not read as predatory? And if not that, at least one person would assume Valentina had gotten the job for reasons other than being a promising, young chef.

Jesus Christ.

How had this gotten so far out of control in a matter of... what, weeks? Days?

Her 7 a.m. alarm blared—the default *Radar* ring unpleasant and insistent enough to always get her out of bed without hitting snooze. She shut it off with a blind stretch of one hand and sat upright, swinging her legs off the edge of the bed as she clutched the fabric of her duvet in both palms.

There was only one way out of this thing with Valentina, one way that she got to live the dream Mr. and Mrs. Rosas had mentioned three days ago. Had it only been three days?

The memory of their thick accents and kind faces seemed fainter somehow. Months away.

She had her father's eyes. Valentina. Somewhere between cinnamon and dark chocolate. Her mother's nose, though. Not scientifically perfect for all that 106-degree tip rotation nonsense. But perfect nonetheless—the kind of perfect that inspired butterfly kisses and lazy mornings in bed with their faces ever-touching.

This only ends one way, Jenn reminded herself, and her current train of thought was every kind of counterproductive. She *would* fix this. Hopefully, an emergency meeting with Avery and Mel was all it would it take. But first...

She stood, crossing her bedroom toward her closet.

A walk.

And a call with Nonna. Breakfast optional.

UNLOCKING the doors to Gia felt like entering a strange sort of purgatory. This place that Jenn loved like a living, breathing part of her, that had kept her together more times than she could count. Certainly through the hardest time in her life. She hated the crushing sense of vulnerability that came with missing her mom. Even after almost four years, she never could decide what to do with the grief; had never settled on what to believe in. Her mind processed strange concepts of her mother watching over her from...*somewhere* like stories told to pacify people in denial. Her mom was gone—that was certain—but she never liked to believe that she was just nowhere, only persisting as a figment of Jenn's imagination. Days like this, she would give anything to talk to her for a single minute, especially now that the one place she could always go to escape had started to feel like something she needed an escape from.

The smell of fresh bread wafted through the main dining room from the bakery. Traces of butter and honey most potent. Within the hour, the bread rack would be loaded with everything from focaccia to Brioche col Tuppo. For the first time all morning, Jenn's stomach stirred with a craving for at least a cup of coffee and a roll. Maybe not coffee. Maybe a steaming cup of Chocolate Abuelita, and she didn't have any on hand, but she would hazard a guess she knew someone who did.

The door to the kitchen budged, revealing Avery, shouldering it open with both hands clutched around a mug. "Hey, Jenn." She offered a casual smile, hair neatly swept out of her face and makeup pristine to match her flowy monogram blouse, ankle pants and pumps. "Mel's on her way already, but I just made a full carafe if you feel like coffee."

"Thank you." Jenn nodded. "Maybe later."

Avery's brows drew closer in that way they always did whenever she was trying to get a read on Jenn. She brought her cup to her lips, asking, "How are you?" before taking a sip, her eyes fixed Jenn's way.

"Good. And you?"

"More concerned that you're actually attempting to make small talk right now than I am that you called an emergency meeting at 10 on a Friday. What's up?"

Jenn forced a chuckle. "I'd rather not say until Mel's here. No need to go over it twice."

"As if I'm going to let you give me the same speech you give Mel."

"This is work related, Ave." Jenn sighed, starting toward her office as Avery fell into step next to her. "And in matters of work, you and Mel are equal. You don't get to pull friendship rank."

"The hell I don't."

She twisted the lock on her door and went in, flipping a light on.

"And why do you look like you haven't slept?"

Her eyes narrowed to her desk. The image of herself lying there with her shirt open set in like cold water in her veins. Why hadn't she gone for Avery and Mel's office instead?

"Jenn?" Avery rounded on her and leaned one hip against the desk, her neatly arched brows impatiently raised.

Jenn tried not to wince at the sight of her in the exact same spot that Valentina had kissed her—first like a cautious meeting of strangers, exploratory and gracious, then with the confidence of someone who had kissed Jenn a hundred times, who knew her secrets between the sheets and out. Jenn shifted some papers around on her desk. Invoices she'd already been through. Three times. "I had a rough night. Didn't get much sleep. But I *did* listen to another two episodes of that podcast for restaurant people."

"Mhm?"

"I like the idea of letting the staff each run a team meeting where they give a quick tip on their primary role. The grocery program is great too. I think they'd like that." She rolled back her chair and slid into it, reaching for her laptop, if only to get Avery to change gears to something Gia-related. Days like this, she'd kill for a window in here, when warm lights and cool colored walls did nothing to quell her craving for a view of the ocean, even the mindlessness of traversing pedestrians and flowing traffic.

Avery moved toward the pair of armchairs and got

settled into one, crossing her legs at the knees then taking another sip of her coffee. "How'd the doctor's appointment go? Didn't think you'd wind up taking the day off."

This, at least, she'd expected since she hadn't told Avery she wouldn't be in for the rest of shift, and by the time she'd shown up at almost ten last night, Avery had already gone home. Still, "I didn't tell you it was a doctor's appointment."

"You didn't need to."

Jenn narrowed her gaze to Avery's for a moment, just long enough to make sense of exactly how she could possibly know that. "I liked it better when Rachel thought you were someone she needed to worry about."

"No, you didn't. You're about as allergic to drama as I am to pollen. Besides, it was never me she hated. It was that you *sometimes*"—she emphasized—"spent more time with me than you did with her."

Jenn shot her a look.

"*Don't* shoot the messenger."

"I didn't ask for any messages. The message is old. Delivered, processed, archived. How am I ever supposed to move on if everyone keeps trying to remind me of it?"

"Hey." Avery slid to the edge of her chair, lips and brows drawn in concern. "What's going on? Who is everyone?"

Jenn rubbed her thumb against her forefinger in a compulsive motion. "No one. I was being hyperbolic. I had a talk with Rach yesterday. She may have mentioned something."

Avery hummed, seemingly processing the words.

Jenn had never resented Avery and Rachel growing closer toward the end of her relationship with Rachel. There was just something about this constant mention of how busy she'd always been at Gia that rubbed her the wrong way, especially with them both bringing it up within twenty-four hours of the other. Especially now that Jenn had managed to screw up in other ways. She owned restaurants in two of the restaurant capitals of the country. Had five Michelin stars to her name. Did either of them think something like that just happened? Besides, Rachel had moved on. Didn't Jenn deserve that too?

"You met someone." Avery said the words like a matter of fact. No two ways about it.

Jenn blinked. "What?"

"Two years. Two years you and Rach have been done and this is literally the first time I've heard you even mention the words 'move on'."

Valentina's face popped into her head like a montage—the day they'd met when she tripped and Jenn had caught her, the morning of the food drive with her dark hair framing her face in long waves, the sliver of tan skin left on display by her crumpled shirt, beauty marks on her cheeks, the way she chewed her bottom lip…

Jenn shook her head. "It's a figure of speech."

"Right." Avery squinted. "Well, all I'm saying is you're young—"

"Thirty-seven—"

"And hot and powerful, and if you were ready to get back out there, I would be happy for you." She paused almost as if to make sure Jenn paid careful attention to her next words. "No matter who she is."

Jenn sat up straighter in her chair, searching Avery's gaze for something unstated between them. Her chest tightened, compounding the relentless churn in her stomach. Avery knew her well, but she didn't know her *that* well. She couldn't possibly know about—

A series of raps sounded from the door seconds before it swung open, and Mel rushed in. "Sorry. Quinten decided he didn't want to wear shoes to his grandparents' today. We settled on Crocs." She pushed the door shut behind her, a few strands of her curly red hair clinging to the light sheen of sweat on her pale forehead, her chef's coat a blinding white. Then, she plopped down into the chair next to a chuckling Avery. "My takeaway? Five-year-olds are argumentative little shits."

Jenn laughed. "Yeah, well, Tommy turns fourteen next month and I can tell you it only gets worse as they get older. You're also not late, so don't worry about it."

"You two were already here. Plus, your emergency meeting text was pretty ominous. Makes me feel like someone's getting fired."

Avery's eyes widened. "Oh my God, is this a firing meeting?"

"*No one* is getting fired. I mean, I don't think so."

"Yeah, this totally feels less ominous." Avery leaned back in her chair and crossed her legs.

Jenn sighed. This didn't have to be complicated or burdensome as long as she ignored the tiny, aching part of herself that didn't want to do it. It was for the best, though. This was how she protected Valentina, how she gave her the chance she deserved. "I need to take some time off."

"Time off?" Mel regurgitated the words like they just didn't compute.

Coming from Jenn, they probably didn't. What had she taken? Two full days off in the last two years. Not that it was time off exactly. Then again, maybe she should take a few days. Spend some time with Tommy. Wake up at midday. Go to the beach. Do...whatever other people did in the summer. Either way, "I think I'm going to go to New York. Check in on Gia, Manhattan."

"You *think*?" asked Avery.

"Yes. Why do you both keep repeating my words like that?"

Mel glanced at Avery, almost as if to say *this one's yours*. Avery opened then shut her mouth, shaking her head as she said, "We're just a little...concerned. You usually plan your absences months in advance. Did something happen in Manhattan? Is there some kind of emergency?"

"No. I just—" How could she explain that she simply had to go? That there was no being in the same building, let alone the same kitchen with Valentina right now. That she didn't trust herself to be objective. That she didn't *know* herself for that matter. "I need to go. I know the place is in excellent hands with Kathy, but it gives me peace of mind to drop in every now and then."

"Okay..."

"There's one more thing." Tension built in her throat, and she fought to force it down. "I need you to observe Rosas while I'm gone. Make sure she's a good fit for Gia."

"Rosas?" Mel frowned. "I thought we were permanently taking her on next week."

"She needs to go through the six-week stage," Jenn insisted.

"Why? I mean, do you have concerns? She has everything we usually look for. The knowledge and talent, charisma, eagerness to learn. Tries to overcompensate sometimes, but she's fit right in with the team—"

"It doesn't matter." Jenn caught the clip in her tone and softened it quickly. "I need to be sure, Mel. And I can't be here, so I need you to be my eyes and ears. I need you to look after her. If she's cut out for this, another two weeks won't hurt."

Like earlier, before Mel had come in, Avery watched Jenn with obvious scrutiny—her eyes reflecting everything from confusion to knowing. And then she shrugged. "It is in the contract. Four to six weeks. It won't come as too much of a surprise if she doesn't get the offer next week."

"Okay." Mel crossed her arms over her chest, despite her acquiescence.

Jenn could tell she thought the additional two weeks were a waste of time. Maybe that should have been enough to quell Jenn's concerns about offering Valentina a permanent position right then, but it wasn't. She needed to remove herself from the equation, for Valentina to prove herself in Jenn's absence and leave no questions about it. For her own good as much as Jenn's.

"So, when does this time off begin?" Mel asked.

"Today."

Avery cocked her head to one side. "Today as in you're here tonight and off tomorrow?"

"Today as in I'm leaving as soon as we get done here. Of course, I'll be fully accessible via call, text or email for whatever may come up."

"Great."

"Sounds good to me."

"Perfect." Jenn rolled her chair back, glancing at her watch. Just after eleven. If she left now, she could avoid running into Valentina, or the likelihood of Valentina seeking her out to talk. Assuming she wanted anything to do with Jenn on a personal level after last night. There would come a time where they'd have to talk about it—what had happened, why it was better for it not to happen again—but today didn't feel right. Something told her Valentina wouldn't understand anyway. "If there are no other concerns on your part, I'll let you two get ready for the pre-shift meeting."

"I'm good." Mel stood in readiness to leave the office, glancing Avery's way, likely expecting her to follow suit.

Avery took the hint and they both started toward the door, though she clearly appeared to be in less of a hurry to leave than Mel. When Mel had left the room, she hovered by the door, and Jenn almost expected her to pick up their earlier talk about Jenn moving on. Instead, she tapped the nails of one hand against the door jamb, eyes momentarily trained on her feet before she looked up. "I hope you know what you're doing, Jenn."

And Jenn wasn't sure what Avery meant, but all she could think was, *me too*.

CHAPTER 13

"Okay," Zoe's voice carried a nervous pitch over Val's earbuds. "So, I know I agreed clearing the air between you two would be a good idea, but I'm starting to think this is absolutely not the way."

Val stared up at the two-story Edwardian in front of her, its walls painted a deep Carolina blue but for the white trimmings and large bay windows. The wrought iron grill barring the first-floor windows and modest patio probably had more to do with the area—lots of houses in the Mission had them, despite a relatively low rate of break-ins—but somehow, this wasn't the kind of home she imagined Jenn would live in. Although, the adjoining sunflower yellow complex Avery had mentioned told Val she was in exactly the right place. "It's simpler than I thought," she mumbled.

"Showing up at your boss's home unannounced isn't supposed to be simple."

"What?" Val blinked. "I mean, the house, Zo."

"Well, it's the Mission, V, not Billionaire's Row."

"You know what I mean."

"Yes, yes, she's a big shot chef, and whatever humble digs

you're staring at right now is probably making you twice as hot for her but remember why you're there."

Because yesterday Mel had announced Jenn would be taking some time off for an unspecified length of time, and as much as Val should've been satisfied that neither Avery nor Mel had mentioned anything about her losing her stage, Jenn's sudden absence didn't sit well with her. Not the night after she—after they almost—Val swallowed. "My insides feel all quivery."

"Maybe we were wrong," Zoe chimed in. "Talking is overrated. If you were fired, someone would've said something."

"You're not helping, Zo."

"You know I get second-hand anxiety."

"Which literally makes you the worst kind of moral support right now."

"Or the best. Who else would understand exactly how you're feeling?"

"No one." Most days, Zoe was more of a sister than a best friend, like they shared one brain. Val blew out a breath, glancing over her shoulder as a woman zoomed by on a motorcycle. "I just…I have to know, Zo."

Zoe sighed. "Then you know what you've got to do, babe."

"Yeah." Val reached for the latch on the gate, her pulse racing that much more at the feel of the warm metal beneath her fingers. "I'll let you know how it goes." She exchanged a quick goodbye with Zoe then jogged up the stairs to the front door and knocked twice. Any further delays and she'd just turn around and continue the five-minute drive to Gia. Nerves coursed through her from head to toe. She found herself examining the immediate area again, just to give herself even the notion of something else to occupy her mind. The small tree on the curb, maintenance pickup truck parked across the street—

"Yes?"

Val spun at the sound of an unexpected voice. "Um." She flinched back slightly. The teenage boy standing before her with skin a richer shade of brown than Jenn's and the height and build of a traditional athlete was the last person she'd been expecting. Didn't Jenn live *alone*? Her eyes widened and she took a step back. *Shit*. Was this the wrong house?

The boy's brows rose toward his razor-sharp hairline, his tone dry with impatience when he asked, "You here for my mom?"

"Your...mom?"

"You work at Gia, right?" He gestured toward the t-shirt Avery had asserted in no uncertain terms was *just merch, not uniform*.

"Yeah. I do. I am...here for your mom, I guess?"

"Okay?" His face scrunched up as if he was trying to get a read on the weirdo on his doorstep. "Come in. I'll let her know you're here. Who should I say?"

Val stared at him. He didn't really look like Jenn. Not that that meant anything.

"Your name?"

"Right." She blinked, jerking over the threshold into the house. "Val. Valentina. Sorry."

"Cool." He shut the door behind her then started up a flight of stairs.

Val stood in the narrow entryway, taking in the all-white walls and three-painting array that occupied the space just above the handrail. A part of her wanted to open the door and disappear onto the street as if she'd never been there, but after giving her name, running seemed worse. Why hadn't she just pretended to be in the wrong place? And why the hell hadn't anyone mentioned that Jenn had a teenage son? Val went over the math in her head—Jenn couldn't be older than thirty-five. Thirty-six? Unless he was adopted.

She slapped a palm to her forehead. *Priorities, Val.* She was there to talk, not analyze Jenn's obviously very private, personal life. Well, talking was out the window now. Unless she wanted to be like, *Hey, remember two nights ago when we almost had toe-curling sex in your office?* with a teenage boy in the other room. And okay, she didn't imagine getting involved with her boss would be simple, but did it have to be *this* complicated?

The sound of footsteps drew her attention to the top of the stairs, and she looked up to see a woman—skin with the same reddish-brown undertones as the boy's, hair in long braids all the way down to her chest. Maybe it was the full flight of stairs between them, but Val could've sworn the woman had looked her up and down before offering, "Come on up. Jenn's just out back on a call."

"Um." Val hesitated, clearing her throat. "Thank you." She started in purposefully slow steps, hoping to give herself time for her stomach to settle, or the tingle in her hands to pass. If her guess was right, this woman was also the boy's mom, which made her what? The girlfriend or wife Jenn had claimed not to have? Worse, an ex?

Ugh.

Val did not do exes. She didn't do any of this. Yet, as she got to the landing, the woman took a step back toward a gorgeous living room—walls the same shade of white as the entryway, an elegant sofa accented with two pairs of mismatched pillows set in front of a smooth coffee table and brick fireplace. Daylight streamed in from the sizable trio of bay windows, casting a glow over the pristine room and adding to its charm. Val couldn't help thinking she'd been wrong before. She couldn't explain it, but this place gave off the sort of reserved luxury that *felt* like Jenn.

"You must be new."

Val abandoned her appreciation of the space to look at the woman. "Sorry?"

"At the restaurant," she clarified. "I know all the staff. So, you must be new." Her forehead creased in a way that made Val feel like her explanation was more for herself than for Val's benefit.

That night, Jenn had mentioned having only three people in her life who she trusted enough to talk to. Since one worked at Gia and the other had to be much older than the beautiful if slightly intimidating, woman standing in front of her now, that only left one person. "You must be Rachel."

Her brows inched up and she crossed her arms over her chest before Val even had time to question why she hadn't just waited for an awkward introduction. "What have you heard and from whom?"

"Um." Why did that feel like a trick question? Another set of footsteps beckoned her gaze to the right, where the room opened to a six-person dining table, an island counter for two and the kitchen further back. Jenn emerged through an archway with signs of panic on her face—widened eyes a burning hazel, mouth slightly agape. Val's chest tightened, the beat of her heart imposing and unsteady. Showing up this way really wasn't a good idea—she knew that now more than ever—but how could she regret the sight of Jenn like this? Hair in messy waves down to her chest, dressed in a tight cami and flowy lounge pants with her feet bare.

"Valentina?" Even after a full thirty seconds of just looking at each other, Jenn uttered her name as if she wasn't convinced Val had really been standing there.

"Yeah, um, sorry." Val glanced from Jenn's son—God, would her brain ever get used to that?—to Rachel, whose scrutiny had somehow gotten more intense. "I should—I can come back, or just see you at work. Yeah. I'll see you at work."

"It's okay." Jenn shook her head. "Let's...step out back." She gestured for Val to follow and started in the direction she'd come.

Val ignored the pair of eyes on her and followed Jenn's path, through the kitchen she didn't have time to appreciate to a door that led to a back patio. Palms and potted plants Val couldn't identify gave the space a tropical feel, despite the abundance of concrete. A high-end grill stood off to one corner and an outdoor dining set occupied the center.

Jenn stopped by the table, back turned to Val as she asked, "Would you like to sit?" despite remaining on her feet.

"Not really." Something in the way she hadn't looked at Val the whole way there, the way she still hadn't looked at Val, made her question her intrusion again. "I'm sorry. For just showing up here."

"Are you?"

"Jenn..." Val took a step closer but stopped. "I don't want to have this conversation staring at your back the whole time." However nice of a back it was—all smooth lines and curves from her shoulders to her hips. A moment passed, Val keeping time with the beat of her own heart, ignoring a rustle in the trees.

Jenn turned, gaze shifting everywhere but the single inch of space Val currently occupied.

"You're really not going to look at me?"

"You should not have come here, Valentina."

"Yeah, so you keep saying."

Jenn's eyes darted to hers and stayed there. "This is my *home*."

"Yes, I know," Val breathed, moving closer. "And I am really, really sorry for showing up here like this. If you ask me to leave, I will turn around and go right now, but..." The memory of Jenn asking her to leave that night looped in her head, the memory of everything from their talk to their kiss to the rapid escalation of her hands on Jenn, Jenn tugging, needing her closer. "I would really like to know what happened two nights ago."

Jenn's jaw tensed then relaxed as she glanced at her feet. When her eyes returned to Val's, they spoke of distance and aloofness. "Something that shouldn't have happened. It was —*I* was irresponsible, and I took advantage of the situation. I took advantage of..." A gulp slid down her throat. "You, Valentina."

Val scoffed, biting down on her bottom lip. "Because I'm so impressionable."

"That's not what I meant."

"What *did* you mean, Jenn?"

"Valentina, you are my employee."

"And you're not some sleazy boss who tried to stick your hand up my skirt."

"That doesn't make it right."

"I—" Val cut herself off, suddenly aware of how short her breaths had gotten, how she'd made it close enough to make out the flecks of gold in Jenn's eyes. Her eyes dropped to Jenn's lips, and she dug her heels in to not move an inch further, despite the way Jenn's eyes had darkened with their proximity. Somehow, she felt finishing the sentence lingering on her tongue could cost her everything. And yet... "I *wanted* you to kiss me." In truth, she might've done it a week ago if she'd known Jenn would kiss her the way she had that night.

"Valentina." Her eyes fell shut. "You're young—"

"Not much younger than you."

"You can actually have a future in this field, probably with Gia, probably anywhere you'd like. Do not jeopardize your career for an infatuation with someone you know nothing about. Certainly, not for someone who is not willing to do the same for you."

The words hit like a bucket of cold water, nudging Val back right out of Jenn's personal space. So, there it was. It was never about Jenn taking advantage of a situation. It wasn't noble. It wasn't about exercising restraint or discipline. Valentina simply wasn't worth the stain on her name that Jenn would attract for sleeping with an intern. "Well..." She ignored her slowing pulse, the way she felt weaker for just standing there and she gulped against the aching tautness in her throat. "That's all you had to say. See you at work, Chef Coleman."

CHAPTER 14

Val dragged her feet along the side alley next to Gia, her body physically weighed down with exhaustion. Well, and the thirteen miles she'd done this morning. Running her feet numb had been meant to clear her mind, but coming across Joey on her way back past Dolores Park had only added to the myriad of thoughts that had kept her restless. Last night, he'd been back in the park again with the shelters full, and she was beginning to think there must be more she could do than give him food and a twenty whenever they'd crossed paths.

There had been something about him since the first morning she'd bumped into him—her in a steady jog as she glanced over her shoulder at the fluffiest golden retriever, and him casually folding a blanket as if standing in his own bedroom. Something beyond the heartbreaking realization that it had probably been the only thing to keep him warm the night before, and his kind eyes and polite manners. Today, when they sat on a bench, eating their food truck breakfast and he kept fidgeting with his shirt, along his chest, she'd begun to understand what it was...even before he'd hung his head and murmured nearly inaudibly, "My dad burned all my binders the day he kicked me out."

"Oh." Val had felt stupid, useless for it, but she couldn't think of a single other thing to say.

"Yeah." He'd taken a healthy bite from his panini.

Val's stomach churned, though she suddenly had zero interest in her food. "How old are you?"

"Seventeen."

The faraway look on his face looped in her mind. Seventeen and homeless. For what? Not feeling comfortable in the body he'd been born in?

She paused with a hand on the door outside of Gia. Getting lost in the rush of another Friday shift felt like exactly what she needed, even if it had been a week since Jenn had come in, since she'd stood in the kitchen calling orders yet giving soft directives to Val, since she'd told Val they were better focused on their careers instead of this *infatuation*. In a way, Val was grateful—if anything, her focus had been laser sharp this week with Jenn across the country instead of the kitchen—but right now, she had the strangest urge to reach into her pocket for her phone and FaceTime her parents. If only for the drama over how she hadn't called in a day, or how Mami doesn't put enough cream on the picaditas, or how, "Tu padre come demasiada crema, Vale." If only to say she loved them, even if it had taken them a while to understand her attraction to men *and* women, because some parents...some parents just never got it. Ever.

"Val?"

Val glanced behind her to find Avery approaching, her heels only now a noticeable tap against the cracked concrete. She sidestepped a puddle then came to a stop next to Val with her handbag in the crook of her elbow.

Val's mind went off in search of that one *Cosmo* article

about the way women carry their bags saying something about them. The details were foggy, but the words "high maintenance" lit up like a billboard neon sign, and she couldn't help but smile. "Hey, Avery."

"Hey, yourself." She beamed, bobbing her head toward the door. "Everything okay?"

"What do you mean?"

"I mean…I watched you all the way from the curb, and you've just been standing here. So, one more time. Is everything okay?"

"Yeah." Val furrowed her brows, shaking her head. "Think I'm just tired. And I had a hard conversation with this kid I met in the park a few weeks back. His dad kicked him out, so he's been pretty much living in parks and shelters for almost two months."

Avery flinched. "That's tough. I'm guessing you're thinking of trying to help him?"

"Yeah. I just need to figure out the best way."

"I'm sure you will." She placed a hand on Val's arm. "And let us know how we can help. Jenn, too. She really cares about things like this."

The first thought to enter Val's mind was, *doesn't everyone?* Care about things like this. But if everyone did, Joey's dad wouldn't have kicked him out in the first place.

Then, she thought of the food drive, and how every night Postmates showed up to Gia to collect excess food and deliver them to shelters in need, because Jenn, as Mel had put it, had signed up for the program the day it started three years ago. Val knew Avery was right. Jenn did care. And maybe next to calling her parents, Val wanted nothing more than to be able to stay well after closing, or show up two hours early, just to tell Jenn all about her talk with Joey and so much more.

Jenn *did* care.

Except about what she and Val had.

What they could've had.

"Yeah." Val glanced at her feet, swallowing hard. "I'll let you know."

"Hmm," Avery hummed. "Seems like there's something else."

"No. Just tired, like I said." Talking about Joey was one thing, but she wasn't about to word vomit her feelings about Jenn all over Avery's high neck, lace trim top. Especially when she knew for a fact they were friends. Good friends.

"This isn't on the record or anything, but you're going to get it, you know?"

Val frowned, tilting her head.

"The job." She rolled her eyes, sighing dramatically. "I know once it gets to that three-week mark, it's all anticipation and panic, especially when three weeks turn into five and you haven't exactly heard anything. But it's pretty much set in stone already."

The weight on Val's chest, in her limbs, shifted and for a second, genuine euphoria washed over her. She'd imagined the moment those words would come. She'd expected them a week ago, had hoped to fall on the lower end of the four-to-six-week assessment scale. Hearing them in week five was bittersweet. Hearing them from anyone but Jenn... Well, she didn't quite know how to feel about that. "Wow," she breathed.

"It's not just that I watched you stand by the door for half an hour." Avery chuckled at her own exaggeration. "You seemed a little down this week. And obviously, I have to wait for the go ahead from Jenn and Mel before I call you in with the official offer, but if the not knowing has anything to do with why you haven't been your charmingly social self, consider this my *unofficial* welcome to the team."

Val laughed. "Thank you. As long as you don't make me dance the Twist again."

"Hey, you got off easy. Jenn had to Dougie!"

"Now that must have been hysterical."

"It was, trust me."

The laughter died down between them—Val stuck in this constant flux of content and dejected with every mention of Jenn. Like she had to remind herself each time that yes, Jenn was as beautiful as she was awkward, but Val would probably never get close enough to get to know her the way Avery did. *Better* than Avery did.

"You know," Avery started, "It's also okay if..." she trailed off, her eyes wandering skyward as if in search of the words. "If *something* just feels missing right now."

"Um." Val narrowed her gaze to Avery's. Was it her, or did Avery seem to be hinting at a very specific something? Someone? "I'm not sure I know what you mea—"

"Getting to know your future in-law, Val?"

Avery rolled her eyes and they both turned to see Landon approaching, chin high and shoulders square. As he slowed next to them, he grabbed the strap of his backpack in a way that literally flexed his bicep. Not that he needed to with the plain white t-shirt he wore being about two sizes too small.

"Oh, Brother." Avery sighed. "I'm just going to say it since Val is clearly too sweet. Your frat boy charm isn't valid currency here. So, quit it, or I will personally point her to our harassment policy."

Landon scrunched up his face. "I'm not—I'm just kidding. We're cool." He turned to Val, eyes widened with alarm. "We *are* cool, right? I'm not, like—Am I harassing you?"

Val laughed, shaking her head. Truth be told, she hardly took his jokes seriously anymore. He was so far in the friend zone, she didn't know what it would take for them to end up together. And it was either friendship or distraction sex. She didn't see much of a middle ground, especially not with Landon. Although, he had been nice enough to bring her chocolate truffles last week after she'd faked cramps to get out of their misguided group plans to go drinking at 1 a.m.

The look on Jenn's face—shock, maybe with a hint of muted delight—when she saw Val outside of her office door pulsed behind Val's eyes again.

She drew herself back to Avery and Landon. "Yes, Lan, we're cool." She turned to Avery. "Nice to know whose side you're on though."

"Oh, no question," answered Avery. "He may be my brother, but women get enough shit in the workplace as it is."

"Hey, I'm a feminist, okay?"

"I *drag* him to one Women's March and he thinks he's a feminist."

"You didn't drag me." He shrugged, taking on an expression of feigned nonchalance. "Val, she didn't drag me."

"Uh huh." A smile took shape on Val's face as she watched them, remembering the night at the pier, when Landon had mentioned Avery was his sister. His twin, at that. He didn't share Avery's olive complexion or almond shaped eyes, but they had the same sleek black hair and aquiline nose, and that way of relating that was so brother and sister.

"Anyway, not that this back-alley chat isn't totally

conducive to bonding, but should we maybe get inside before any weird smells start to cling?"

Landon scoffed. "You're such a diva."

Avery smirked, winking at him. "Back at you, queen."

All Val could do was reach for the door with a constant chuckle simmering in her stomach. Maybe Jenn wasn't here, and maybe Val couldn't really say she missed her, but at least she had *this*. *"It's pretty much set in stone,"* Avery had said. At least Val had the job of her dreams, and the most ridiculous coworkers who she'd fallen for just as fast and hard as working at Gia. Even if she could never have Jenn.

CHAPTER 15

Jenn glanced between Avery and Mel—each seated in one of the accent chairs across from her desk, their expressions running the gamut from shock to disapproval. She hadn't expected them to take the news particularly well, especially after her meeting with them two weeks ago regarding extending Valentina's stage while she was in New York. Still, Mel's ginger brows drawn low over her blinking green eyes and Avery's grimace as she stood and started a slow stride toward a potted plant in the corner of the office had Jenn doubting the decision she'd made.

Again.

Ten days. She'd spent nearly ten days thinking it over after the idea had struck on her first drop in at Gia, Manhattan. She'd turned up without a word—in the middle of dinner service on a Sunday, at that—but had found everything running like a well-oiled machine. Unsurprisingly. With Kathy at the helm, Jenn might as well have been running the place herself. They shared the same need for precision, structure, dedication.

"Jenn…" Avery's gaze narrowed at Jenn, her tone clipped with the sharpness of someone who intended to not hold anything back. "This is a joke, right?"

Mel scoffed. "Yeah. That's exactly the vibe I'm getting, Ave."

"I understand you two are upset—"

"Not as upset as Val will be."

Jenn clenched her teeth. "She is getting the job, Avery. Her *first* job out of culinary school in a Michelin-starred restaurant. Why are we all pretending that's a bad thing?"

"In Manhattan, Jenn! You insist on the six-week process, after we all agreed she was perfect for the role, and then you come back with the grand idea to send her to Manhattan?"

"The contract promises a job at Gia. It doesn't say anything about it having to be in one location or the other."

Avery scoffed. "That's bullshit and you know it. She moved across the country for this stage."

"Sounds like you two have gotten real close. Or did you hear that from Landon?"

"Okay! Let's all take a breath." Mel stood, both hands raised to position one palm in either of their directions. "Ave, remember where you are," she said softly.

The underlying implication was clear. Remember who pays your salary. Mel meant well—she was trying to douse a clearly heated situation before either Avery or Jenn had gone even further—but somehow, Jenn didn't like the comment. She didn't like people fighting her battles for her, or Mel handing down reprimands on her behalf. Besides, lines always blurred when working relationships were also personal, and Avery was her closest friend. Wasn't that why she *had* to offer Valentina the junior chef position in Manhattan instead? Because like she and Avery had gone off on each other like friends only seconds ago—chain of command be damned—things between Jenn and Valentina could never be separated. How could she walk into Gia with this gnawing sense of yearning, of wanting, every day and be Valentina's boss, too?

"Mel, can you give us a sec?" Avery asked, eyes unwaveringly trained on Jenn.

Mel glanced at Jenn as if in search of confirmation.

The word *no* rested on the tip of Jenn's tongue. If anyone could get the truth about why she seemed intent on turning Valentina's life upside down by forcing her to move across the country for the second time in months, it was Avery. But this was for the best, and Avery would only try to change her mind. She knew that. And yet, she dragged in a slow breath, nodding. "It's okay, Mel."

Mel exchanged a look with Avery that could only pass as hopeful, lowering her head as she started toward the door.

A series of raps echoed through the room then stopped.

Jenn frowned, waiting. Her policy on staff visiting her office had always been the same. Knock and come in. She had a "Do not disturb" sign stashed away in the bottom drawer of her desk but had never used it for fear of someone taking it too literally and not informing her of some important happening in the restaurant. 100% availability 100% of the time had landed her in many an argument with Rachel, but she'd never not been informed of an incident. Be it smoothing over a server misgendering the Mayoral candidate's daughter, getting a plumber capable of fixing a set of burst pipes in time for opening, or rolling up the sleeves of her chef's coat and taking over in the dish pit herself when the escuelerie tried to work through a bad case of the stomach flu. "Come in!" she called out.

The door opened slowly and the weight in Jenn's chest shifted.

"Valentina." Their eyes met for the briefest second—Jenn clinging to the way Valentina still couldn't keep her hair in a ponytail that didn't leave strands dangling in her face, how her skin forever looked sun kissed as if she didn't spend all her best hours working in a kitchen with a total of two windows, her bottom lip tucked between her teeth.

"Sorry." She glanced at Mel then Avery before locking eyes with Jenn once more. "Your message said as soon as I got in."

"Right. We were just finishing up here." The sooner they got this over with, the better.

"Actually, Val," Avery put in. "If it's all the same to you, I'd like to have a word with Jenn before your meeting."

Val shrugged, already turning to leave. "Of course."

"Valentina," Jenn called, prompting Val to a halt.

"Jenn..."

"Avery, please. Let's talk about it later."

"Jenn—"

"Avery," Jenn gritted out. For a moment, their gazes held—Avery's firm with defiance, Jenn's unrelenting. Thirty seconds ago, she'd been ready, at the very least willing to have this fight with Avery. To allow her resolve to be questioned and tested until Avery understood why Valentina going to Gia, Manhattan, was better for them both. She would have to tell Avery why, but that was okay. There was little point denying something she was sure Avery already knew. At least suspected. It's not as if she could hide it when her basic instincts drew her to Valentina whenever she was near. She couldn't not stare, not stand too close when they spoke or brush by Valentina in the kitchen. Not to mention how her dislike for Landon, a perfectly capable if not talented station chef in her own kitchen, was growing by the day.

It was all so, so...incredibly unprofessional, she hardly recognized herself.

"Sure, Jenn." Avery's heels hit the tiles with pronounced force as she crossed the room, snatched her tablet from Jenn's desk and made for the door. "Excuse me."

Mel looked up at Jenn. "I'll talk to her."

"*I'll* talk to her," Jenn insisted. "Let her cool down for now. But please take care of pre-shift."

Mel answered with a curt nod, "Of course," then rushed by Valentina, her gaze averted.

Valentina looked after her before facing Jenn and stepping into the office. "That looked intense," she started dryly.

"That's Avery."

"Is everything okay?" she asked, shutting the door behind her.

Jenn gestured to the chair Mel previously occupied. "Sit. Please."

"Am I in some kind of trouble?"

"Not at all." Jenn flattened her palms against the small stack of papers on her desk, closing her eyes for a moment. Somehow, now that they were alone in the place where everything had changed, she couldn't seem to gather her thoughts. *Apples*. Valentina had tasted like apples when they kissed—exhilaratingly sweet even as everything about her grip, the press of her hips and lips screamed that she was the kind of dominant Jenn had never experienced in bed.

"Jenn?"

"Yes." Her eyes sprung open, her head pounding. "Valentina, I—*We* would like to make you an offer for commis chef. Of course, with your aptitude it's only a matter of time before you move up to—"

"Wait, I'm not getting fired?"

Jenn gaped, furrowing her brows. "Fired?"

"I just thought because of—" She cut herself off, leaving Jenn to fill the blanks.

Because what? Because Jenn had had a panic attack the same day they'd kissed and had held on to Valentina like she was the only thing keeping her breathing on both occasions?

"I would never fire you because of what happened between us, Valentina. Like I said when you came to my house, I take full responsibility for how it happened."

Valentina stared, something unreadable in her eyes, and then she nodded, dropping her gaze to her lap. "I get to work at Gia," she whispered to herself. Her smile gradually turned to a full-on grin. "I get to work at Gia."

A smile bloomed on Jenn's face too, Valentina's quiet content contagious like everything about her, only to be snuffed out near immediately by what she knew would come next. Saying the words with her desk between them felt impersonal and cowardly, but if she didn't spit them out now, she never would. "There's only one thing."

Valentina's smile faded as slowly as it had emerged. The moment dragged. She said nothing.

"The role is for Manhattan."

She flinched back slightly. "Wait—No—What?"

"It's for Manhattan, Valentina. If you want it."

"No." She shook her head, standing. "Avery said—Avery said I got it. It was set in stone."

Jenn sighed, getting to her feet too, but planting them to the spot. "Avery shouldn't have told you that. But—" She held up a hand. "It doesn't matter. You did get it. Just not here."

"Why?"

Jenn blinked, furrowing her brows. "Why, what?"

"Why not here?"

"Valentina..."

"You did this." The weight of those three words hit Jenn like a brick—the traces of disappointment, displeasure, dissociation in them. "You won't fire me, but you will do anything to make sure I'm not here."

Jenn sighed, rounding the desk to face her. "Valentina, you have to understand that this is what's best for us both."

"You mean what's best for you."

"No." Jenn shook her head slowly, ignoring the tightness in her throat. "No."

"Are you that afraid of having me here?"

"Yes."

"Jesus, Jenn, I told you! I won't say anything. You were very clear at your house. Trust me, my *infatuation*..." she snarled, venom in every syllable of the word. "Consider it in check."

"You still don't understand." Jenn moved closer, all but eradicating the space between them, Valentina's deep brown eyes glossy with rage and something else. Something Jenn had seen in her eyes before—in the break room when she'd cut her hand, in Jenn's car two weeks ago, especially the night they'd kissed.

"What?" she asked softly. "What don't I understand?"

"Valentina, I can't—" Jenn frowned, the words prickling at the forefront of her mind difficult to process even for her. She'd thought about it all through her trip to New York, but saying it out loud hit harder somehow. Made her question everything she knew about herself. "I can't *trust* myself around you. I can't trust myself to be objective, to not wonder how you're doing on shift, give you special attention, or—" She swept a strand of hair behind Valentina's ear, only for it to fall out of place again. "Do this when your hair does that."

"Jenn..."

She brushed the back of her hand in a gentle stroke against Valentina's cheek. "So, maybe you're right. Maybe it is for me, but it's also because...God knows there's so much of you for me to know, so much I wish I could know, but I can't let you be the kind of person who gets swept up in—"

This time, it was Valentina—Valentina who leaned in to press her lips against Jenn's, making her breath catch and her pulse race. But it was Jenn who cradled Valentina's face in both hands and kissed her deeper, slower, longer. Because maybe they couldn't have it all, but maybe she could let herself have the memory of what could've been.

Valentina hummed, wrapping her arms around Jenn's waist, holding her close.

The unlocked door flashed in Jenn's mind. Her knock-then-open policy. Pre-shift when Mel or Avery, any of the kitchen staff or servers could pop in with a question or concern. And yet, she couldn't bring herself to pull away—not with the glide of Valentina's lips and tongue against hers, the silky strands of her hair unraveling between her fingers, the coil low in her stomach.

Valentina pulled away—too soon, much too soon—keeping Jenn close as she whispered, "I would show you everything about me, if you just asked."

Jenn kept her eyes closed, breathing in the traces of shea on Valentina's skin, the fruity scent of her hair. "And what about your career?"

"I don't see why you think I have to choose."

"Because if we do this, Valentina, people start doubting that you got wherever you are because you're you and start thinking it's because you're Jenn Coleman's girlfriend."

"People can think whatever they want."

Jenn sighed, smiling. "That's either really brave or incredibly naïve. And I think you know where I stand."

Valentina flinched back, putting space between them as she glared at Jenn. "It's still my decision to make, Jenn."

"It is." Jenn nodded, fisting both hands, grounding herself in the plush of the rug beneath her feet. "But I do need your answer by Friday so I can inform Manhattan. If you'd like to go, we can arrange accommodations until you can find your own."

Valentina's brows inched up, her eyes widening. She took a step back, another, then shook her head and started toward the door. "You know…You keep saying you're doing this for me. For my career. To protect *me*. But you haven't even asked me what I want. Not once."

Jenn gripped the edge of her desk with both hands, closing her eyes. *Just let her go.*

"You know what I think?"

No, she thought. *Because you're right. Because I never asked.*

"I think you're terrified of anything that doesn't make you feel completely, contentedly in control." The door clicked open. "I'll let you know what I decide."

CHAPTER 16

*J*enn rested her forearms against the guardrail and leaned forward, closing her eyes against the gentle whip of the wind sweeping through the Mission. This was the closest she'd ever get to the calm of being near the ocean—the escape she rarely ever needed but was grateful to have at Gia. Luckily, the rest of the staff never frequented the roof. Probably not a tempting enough view with the building a mere three stories. For Jenn, things simply made more sense this way, when she could stand apart and observe it all. The focused or casual stride of passersby, cars zooming up and down the intersection, even the grand expanse of soccer field across the street. All so purposefully designed.

Lately, being amongst it all had rendered her confused and out of place. In her own damn restaurant at that. Was sending Valentina to Manhattan really the answer, or merely a hideous ultimatum disguised as a choice? How did this make her better than *him* for what he'd done to her mother?

Her eyes sprung open as she pushed the thought from

her mind—never wanting to give him more space there than he deserved, which was none at all. She *wasn't* him. She wasn't doing any of this to hurt Valentina, or simply because she could. She was doing it *for* her. Because a career in the culinary industry was hard enough for women as it was—especially Black and Latina women—and Valentina deserved all the success she was destined for without Jenn in her way.

The sound of Valentina's voice carried like ghosts in the wind—enchanting, spine-tingling. *"I would show you everything about me, if you just asked."* A part of Jenn knew the answer to the prisoner's dilemma she'd created for herself. She'd always considered her brain and heart to be equally rational, but she was starting to think neither would cooperate very easily with this plan of having Valentina leave. Which was why no matter how badly she wanted to march into the kitchen and tell Valentina she was sorry, that she could stay—that she *deserved* to stay—Jenn needed to interact with her as little as possible. Clean break. By Friday, things would be more settled and then she could regain some semblance of control. Valentina would be on a flight to New York this weekend or decline, staying in San Francisco in search of other opportunities. It was a big city. Maybe they'd never see each other again. Or maybe, she and Landon would lend truth to all the gossip about them buzzing through Gia and get together once and for all.

Jenn's stomach roiled. *It's for the best,* she told herself.

The door to the roof clanked open and Jenn straightened, turning toward it to find Avery carefully planting a stilettoed-foot over the threshold. "You know"—she smoothed her top, casting an apprehensive glance toward the building just right of Gia—"I don't need to remind you that being up here is a safety hazard, but making me come find you, while I'm dressed in five-inch heels is positively endangerment."

Jenn raised a brow at her. "Making you come find me?"

Avery gave an impatient wave of her hand, side-stepping a spatter of what Jenn assumed to be bird feces. "Okay. You didn't make me, exactly, since we're getting technical." She frowned, attempting to peer over the ledge from a clear ten feet away. "Can you step away from there?"

Jenn chuckled but acquiesced. "Why did you even bother coming up here when you hate heights?"

"I don't hate heights, from, like, the safety of an enclosed plane. But I just dropped by the kitchen for a coffee top-up, and based on the way Val was chopping those vegetables and you being MIA, I'm guessing she wasn't happy about Manhattan."

A sigh escaped Jenn's lips. "She's going to cut herself again if she keeps that up."

"I wouldn't worry about it. She's been pretty...different lately."

"Different? Different how?" Jenn narrowed her gaze to Avery's.

Mel's report on Valentina for the two weeks Jenn had been in New York was good. "Focused, diligent, creative. Exactly what we're looking for," she'd said.

Avery hummed, wincing in consideration. "Like...sort of single-minded. Not as social. Less like Val, you know?"

"Oh." Jenn took a step back then turned toward the ledge again.

"What's going on, Jenn? I hate to say it, because you're you, so it's so hard to even imagine. I've been kind of telling myself that I wasn't seeing what I thought I was seeing since the first week she's been here. That day Lan said whatever he said to warrant an apology and you just couldn't take your eyes off them—"

"Avery..."

"But a lot of things are starting to add up here. Including her asking for your address to drop-off some weird grandma chocolate."

Jenn smiled to herself. *Chocolate Abuelita.*

"Your impromptu visit to Manhattan, her deflated mood."

"Avery—"

"What happened between you two? And don't say nothing because I'm probably the one person in this building you never need to lie to."

Jenn huffed, signs of a headache pulsing behind her eyes. "You know I'm not any good at lying." Which was probably what had gotten her into this mess to begin with.

"Disclaimer. Just in case you felt like this time you needed to try. Besides..." Avery took a step forward, seemingly unconcerned about the height for the first time since she'd exited the building onto the roof. "I'm not asking as your HR or admin. I'm asking as your best friend."

Jenn dragged in a deep breath, despite the tightness in her chest. Avery wouldn't judge her—she knew that—but it was like she'd said earlier. She knew Jenn, knew what she had probably guessed was something so unlike Jenn it seemed near impossible. But she had... acted unprofessionally in almost every capacity. And she'd thought it over for weeks, but she had yet to make sense of why she'd asked Valentina into her office at 1 a.m. to say something that could have been relayed on a walk to her car. Somewhere, in her subconscious, she must have known she would have—She squeezed her eyes shut before the onslaught of memories emerged. "We kissed." Her lips pressed into a line. "*I* kissed her."

"At your house?"

"In my office. The night before I told you and Mel I was going to Manhattan. And then..." She trailed off, forcing her eyes open to meet Avery's expectant gaze. "This morning."

Avery's eyes widened. "This morning?"

"I know it was unprofessional—"

"But consensual."

"Of course," Jenn asserted, though Avery hadn't phrased it as a question.

"That's why you forced the six-week stage and left. To make the decision Mel's instead of yours," she said more to herself than Jenn. "But Jenn..." She turned to Jenn with a sigh. "You can't just send her across the country because you have feelings for each other."

"I'm her boss, Avery."

"Which makes things complicated, not impossible."

Jenn huffed, turning away from Avery again. "What are you saying, Ave?" A part of her knew exactly what Avery was suggesting—the same part of her that had willfully given the idea no consideration. That kind of thought would scatter seeds of hope and leave them to bloom all through her already conflicted mind and heart, would leave her thinking maybe her restaurant, her son and a broken-romance-turned-friendship with her ex wouldn't have to be all she wanted for herself. All she had. But Valentina was the first person in two years who had unearthed this yearning for more; for the thrill of getting to know someone and still wanting to know more, of being warmed and inspired by their very presence, brush of their lips, and touch of their hands. Something that vaguely hinted of a feeling she'd lost even before she and Rachel had separated. Passion.

The subtle tap of heels gave away Avery's approach before her hand landed on Jenn's arm, willing Jenn to face her. "I'm saying the look in your eyes, that glimmer of losing something that wasn't even yours, is rare, Jenn. Especially for you. So, sign a fucking consensual relationship agreement, let Mel do what Mel does in the kitchen and go get your girl." She tilted her head to one side. "Just...Later, maybe. We're in the middle of lunch service now."

Jenn breathed a chuckle, almost immediately becoming subdued again. Were things ever that simple? What if Valentina didn't even want to stay after Jenn essentially put her on a plane to New York? Besides, there were other factors to consider here. Valentina had kissed her, held her, promised to let her in if she only asked, but there was still...*something* between her and Landon, and Jenn wasn't quite sure what to make of that. "You know your brother is interested in her."

Avery's brows knit and she waved off the implication. "Lan will be fine. His ego could actually use a little bruise."

"And if Valentina is interested in him?"

"She's not."

"You can't know that."

"I *do* know that. Trust me, if something was going to happen between them, it would've happened already. If anything, she's keeping her options open."

Jenn's stomach dropped. She didn't like the sound of that —the implication that she was so disposable, Valentina could simply move on to the next best thing—especially when no one else had entered her own mind. Maybe this was what it was like getting involved with someone in their twenties. Maybe Valentina didn't want serious. But serious was all Jenn knew.

"Listen..." Avery gave her arm a gentle squeeze. "Think

about it, but you may want to remember the timer you put yourself on. It gets that much more complicated if you let her get on that plane. Either way, if it's serious enough to get Jenn Coleman out of the kitchen in the middle of shift, it's at least worth a conversation."

A smile tugged at Jenn's lips, her brows knitting together as a faint buzzing forced her to reach into her pocket and grab her phone.

Dr. O'Connell's office.

The creases in her forehead deepened and her pulse matched the pounding in her ears. "Uh—" She swallowed.

"Take it," muttered Avery, already turning to leave. "And talk to Val!"

Jenn mumbled something unintelligible in assent as she answered the phone and brought it to her ear. "Dr. O'Connell."

"Jennifer, hi," he droned. "Your results are in. I'd like to discuss them in person. How's Thursday at 3 p.m.?"

"Is everything okay?"

"Nothing too concerning. We just actually need to take another sample. Can you come in?"

"Of course." Dr. O'Connell pulsed in her mind like a middle-aged effigy—his stern, tightly drawn features and greying hair, the unnervingly long needle attached to the syringe in his dependable grasp as she lay there alone, waiting. She blinked away the image. "I'll be there."

"Good. Talk then."

The call disconnected with a beep and Jenn slowly drew the phone from her ear, unsure what to make of O'Connell's brusqueness. What did "nothing too concerning" even mean? Was there something to be concerned about? The answer came to her nearly the second she'd asked herself the question. Of course, there was. There would always be.

The very diagnosis O'Connell had given, fibrocystic breast disease, would leave her in a constant state of questioning every sign of a lump for the rest of her life. That coupled with her family history. She'd never escape the fear of the dreaded C-word—the tension in her neck and feeling that she couldn't breathe before and after every doctor's visit. This time, she'd have to wait three days to find out exactly what she was expected to be not too concerned about.

She never really had those bursts of inspiration about life being short and all that—life was sort of just life. Long, short, something between. She'd never given much thought to chasing everything she wanted in case she couldn't someday. But in the midst of the fear twisting its way up her spine, Valentina's face and Avery's words resonated in her mind, and for the first time, she couldn't help but think...

Maybe life *was* too short, and maybe she did want more than Gia and her family.

Maybe she wanted Valentina to stay.

CHAPTER 17

Val unclasped the chain around her neck and slipped her key into the door lock to her apartment. Her body thrummed with residual bursts of energy, her breaths short and quick but heading toward normal after a brutal twelve miles. The buzz wouldn't last—it never did—especially after another long shift at Gia and a restless night. But she needed something to take her mind off the last three days, to give her at least an hour of reprieve from Jenn and Manhattan, even if it meant literally running herself ragged.

The chill of the air conditioning hit her sweat dampened skin the second she pushed the door open.

Zoe hopped to her feet, almost as if she'd been sitting on her bed the whole time, waiting for Val's return. "I've thought about it, and I just started at Cakes and Stuff. So, maybe we *should* just go back to New York."

Val heeled off her sneakers, sighing as she headed for the refrigerator. "Zo, come on. You know that's not what I want."

"Yeah, but we promised to do this together. And if you

have to go, then so will I. I didn't come all the way to San Francisco to live out *our* dream alone."

The distinct sound of a toilet being flushed drew Val's gaze toward the closed bathroom door as she reached into the fridge and grabbed the water jug.

"It's just Warren." Zoe shook her head, crossing the living room. "I'm serious, Val."

Halfway between them, the door to the bathroom opened and Warren strolled out, dressed in the same t-shirt and jeans he'd worn to work yesterday, head hung as he mumbled, "Morning, Val."

Val raised her brows at him, taking a sip of her water. "Are we going to do this every time you sleep over?"

He scanned the end table next to Zoe's bed. A pair of keys jangled. "Do what?"

"This thing where you refuse to look me in the eyes the morning after, even though I'll just run into you at work in a couple of hours." She tried to ignore the way her chest tightened. It wouldn't be long before she lost the ability to pull Warren's leg this way. Two shifts, actually. Today then tomorrow, and she'd be seeing significantly less of him. One way or another. She fought to keep the mood light anyway. "You know Zo tells me everything, right? Literally, everything. Including that thing you do with your—"

"I gotta go," Warren cut in. "Promised my aunt I'd grab groceries for her before work."

Val tossed her head back in a laugh.

He rested a hand on the small of Zoe's back, bending to kiss her lightly on the cheek. "Call you before shift?"

Zoe nodded, blue-grey eyes glimmering up at him. "Yes, please."

"Cool." He bobbed his head in Val's direction, rushing by her on his way out. "See you, Val."

"Bye, Warren."

Zoe rolled her eyes as the door shut behind him. "You are so terrible."

"Learned from the master." Val beamed, drawing a smile from Zoe too. The moment dragged on—the kind of content she only ever found with her best friend, that she'd never imagined ever having to give up. In her mind, they'd forever be this close, even if they didn't live together. Zoe would never be too far away. Certainly not in another time zone. Val pushed the thought away. "It's nice. Seeing you happy."

Zoe's smile widened to a grin. "Is happy code for monogamous? Because I was always happy."

"Touché, my friend." Val raised her glass in mock cheers. "Touché."

"V, you know I'm serious, right?" Zoe repeated.

"Zo—"

"No. If Coleman wants to be an idiot about this and risk losing you in more ways than one, then it's about to be a broken hearts parade all over the damn Mission, because it's going to lose me too."

"You quoting Good Charlotte reminds me how desperately we wanted to be angsty teenagers but were actually really bad at it." Val lowered her glass to the counter, taking a moment to really let the words set in. "Probably won't be a parade, Zo, but I know at least one person who would really hate to see you go."

Zoe slumped down into the sofa. "I know. I know. And I really like him, too."

"So, stay."

She pressed her lips together, wrinkling her nose in that way she always did whenever she was conflicted. "You know, you don't have to go."

"That's the thing, Z. I think I've already decided to."

VAL PULLED her knees up to her chest as salty air whipped around her, the bite in the breeze enough to keep her arms tightly wrapped around herself, despite the glow of the setting sun. She'd never seen Golden Gate Bridge this way—a striking backdrop to the waves cresting against the shore, the sky a kaleidoscope of burnt orange bleeding into pewter grey, thunder clouds rolling in on the horizon.

Two whole months, and this was the first time she'd even set foot on Crissy Field East Beach. They'd promised to come together. She and Zoe. But they'd packed up and left their lives in New York in pursuit of a dream. A dream that had wound her up and tossed her into the mouth of a whirlwind only to spit her out where it had all started. They'd hadn't had time for the beach or the nights of restaurant hopping they'd promised themselves. Getting immersed in the culture and food in one of the most beautiful cities in the country. She'd never questioned it. She'd just always figured they'd have time.

She closed her eyes, scoffing at herself. *No one is dying, Val. It's just...long distance.*

Her stomach sank at the thought. What would she do without Zoe by her side to scold her then turn around and validate all her bad decisions? But she couldn't ask Zoe to follow her back to New York. She had a life in San Francisco now. A promising job at Cake and Stuff. A perfect, if mismarketed apartment they'd both grown to love. Warren.

One year would fly by in a snap, wouldn't it?

One year at Gia, Manhattan, and Val could come back and have her pick of restaurants. Maybe even the one she was leaving. If they would have her.

A drop hit her cheek and she looked to the darkening

sky. This was a shit day for the beach, but after she'd signed those papers back at Gia and Mel had offered her the rest of the day off, she couldn't think of anywhere else to go. Finishing her shift would have been torture, and with Zoe not at home, the pillow fort she had in mind just seemed depressing. Much like sitting on the beach alone on a rainy day.

The droplets fell faster and the two dozen or so people still milling around began scrambling for their belongings.

Val dragged herself to her feet, despite the unexplained weight of her body and sinking feeling in her stomach. As she started toward her car, she tried to remind herself...

There are beaches in New York, too.

She tried—failed—not to think about the things that weren't.

Zoe, who knew and understood her better than anyone. Landon's terrible jokes. Avery taking every opportunity to check him. Warren's benevolence and bashfulness.

Jenn.

Jenn.

Jenn.

CHAPTER 18

Despite the sudden relentless downpour, Val drove the long way home by the Presidio Golf Course onto Geary Boulevard. She'd had her trusty, third-hand Prius serviced a little over two weeks ago, and if she ignored the momentary sputter of the engine before it sparked to life when she turned the key, it almost ran like new. Her doubts it would leave her stranded in the rain were few, but maybe it was time she found it a new owner. Having a car through her years at culinary school at the Institute had been convenient for driving into the city once in a while, but she didn't imagine she'd have much use for it living *in* the city. Not when the subway took half the time to get almost anywhere.

Maybe she could leave it to Zoe.

She slowed in a line of traffic, glancing at the time. 7:02 p.m. Just outside peak hour. Rain hammered against the roof of her car and splattered onto the pavement, the shower almost enough to drown out the pop ballad playing softly over her radio.

She closed her eyes, breathing in as she brought her

forehead to the steering wheel only a second before her phone chimed, drawing her attention to where it sat in the holder on her dashboard. The words on the screen crept into her chest and squeezed.

Jenn (7:03 p.m.)

I won't be in for the rest of shift. Please see me when you're in tomorrow.

Another chime.

I'd like to talk.

About Manhattan.

Val's brows drew together. She hated the way just the sight of Jenn's name on her phone sent her pulse racing. Although, Jenn had only messaged her a total of one time before today—Monday, when she'd asked Val to come to her office, where she'd delivered the news that Val would not be given an offer for Gia, San Francisco. And maybe Val was *supposed* to be grateful to have been offered a spot in Manhattan, where she'd be exposed to the pinnacle of Italian haute cuisine and celebrity clientele. But she'd fallen in love with Gia, San Francisco, because it wasn't just haute cuisine, even if the Italian-Mexican fusion was considered by some to be the less sophisticated of the two.

A honk blared, alerting her to the green light ahead.

Thoughts of Jenn swirled in her mind. Their argument three days ago. She couldn't reconcile the way Jenn had kissed her—not the first or second time—with Jenn asking her to leave. Phantom traces of her hands lingered on Val's face, the back of her neck, in her hair, their lips every kind of hesitant and desperate all at once.

Jenn's first text flashed in her mind again. '*I won't be in for the rest of shift.*' Her gaze swept around the street she was on. Harrison. The polished wooden sign of Gia glowed in the distance.

She took a left at the next stop sign, her wipers struggling to keep the windshield clear as she ignored all the reasons why she should've gone right instead, why what she was thinking wasn't a good idea.

It was a five-minute drive, but it was only three minutes before the two-story Edwardian came into view, the Carolina blue facade darker beneath the roar of the storm, despite the porch lights being on. Val sat in her car, staring, her grip on the steering wheel painfully tight, her left foot in a constant tap against the floor of her car. *Turn around. Turn around and go home.* The words echoed in her head like a mantra for a full twenty-three seconds before she huffed, "Fuck it," shifted into park and shut off the engine.

She pulled the hood of her cropped hoodie over her head, slamming the car door shut as she rushed toward the wrought iron gate, only to find it locked. Her forehead creased as she frowned down at the call button next to it—she hadn't needed to use that last time. Before she could second guess it, round on this shitty idea and get back into her car, she pressed the call button and waited.

Rain pelted against her shoulders and back, soaking her down to the pair of Chucks on her feet.

A crackle sounded from the speaker. "Yes?"

She peered up at the house almost defiantly. A woman's silhouette emerged in the center of a trio of bay windows. "It's Valentina."

A fresh burst of static sparked from the speakers—words she couldn't make out—then the gate buzzed open.

She darted up the stairs onto the porch right in time for the door to swing open, revealing Jenn in a pair of plain lounge pants, just like last time, and a white sweatshirt with Le Cordon Bleu printed across the left breast. Her hair had been swept in a messy bun and not for the first time, Val understood her affinity for tucking loose strands away from her beautifully freckled face, her eyes a fiery mix of perplexity and wonder. "Valentina, what—Is everything okay?"

"Are you alone?"

"What?" She shook her head, adding, "Yes, of course," as if it was the most ridiculous thing.

Val had to ask though, because last time... Last time Val had been met by Jenn's kid and her not-so-welcoming...Rachel, and if she had any idea what was good for her, she probably wouldn't be here right now. "I know this is your home. I know I shouldn't be here, and I meant what I said, if you want me to go, all you have to do is ask. But I—"

"Valentina, please, you must be freezing." Jenn reached for her, pulling her into the house and shutting the door behind them.

"I signed the transfer."

"You—" She faced Val, lips slightly agape. Closed. Open. "What?"

"I signed it, Jenn. I'll go." She took a step closer, gaze trained downward as she brushed the fingers of one hand against Jenn's, the touch like a burst of electricity straight to her toes. "I just..." She looked up at Jenn. "Needed to do this one last time." She barely got the words out before Jenn's lips captured hers, arms wrapped around her neck.

Val's hands shot to Jenn's hips, the momentum forcing her against the door with a thud. She breathed a moan, unearthing something primal in the depths of Val's stomach before it settled between her thighs, making her hypersensitive to Jenn's fingers tangling into her hair, the smell of Jenn's skin and faint traces of wine on her tongue. And all Val wanted was to get her out of every piece of clothes covering her silken skin, count those damn freckles with her lips, while she—

"Wait. Sorry. I should've asked—Are you…" Jenn pulled away, eyes darker than Val had ever seen, breaths quick against her lips. "Are you sure about this?"

Val slipped one hand beneath Jenn's sweatshirt, in love with the way Jenn's stomach tensed beneath her palm as she pressed a kiss to her neck. "Define *this*."

"*Valentina*."

"If it's more of you saying my name like that, then yes." Another kiss, just beneath the lobe of her ear. "Absolutely yes."

"If we do this, there's no taking it back."

She pulled away enough to make eye contact, hands planted on the door, either side of Jenn. "I know. I don't want to take it back. Not anything that's happened between us before, or anything that…" Her heart pounded, her body hot beneath her drenched clothes. "Or anything that might happen here. Tonight."

"God." Jenn closed her eyes, dropping her head against Val's shoulder.

Val braced herself for another abrupt stop, another speech about why this wasn't right, why they shouldn't.

Jenn cradled her face in both hands and kissed her softly, the gentlest press of her lips. Then, she brushed her nose against Val's and leaned against the door, the command almost inaudible when she murmured, "Take off your clothes."

A slow gulp slid down Val's throat, but she started with her shoes, heeling them off one after the other before reaching for the hem of her shirt.

Jenn's gaze swept over her newly exposed skin, her breasts hugged in a simple sports bra that made her wish she'd planned for this moment. Something lace, or strappy, maybe both. As she reached for the button of her jeans and pushed them down her legs, she found herself wondering if Jenn even liked lingerie. Her fixed gaze and slightly parted lips suggested she didn't much mind practical. Val's hands went for her bra and Jenn surged forward, stopping her.

"You can—" Her chest rose and fell in short breaths, her eyes trailing Val's body. Head to toe then up again. "You can keep that on."

Val licked her lips.

Jenn took her hand, "Come here," and started toward the stairs.

Val envisioned her own compliance—following in silence, only the light taps of their feet on the hardwood and what sounded like a news reporter on the TV in the living room, her eyes glued to the swing of Jenn's hips, intensifying her need to touch her—*really* touch her—but her hands ached with the need to explore every inch of Jenn *now*.

She tugged on Jenn's shirt, already set to meet her lips the second they were face-to-face again. "Promise me something." Val broke their kiss only to pull Jenn's shirt over her head.

"Anything."

Val smiled against her lips, one hand on Jenn's face as their eyes met. "No holding back. Tonight, I'm not your stage, or your commis chef. Tonight, Gia doesn't even exist to us. Just you, me, and this. Is that okay?"

"Yes." Jenn closed her eyes, breathing in, her hands wandering upward, just beneath Val's bra then down to the hem of her basic bikini cut underwear. "You are so...God, I don't even know where to begin."

Val breathed a laugh, backing Jenn against the banister of the stairs as she kissed a trail down the column of her neck. "I can think of a few places." She nipped at her shoulder, loving the way Jenn's breath caught and her grip tightened—one hand low on Val's back, the other tangled in her hair. And exerting dominance in the bedroom, or out of it, had always come naturally to Val, but there was something about having Jenn so completely at her will that had her blood rushing and her clit throbbing before she'd imagined all the ways she wanted to hear Jenn plead, and moan, and scream her name.

Jenn released a shuddering breath. "Valentina, we won't make it to my bed if you keep that up."

Val reached behind Jenn to unhook her bra before tugging it off and dropping it to the floor. She took a second to appreciate Jenn's breasts, her nipples ready and keening for Val's lips. "What if I wanted you here?"

Jenn's brows inched up, but something flashed in her eyes. "Here?"

Val pressed a kiss to her lips, taking her breasts in both hands, caressing, teasing. "Yes, Jenn. Here. Then your bed. What if I wanted you on every inch of this place?"

"I—Valentina..."

Val slipped a leg between her thighs and rocked forward slightly. "Whatever you want. But you're going to have to say it."

"You." Jenn wrapped both arms around Val's neck, breathing the words into her mouth. "Here. My bed. Wherever. Just—"

Val rocked into her again, nipples between her fingers.

Jenn moaned her name. "*Yes.*"

Val kept up the motion for a minute, longer, enough for Jenn's lips to attain that delicious bruising red from not-enough kissing and a light sheen of sweat to gather on her chest, breaths and hands shaky. And then she pulled away.

Jenn tried to pull her back in. "Don't—"

Val pressed a thumb to her bottom lip, reveling in the touch, the hint of indelible abandon in Jenn's eyes. "If you think the first time you come for me, you'll still be wearing those really flattering yoga pants, you're out of your mind."

Jenn breathed a laugh. "I think I am. A little bit."

"Not yet." Val grinned, shaking her head as she pushed Jenn's pants over her ass. "But you just might be when we're done."

"That is..." Jenn rushed to step out of her pants, stumbling slightly.

Val caught her, eyes roaming her face, momentarily stuck on the delicate cut of her jaw and cupid's bow of her lips, hair now in messy, sexy, dark waves down to her chest, though Val had no recollection of freeing it from its bun. The last time she'd stopped to appreciate Jenn like this— acknowledge the way everything about her body and mind inspired awe—their physical connection had come to a screeching halt, leaving her all wound up and turned on and too frustrated to even do anything about it when she'd crawled into bed that night, wondering what the hell had happened.

"Valentina," Jenn whispered, hands wandering over Val's body—over her bra-clad breasts, the center of her abdomen to that spot just beneath her belly button piercing that made her toes curl and her body ache with want. "About Manhattan."

Val shook her head. "Not tonight, remember? Tell me you want me, tell me you don't, but not that. I can't think about how this may be the only night I'll ever get to have you like this."

"You don't understand."

"So you keep telling me."

"I do...*want* you, Valentina. I don't know if I've ever—" She stumbled again, her groan more frustration than pleasure.

Val's grip tightened as her gaze fell to the yoga pants still tangled around Jenn's ankles. "Let me help with those." She leaned in, placing both Jenn's hands on the banister—fixing her with a stare that said *don't move*—and she bent to free her feet completely, gazing at her long, toned legs, trailing her hands from her toes to the wet spot on her navy underwear. "These, too."

Jenn tossed her head back as Val kissed her inner thigh, nudging her legs apart.

It was every bit of her nature to tease a little bit more, as much as Jenn could take, but she was drawn in by everything from the intoxicating wave of arousal beckoning her closer to the slight, keening jut of Jenn's hips to the white-knuckled grip she had on the rail. Val dragged an unsteady finger from her clit to her core just to assure herself Jenn was exactly as wet and molten as she thought.

"Valentina, *please*."

Just to hear her whimper like *that*.

And then she took her clit between her lips, lavishing it with all the attention she'd denied since the second Jenn had kissed her tonight. She built her up slowly anyway, relished every second of Jenn's evident conflict between opening her legs wider or closing them. Then, she made it easy for her by leveling one over her shoulder, holding it there with a steady grip on Jenn's ass, nails of her other hand scratching lightly down Jenn's stomach.

"Val—Yes—" A hand landed on the back of Val's head, tangling in her hair. "Valentina!" Her thighs tremored, trapping Val's head between them, cutting off any hint of oxygen.

The hardwood dug into Val's knees. She couldn't breathe, but she would happily never take another breath if this was how it ended, with Jenn's release on her tongue and her body on edge with the very intensity of the moment. She slipped Jenn's leg off her shoulder, working her way up Jenn's body to a bruising crash of lips and tongue and teeth.

"You are—*oh*."

"Fuck." She slipped her hands between Jenn's thighs, rubbing over her clit before slipping inside her. "Is that okay?"

"Yes. God, yes." Jenn's hips bucked, her moan guttural, hands clutching at Val's shoulders.

Pressure built low in Val's stomach, her own clit throbbing with an almost painful lack of release. Her knees ached from kneeling on the hardwood staircase for a length of time she had no concept of and her back stung in a way that told her she'd been marked. A lot. She added a second finger, deepening her thrusts and their kiss, until breathing made it impossible to sustain. Jenn's head fell to her shoulder, her murmurs of *yes, please, God, Valentina* muffled, and she clenched Val's fingers tighter, barreling into another orgasm as she bit down on Val's shoulder.

Val almost, almost came right there with her.

She let her ride it out, nothing but soft strokes of her hips and kisses on the side of her head. She didn't know how long it was that they'd just stood there, holding onto each other like they never wanted to let go. And she didn't, but when Jenn pulled away to look at her—eyes glossy and pupils blown, the kind of just-fucked-beautiful Val could absolutely, hopelessly, irreversibly fall in love with—she tried not to think about how they *would* have to let go. Tomorrow, if not now.

Jenn brushed her nose against Val's, the way she always

did after every kiss. "You're going to have to give me a minute before I even attempt to replicate whatever you just did to me."

A laugh bubbled up in Val's chest, and she kissed her softly. "Now we go to bed."

CHAPTER 19

Jenn threaded her fingers through Valentina's hair, stroking gently as she stared down at her —head snuggled between Jenn's thigh and hip bone, features serene with her eyes closed and her breathing even for the first time in hours. The contrast of her chocolate brown hair nestled against her olive complexion, thin scratches scattered across the prominent arch of her back, the curve of her ass, legs that seemed to go on forever despite her only being as tall as Jenn—a comfortable five feet, six inches... Jenn didn't see how she would ever walk into Gia again and not think of her *exactly* like this. Not think of the way she'd been inside her, reduced Jenn to a sum of moans and pleas, and still leave her craving more.

"You think we could just stay like this?" Valentina muttered the words with her eyes still closed, breath warm and too close to where her mouth had been for what felt like an eternity mere minutes ago.

Jenn's fingers laced deeper into her hair, and she shifted

her thighs closer, the friction making it worse. Or better. She couldn't decide. "*Exactly* like this?"

Long lashes fluttered as Valentina's eyes opened. She pressed a kiss to Jenn's center, eliciting a groan of her name, working her way up to Jenn's lips before resting on one elbow and tracing Jenn's jaw with her fingers. "Have I mentioned that I love how responsive you are?"

Jenn wavered between closing her eyes to savor the touch and simply staring up at Valentina, only for the latter to win out. "I'm not always." Her gaze faltered. "I don't—What we did, in the stairway—I don't..."

"Tell me," whispered Valentina.

"Things have a place in my mind."

She nodded. "Is that why you wanted to come to your bedroom?"

"Yes, but in my office that night, I was so close to just letting you..." Jenn trailed off, her heart racing, her body taut with so much unsaid, unexpressed. "Valentina, I feel so out of control with you."

"Is that so bad?"

"As your boss, yes."

Valentina glanced downward.

Jenn brought a hand to her chin, needing unwavering eye-contact between them for this part, for words she would've said the second Valentina had showed up on her doorstep if Valentina hadn't been so relentless, if her body hadn't welcomed every second of it. "I should have asked you what you wanted. Regarding Manhattan. I was thinking about your career, because you can go so far with the love and talent you have for food. For cooking. And because I knew someone who spent her life professionally stuck because she fell in love with her boss. But I guess it was also for me. Because after everything that's happened, especially tonight, I don't know that I have the will to stay away from you anymore."

"Then don't." She shuffled closer, intertwining their legs as she breathed the words onto Jenn's lips. "Don't stay away."

"Valentina—"

"I've decided to go to Manhattan for a year. I understand why it could be good for me, I do. That's why I signed the transfer. And we don't have to tell anyone about us. Just…We can have this, Jenn."

Jenn smiled, breathing her in. "Secrets never really stay secrets, but I would be lying if I told you I didn't want to try. So, yes, if it's what you want."

"It is."

"Then, we'll consider it a calculated risk."

Valentina nuzzled Jenn's neck, trailing a hand between her breasts to her stomach. "It's so much sexier when you rationalize with your clothes off."

Jenn chuckled. "Then you should find it irresistible that my mind is already doing travel math. I have a lot of miles and a built-in reason to be in Manhattan"—she wound her hands around Valentina's lower back, brushing their lips together—"very, very often."

"Yeah?"

She tightened her grip and used the momentum to flip Valentina onto her back, her stomach fluttering at the way Valentina's breath caught and her eyes darkened to an almost pitch black. Jenn didn't recognize herself—her raging libido, the words coming out of her mouth—but it seemed like a consequence for any other moment but this one. "Or you could stay," she said.

Valentina's forehead creased and her gaze turned scrutinizing. "I'm sensitive for a hundred reasons right now. You cannot say words to me that you don't mean."

"Stay, Valentina," she repeated. "Avery thinks we should sign a consensual relationship agreement, but—"

"You talked to Avery? About us?"

"Yes?" she half-questioned. "I'm sorry if it's uncomfortable because you work together, but she's the only person I trust enough to tell about you. She claimed to have seen it a mile away, but that's beside the point, I suppose."

Valentina shook her head slowly, lips parted as if in awe. She threaded her fingers deep into Jenn's hair, their nipples grazing as their lips met—the kiss a slow waltz of tongues, so deep and sensual Jenn would melt right into Valentina if she could. All she could think was that she'd never been kissed like this, by someone who made their desire so blatantly obvious. She wondered if age was a factor, if it had anything to do with Valentina being nearly a full decade younger, if it had to do with the lithe and tone of her body, or if it was something more instinctive. If she could simply sense that Jenn possessed neither the will nor desire to not let Valentina have her in every way, however or wherever she liked.

Her hand fell to Jenn's ass, and she squeezed, thrusting her hips as she eased back with Jenn's bottom lip trapped between her teeth. "What time does your son get home?"

Jenn groaned, every nerve alive with the burst of pain and pleasure. "He doesn't." Her pulse raced. She didn't understand how her body could feel so untethered and ache with desperation all at once. "He's with Maverick for the night."

"Maverick?"

"His best friend."

"Good."

Jenn barely had time to process why that would be interpreted as good, to realize she had no idea just how insatiable

Valentina could be, or how addictive she found it, and then she was on her back in a blur.

Valentina sat upright, both hands raking her hair back, body in a paralyzing arch as she ground down onto Jenn's thigh, coating it in her arousal with every roll of her hips. "Because I'm not ready for this night to be over."

Jenn stared—helplessly, motionlessly stared—before sitting up too, one hand caressing it's way from the jewel adorning Valentina's navel to her chest, all the way to the base of her neck.

"Yes." Valentina caught her hand and guided it an inch higher, until Jenn had a loose hold around her throat. And Jenn dare not squeeze but—"Fuck. I want you inside me. Now, please."

Jenn did as commanded, slipping two fingers between her folds, deliberate in the pressure against her clit until she was knuckle-deep inside her. Heat bore down on Jenn's skin, her mind hazy with everything from memories to the unraveling of fantasies she never knew she had—the silk and fire of Valentina's skin against hers, sheer power in her lack of reserve, tightening grip on Jenn's fingers. As much as Jenn didn't recognize herself, she could hardly believe this was the same nervous, bumbling stagiaire who had tripped right into her the day they'd met, who had looked utterly adorable in her interpretation of the Twist. And she didn't mean to sound quite as spellbound as she felt, but the words fell from her lips entirely unpermitted when she shook her head and breathed, "Who even are you?"

Valentina shifted the thrust of her hips from back and forth to up and down, and she held Jenn closer, tighter, lips against Jenn's ear when she whispered, "Yours."

Jenn scribbled her signature onto the bottom of the consensual relationship agreement, attempting to disregard Avery's probing eye-contact as she sat behind her desk with arms crossed over her chest and her "Power Red" lips curled in a smirk. The picture of smug. "Don't you think you're enjoying this a little too much?" Jenn asked, leaning into the backrest of the armchair. She shifted slightly, though the chair accommodated her body well enough, then traded it for standing instead. Something about being on this side of the desk niggled at her—unfamiliarity, the power dynamic? A swift visual pass around the room—the glitter font *Work Hard Stay Humble* picture frame in particular—reinforced that this was Avery and Mel's office, and she couldn't just sit wherever she'd like because of her...control issues.

Issues she didn't seem to have last night, or this morning.

Avery raised a brow at her. "Jenn, you just signed a fucking CRA. *You*. Jenn Coleman."

Jenn winced at Avery's pitch, even knowing—*hoping*—there was no one else in the restaurant besides the two of them and Shan, the baker, who was busy in the dough room on the other side of the building. "I did read the form, Ave. I know what I signed."

"No, no, no." Avery rolled her chair back and stood. "You're going to have to put Chef Coleman away for this one. We're not working yet and I—"

"*I'm* not working yet," Jenn specified. "Or have you forgotten what time the office opens?"

"Fine. I'll tend to the million HR crises on my desk right now," Avery deadpanned. "You know you want to tell me."

"I do?"

"Yes, because you're doing that thing with your fingers that you only do when you're on edge and probably should be talking but insist on suppressing all your natural impulses."

"What thing?" Jenn's hand stilled, halting the motion of her thumb rubbing against the tip of her pointer finger the instant the question had left her lips. She fisted her hand then shook it for good measure. "My natural impulse is to *not* talk." She frowned, and crossed the room to sit in the armchair only to immediately stand again. "Has this chair always been like this?"

Avery's brows drew together, her gaze scrutinizing. "Oh. My. God. You slept with her."

A vise tightened in Jenn's chest, and Valentina's face pulsed in her mind—on her knees in the entryway of Jenn's house, deep brown eyes trained up at Jenn, all lust and seduction, on top in Jenn's bed, the untethered arch of her body and moans when Jenn was inside her. An echo of Jenn's own voice shattered the images—pitchy and unrecognizable with Valentina's taste and name on her tongue as Valentina coaxed another orgasm from her against the dryer. The dryer they'd forgotten to turn on, which resulted in Valentina leaving in one of Jenn's shirts and sweatpants, instead of the rain-soaked clothes she'd shown up in last night. Did her voice sound huskier than usual?

"You're not even going to deny it?"

Jenn cleared her throat. "I need you to draft a new contract for when she gets in. She um—" Jenn flushed, her body burning head to toe. "She won't be going to Manhattan."

"That good, huh?"

"Avery." Jenn glared at her. "You are not helping me compartmentalize this very well."

"I'm not trying to help you compartmentalize. I'm trying to help you process, so you don't panic when she walks in, and you can't stop seeing her naked. Then you'll be trying to put her on a plane again and we're back at square one."

Jenn's eyes fell shut and she rubbed at her temples.

A hand wrapped around her wrist, prompting her eyes open to Avery's, that irritating smugness replaced by a sincerity Jenn had witnessed often enough. "This is a good thing. A happy thing."

"I *am*...happy, Ave." She couldn't begin to explain all the feelings buzzing through her. All the same ones as before—concern over how effectively she would be able to do her job, whether she had been correct in all her earlier assumptions that a relationship with her boss wasn't the kind of association Valentina needed this early in her career, but yes, happiness, too. A quiet, unnerving kind of content she already dreaded the possibility of losing. Something beyond all the mind-bending ways Valentina had kissed and touched her. A yearning for the glint in her eyes first thing in the morning—the brown closer to zircon gemstones than their deeper chocolate hue—for tales of Valentina's family, her friendship with Zoe and how she'd discovered her love for cooking. The kind of content Jenn processed like a physical opening of her chest. Rare. Beautiful. Foreboding. Because the thing about her was, once she'd let someone in, really let them in, there was no getting them out. "I am happy," she repeated. "That's kind of what concerns me."

Avery grinned. "That's because you're doing it wrong. Don't overthink it."

Lines drew in Jenn's forehead. "How does one do that exactly?"

A series of raps on the door drew their attention, and Jenn turned to see Valentina stick her head in—eyes and skin radiant, beckoning. Her gaze lingered on Jenn, one corner of her bottom lip disappearing between her teeth, making Jenn's stomach flutter, before she glanced just beyond her to Avery. "Sorry. I'm early."

"You are!" Avery chirped, taking a step forward. She stood next to Jenn and lowered her voice to a whisper. "Think you're getting the hang of it. Just…a little less gawking."

Jenn startled slightly. Was she…gawking?

Jesus.

"You here for me, or the boss?"

"Um." Valentina's eyes shifted from Avery to Jenn as she stepped further into the room, one hand rubbing the back of her neck. Jenn's lips parted at the surplice neckline of her top, the sleeves rolled up to her elbows with the button tabs. "You?" Valentina's utterance screamed uncertainty.

Avery laughed, crossing the room to pat her on the shoulder. "We do have a few things to go over, preferably before the start of shift, but tell you what?" Avery cast a mischievous glance at Jenn before facing Valentina again. "I'm going to go grab coffee. Give you a little more time to be sure you did, in fact, come to *my office* to see *me*."

Jenn forced herself to watch Avery leave, just to prove to herself she was capable of looking at anything but Valentina, but the second the door closed behind Avery, her eyes went in search of Valentina's. Warmth flooded her bloodstream, her heartbeat steady yet imposing. "You were supposed to change when you got home."

Valentina peered down at the blouse she'd left Jenn's place in not even two hours ago. "I know." She glanced back at the closed door then took a measured step forward. And another. "I did change," she whispered. "Then I missed the smell of you. Not that I could ever forget it."

Tiny embers sparked below the surface of Jenn's skin.

"I did actually come looking for Avery." Her gaze fell, her

laugh a nervous parody of the sheer bliss Jenn was used to, had witnessed on her face these last six weeks. Even if it had been Landon in her ear half the time. "Guess I wanted to sign all the paperwork before you changed your mind. Not that you couldn't still change your mind."

Jenn closed the gap between them before she'd even considered it and took Valentina's face in both hands, still not used to the touch of her skin, that she was allowed to touch her at all. When Valentina looked up, chewing on her bottom lip, all Jenn wanted to do was kiss her. Long, slow, reaffirming. Instead, she traced the modest constellation of beauty marks on Valentina's cheek with her thumb, eyes fixed on hers as she shook her head. "I don't know what any of this means yet, but I'm in it, Valentina. And if it's the job you're worried about, it's yours. Not because of last night or anything between us, but because you deserve it. I will never stand between you and your future. I'm not—" She bit down on the word. *Him.* She had happily been all her mother's all her life, and despite her romantic circumstances, she would never be anything like her father. "No matter where this goes, I won't stand in your way. I hope you don't think that's what I was trying to do with Manhattan."

"I don't." Valentina bent her arms to place her hands over Jenn's, holding them against her face. "But why does it sound like we're talking about endings when we've only just begun?"

Jenn smiled, leaning in to press her lips against Valentina's nose—her perfect, 'scientifically' imperfect nose—and she took a moment to breathe her in. *'We've only just begun.'* She needed a moment to process all the wonderfully unusual things those words unearthed in her chest and stomach. "We're not. Talking about endings. Just acknowledging the complexities of our situation."

Valentina hummed. "Sounds pretty serious."

"It is." Jenn pulled back for a look at her. "Serious." She licked her lips, smiling. "So serious I think I really need to leave before I do something entirely inappropriate."

"Wouldn't want that." The way the words slipped from Valentina's lips didn't help, neither did her darkening gaze, slow rise and fall of her chest.

A coil twisted low in Jenn's stomach. She tried to quiet it by tucking an errant strand of hair behind Valentina's ear. "Good luck with the paperwork, and consider this my formal welcome to Gia, San Francisco."

A breathy chuckle resounded as she made to leave, and Valentina caught her hand—just the slightest brush of fingers, a vision of more shared in passing in the hallways and kitchen flashing in Jenn's mind. "Tommy's back later, right?" The look in Valentina's eyes implied exactly what she really wanted to ask, what she sought.

More.

More time alone, more of last night, more of all the things Jenn craved too.

"Yes." Jenn nodded. "I'll actually leave a bit early to go pick him up from Maverick's, but..." She wavered. "I'll text you, if I'm not back for closing. We'll figure something out."

Valentina peered down at their still touching fingers, gently intertwining them before taking a reluctant step back. "I'll be waiting."

CHAPTER 20

Val's feet left the security of Gia's kitchen floors as Warren's arms engulfed her in a tight hug that left her laughing twice as hard. "You're literally a super tall teddy bear."

"I knew Chef Coleman wouldn't let you go." Said by anyone else, Val might have given those words a second thought, but Warren didn't have a sarcastic bone in his body. He lowered her to the floor, grinning as he took a step back. "Glad you're staying, Val."

Val winked at him. "I'm going to take that at face value and pretend all this excitement isn't really because you were scared Zo was going to leave too."

"Well, I mean…" He trailed off. "I can't say I'm mad now she doesn't have to choose."

"Me, too. But, so you know, I would've totally stolen her ID to make her stay."

Warren's gaze shifted downward, his smile equal parts wistful and glad. "You're a great friend."

"I just knew I'd be leaving her in good hands." And Zoe didn't need anyone to take care of her—not when she'd always done so well caring for herself—but the last time she'd liked someone as much as she liked Warren, they'd been undergrads at NYU. Val an Econ major, Zoe undeclared and falling for a trust fund douche enrolled at Cornell. If neither of them never heard the name Kason King again, it would be too fucking soon.

"Think you have a pretty good idea how I feel about this news," Landon put in.

Val turned to face him—his thick dark pompadour caught in a bun with a neon pink hair tie that made him look either sort of adorable or absolutely ridiculous, his smile perhaps the most sincere she'd ever seen it, free of flirtation or ego. And yet, there was something in the way he was looking at her—a softness—that left no question she had to douse any flicker of hope he still had, or that she'd given him.

Warren looked between them, backing away slowly. "I'm going to go, um, grab a bite before things get wild in here."

A pan clanked in the general direction of the dish pit. Mel and two other chefs stood chatting by the expo station. Wednesdays were never wild. They still had prep to do, but Val got the feeling Warren's sixth sense had been tingling from whatever weird energy had been lingering between her and Landon. She couldn't blame him for wanting to get as far away from it as possible.

She faced Landon with a sigh. "Listen, Lan, I know ever since I started here, we've existed in this sort of bizarre limbo of friendly and flirty."

Landon chuckled. "I don't mind that kind of limbo."

Val's smile was tight, unyielding. "It's just...I met someone." She clamped her mouth shut. "I mean, I *am* seeing someone."

His smile faded like a flickering flame.

"I just figured you should know, since—"

"I thought you weren't—I mean…" He shook his head. "I thought you didn't want that right now."

"I didn't. It just kind of…happened?"

"I never understand what people mean by that," he grumbled.

Said by someone who never stayed too late to check on their boss who'd had a panic attack earlier that day, then wound up almost undressing said boss on top of her delightfully sturdy desk. There was a lot to unpack there—including a not-so-dormant fantasy she hadn't realized she'd been harboring—a lot she'd wanted to but still hadn't found the right moment to ask Jenn about. Beginning with why Jenn had been so upset that day, what she'd meant last night about knowing someone who'd spent their life professionally stuck after getting involved with their boss. Had she been involved with another employee before?

"Is it serious?" Landon asked.

The door to main dining opened and Jenn stepped in—impeccable in her whites with her tablet in hand. Her focus faltered as she locked eyes with Val and her gaze softened, flashed with something else, then returned to the device in her hand. "Yeah. I think it is."

Landon scoffed, dragging a hand over faint signs of a five o'clock shadow. "Thanks for telling me, I guess. I hope he makes you happy."

"She."

Creases appeared between his brows. "What?"

"She does make me happy."

"Oh. I didn't know you were gay. I mean, not that I have a problem with that or anything."

"I'm not, but good to know."

"You're not what?"

"Gay."

His frown intensified in a way that reminded her of coming out to her parents. Her traditional, Mexican, nearly sixty-year-old parents. Why a millennial man who spent two-thirds of his nights in bars and clubs in one of the most queer-friendly cities in the country was having trouble processing, she didn't understand. "O-kay. Well, um..." He glanced at the clock above the door Jenn had just come through. "I should probably grab a bite before work, too. For what it's worth, I'm still glad you're staying."

Val surveyed the kitchen once more, slowly, appreciating the moment for what it was. First step in a dream come true. She didn't know how much different things would be now that her role wasn't so speculative anymore, especially with the added element of being with Jenn, but she knew there wasn't a single other place she'd rather be. "Me too."

BEING the newest commis chef at Gia was nothing like staging.

Actually, it was exactly the same, except maybe now that Val had spent the last twelve hours being yelled at by the saucier, Kent, about how to sauté spices and make tomato paste from scratch, she could never make enchilada sauce without a pinch of cinnamon ever again. More than that, the rush of being in the kitchen had altered—it was nothing she could explain. She'd always been driven to excel, always had a hunger for the steady heat of the kitchen, sizzling pans and screaming colleagues, the constant motion of it all. Her name on a contract didn't make being at Gia any more real than it had been the last six weeks, but today she'd felt unstoppable. Capable of absorbing any and everything that would make her a better chef, and never feeling any of the exhaustion.

Then again, Wednesdays had never been all that bad.

And every time Jenn's eyes had caught hers across the kitchen, a new wave of invincibility would wash over her. Her gaze swept over her line station for any perishables that hadn't been taken to the walk-in, one hand slipping into her pocket for her phone. The time stared back at her. A taunting 12:23 a.m. No notifications. No missed calls or messages.

Mel stumbled in from main dining with an arm full of dirty linens clutched to her chest, her green eyes bloodshot beneath the cover of her ginger bangs. "How's everything coming back here?"

Landon's affirmation of "Good, Chef," came with an exuberance Val tried not to take personally. No doubt he was a fan of Mel's more 'here are your assignments for closing' then disappearing act, but Val would give anything to have Jenn hovering with her checklist.

"Rosas?"

Her head snapped in Mel's direction. "Yeah. All good, Chef."

"Great. We just might be out of here before one tonight." Mel turned on her heels, heading in the direction she'd come. "I have to get these to the wash."

Kent's Closing Time playlist looped back to Semisonic—were there even any other songs on that thing? Just over the melody, Landon asked Warren if he wanted to grab a drink before turning in, and Warren declined, explaining how he was headed to Zoe's right after work. Something stirred in Val's chest. All she wanted was to be able to do that too. To just leave work and go to her…

Jenn's.

Go to Jenn's. Lose sleep exploring all the pent-up desire she could only hope Jenn had spent half the day suppressing too. But Jenn's early departure from shift was a stark reminder that the complexities of their relationship didn't only revolve around their dynamic at Gia.

Jenn had a kid. A teenager. She had a...Rachel. Neither of which were exactly a problem. But Val was beginning to think between working twelve-hour shifts and everything else, last night—the freedom of being able to have Jenn so uninhibited—would be a rare luxury.

Her phone buzzed, drawing her attention back to the screen and her pulse to a race.

Jenn (12:27 a.m.)
How are you doing with closing?

The sound from Val's lips echoed half scoff, half amusement.

Val (12:27 a.m.)
Not the sexiest text I've ever gotten at midnight
But I miss you too much to care.

The bubble appeared, signaling Jenn working at an answer. Val watched, waited. The bubble disappeared, leaving her with something she'd never had much of in flirting. Doubt. She never quite knew how forward to be with Jenn, except for last night when everything in Jenn's tone and demeanor screamed surrender. Her fingers swiped across the screen before she'd given her follow up much thought.

Val (12:29 a.m.)
Was that too much?
Saying I miss you.

Jenn (12:29 a.m.)
No.
Not at all.
I'm just trying to decide if I should be concerned you're getting sexy texts from anyone but me.

Val sunk her teeth into her bottom lip.

Val (12:31 a.m.)
Is this your way of saying you want me all to yourself?

Jenn (12:31 a.m.)
Hmm
I don't know.
Last night, when you were on top of me and I was inside you, you told me you were mine...

Val's body heated up at the memory—Jenn's light hold on her neck, her eyes trained on Val with equal parts lust and fascination, lips parted and blush red.

Jenn (12:32 a.m.)
Did I take that too literally? Sometimes, I do take things too literally.

Val (12:32 a.m.)
I can't tell if you're being unfairly adorable, or if you know exactly what you're doing right now.

Jenn (12:32 a.m.)
The truth?

Val (12:32 a.m.)
Always.

Jenn (12:32 a.m.)

It's both.

"Val?"

Val startled, smashing the power button with her thumb as she peered up at Landon. Her heart hammered in her chest, the flush of her skin palpable as she struggled to keep her expression neutral. "What's up?"

Landon's brows drew together in skepticism. "Sexting on the job?"

Val breathed a nervous laugh. "I wish."

"Hey, just be glad Chef OC—"

Val crossed both arms over her chest.

"Coleman," Landon enunciated, his forced recovery a sure sign that he too remembered it—their only disagreement. Val wasn't sure she'd be as amenable to his charm-glazed apology for saying anything less than flattering about Jenn this time. "Just be glad it's Mel who's closing tonight. Coleman doesn't like distractions."

And yet, Val thought, tonight Jenn *was* the distraction. Her phone buzzed in her hand, and she tightened her grip in an effort to not look down.

Landon's gaze drifted to her hand—his lips pursed momentarily—before he looked up again. "You about done here?"

"Yeah. Pretty much." She did a quick visual sweep of her line. "Just about to head back and change."

"Cool. All right. I guess um..." He rapped his knuckles twice against the stainless steel worktable. "Night, then."

Val frowned, watching him cross the kitchen toward the fry station. She had the faintest inkling to stop him and ask if he was okay, but something told her she already knew exactly what that bizarre attempt at a conversation was about.

Her phone vibrated again, and her body tingled with anticipation as she unlocked it.

Jenn (12:35 a.m.)
I did take it literally, because even as new as this is, even with every possibility that it might fail, I do want you to be mine.

I'd be remiss to not acknowledge I'm much older than you are, and maybe more traditional?

I understand if you'd like to keep your options open.
Jenn (12:38 a.m.)
Did I say too much now?

Val (12:40 a.m.)
Later we'll have to talk about everything you just said.
For now, there's only one thing I need you to know.
I don't want options. I just want you.
In every possible way.

Jenn (12:41 a.m.)
Our earlier messages have you labeling words like those as unfair.

Val (12:42 a.m.)
What are the chances I get to see you tonight?

Jenn (12:42 a.m.)
About 10 to 1
Tommy is in full summer mode and wide awake. He has me on a Netflix binge.

Val laughed.

Val (12:42 a.m.)
Is that so?

Jenn (12:42 a.m.)
Yes. Some show called On My Block with teenagers who get into way too much trouble. I don't know if I should be taking hints.

Val (12:43 a.m.)
I'm sure he just wanted to watch TV with his mom.

Jenn (12:43 a.m.)
Maybe.
Let's try for tomorrow?

Val (12:43 a.m.)
Tomorrow.

CHAPTER 21

Jenn stared across Gia's main dining room as she absentmindedly twisted the round pendant of her necklace between her thumb and forefinger, the buzz in the air typical of midweek afternoons. Chuckles, chatter and clinking utensils. Their youngest waiter, Summer, had reverted to sporting a red bowtie with her uniform. Gavin had perhaps leered a bit too much at the four-top occupied by men dressed exclusively in hoodies and horn-rimmed glasses. But the woman by the bar, with gorgeous sun-kissed skin and dark hair in waves down to the middle of her back, had all of Jenn's senses dulling.

Daydreams of Valentina pulsed in her mind. Nearly a week of muted smiles and whispers, brushing hands, middle-of-the-night messages that left Jenn feeling somewhere between painfully aroused and like a lightheaded teenager. Except, she couldn't remember the last time she missed someone like *this*. The last time she *wanted* someone with an acuteness, an aching even, that left her in serious contemplation about breaking every working principle she'd established within the walls of Gia—within anywhere—was probably... Well, never.

"Jenn?" A hand flashed through her line of vision.

She blinked, frowning at the impatience etched on Rachel's face—her routinely groomed brows knitted close together, glare steady. "Sorry. I'm a little tired."

Rachel held her gaze for a moment, seemingly unconvinced, before she forked up another bite of her enchilada lasagna. "You're not sleeping well?"

Jenn glanced down at her own dish. The chicken-avocado caprese quesadillas had always been one of her go to orders for eating in her own restaurant. Yet, after Mel had gone through the trouble of taking the meals out herself, Jenn's stomach no longer seemed interested. "I'm sleeping fine. Better, some nights."

Rachel raised a brow. "Are you about to tell me you're eating fine too?"

"Rach..."

"What?"

Jenn sighed, putting away her fork along with the pretense she had any interest in her food at the moment. "You know I don't like this mothering bit."

"Well, someone has to take care of you."

"Someone does," Jenn asserted. "Me. I care for myself."

"No." Rachel chewed a bite, pointing her fork at Jenn in a decidedly threatening manner. "You take care of everything *but* yourself."

"I thought we were here to talk about Tommy's birthday."

"We were." Rachel shrugged. "Then you checked out on Instagram or movie party."

"Right." Jenn closed her eyes, rubbing away the impending headache at her temples. "Are we sure we want to get behind a social-media themed party? I mean, Tommy has never exactly struggled with friends or popularity, but isn't turning fourteen menacing enough without plastering it all over a platform built on likes and"—Jenn poised her fingers for air quotations—"*living his best life.*"

Rachel chuckled, wiping her lips with a Gia embroidered white napkin. "There is nothing menacing about being fourteen. All he has to worry about is school, sports and girls."

"Or boys," murmured Jenn.

Lines drew in Rachel's forehead as she rested her forearms against the table and leaned forward. "Has he said something?"

Jenn shook her head. "No. I just think it's possible. You see how inseparable he and Maverick are." Not that that necessarily meant anything. Friendships could be so… consuming at that age. Inspiring and grand, especially built on the ideal of an unbreakable bond. A memory of preteen Lizzie cropped up in Jenn's mind—her childhood BFF. But forever could be fragile, especially at that age.

Rachel waved a hand in the air, drawing Jenn back. "Well, whomever he is interested in, I'm sure he'll be fine."

"Said by someone who never had to worry about being liked."

"I was a mathlete." Rachel feigned offense.

"And a cheerleader," Jenn countered.

"So that's a no on the Instagram party then?"

"A movie sounds…" Jenn paused, chasing the word around her mind. "More wholesome."

"Fine. In a second, we'll discuss the logistics of fitting twenty, rowdy teenagers into the living room at the townhouse for a movie, but since when do you care so much about being liked?"

"I don't." Mostly. Sometimes, it was as if Rachel wanted Tommy to take after Jenn as little as possible in all things social, and Jenn was happy he hadn't. Really. The soccer, football, his natural charisma and general willingness to talk to almost anyone made him well-liked. But something about this Instagram party felt...exclusive, vain even, and more like a trend Rachel had picked up on the Internet instead of something Tommy would actually want. There was also the possibility that Jenn was projecting, because she was exactly the kind of kid who would never have been invited to something like that, but still. "And we're hosting at the condo," she clarified.

Rachel scoffed. "Of course we are."

"Rach, we agreed on this a year ago. We share planning and expenses, but I hosted his last birthday. This year, it's you."

"Yes, Jenn. You could still say it less like a commandment and more like a discussion."

Jenn scrunched up her face. "Why would it be a discussion?"

Rachel's sigh echoed frustration. "I don't know, Jenn. Why would anything be a discussion?"

Jenn paused, assessing. The moment read vaguely like one they'd lived before, though it had been quite a few years since. She opened her mouth to respond, only to clamp it shut again at the faint chime coming from her pocket. "Excuse me." She reached into the pair of black slacks for which she traded her whites half an hour ago and came up with her phone. Her nerves sparked at the sight of the notification—the preview enough to display the full message. Both messages.

Valentina (6:38 p.m.)
I know we don't talk like this at work

But I need to see you tonight.

Jenn's gaze drifted to the double doors of the kitchen, one swinging on its hinges as a server rushed out with a steaming tray.

Another chime.

Valentina (6:39 p.m.)
I miss the taste of your lips
The way your body tightens everywhere when we kiss.

"Kitchen on fire?"

Jenn flipped over her phone and slammed it screen down against the table. "No. Just—" She cleared her throat, ignoring the heat creeping up her neck. "An overdue meeting."

Rachel narrowed her gaze, inspecting Jenn for a moment. "You forget that you're the shade of brown that shows a blush."

"Blush?" Jenn sat up a little straighter. "I don't—" She winced at the taste of the word on her tongue. "I never blush." A tingle swept up the back of her neck and fanned across her cheeks.

"Uh huh." Rachel's brows nearly touched.

The lump lodged in Jenn's throat refused to budge. "Should I organize catering from here?"

"Yeah. Just make it less gourmet…and more PG."

"Of course, Rach." Jenn picked up her phone, making a conscious effort to swipe directly to her Notes app, though her fingers itched to tap out a response to Valentina. *Apples.* How did her lips always taste of apples, when her skin hinted of shea and between her thighs—Jenn pressed fingers to her temples again, as if to physically rewire her brain.

"You really need to take care of that headache."

"It's fine." Jenn added *pizzas, tacos and sugary poison* to her *Tommy Turns 14* note. "Will Luna be attending?"

"She will."

"Good. I'll get to meet her."

"You want to meet Luna? My girlfriend?"

"I want to meet the woman who influences our son's nutrition."

Rachel's laugh was part genuine humor, part irony. "Does that mean you'll be inviting that teenager who showed up at your place the weekend you and Tommy left for New York?"

Jenn tilted her head in confusion. "Teenager?" There was only one person who had shown up to the townhouse that weekend, but surely Rachel didn't mean—

"Valentina, was it?" She shifted in her chair, glancing over her shoulder. "In fact, where is she tonight? I'd love to continue our little chat."

Jenn pursed her lips. "Valentina is where she should be. In the kitchen. Working." *Apparently, between teasing text messages.*

"Hmm." Rachel hummed, watching Jenn closely.

"What about a photographer?" Jenn redirected.

"She's your employee."

"I'm aware. Should I call Finley? They did the candids last year."

"She's young, Jenn."

"She's twenty-eight." Jenn added another line to her notes. "I'll check if they're available."

"Did something happen? I know you're stressed over the results of the biopsy. Inconclusive is just that, Jenn. But this...this girl—"

Jenn slammed her palm against the wooden surface of the two-top they occupied. The plates and cutlery rattled.

Heads turned. Jenn's entire body buzzed with quiet rage and mild panic. She waited a beat—enough for a slow inhale, for people to decide there was nothing to see and return to their own conversations. "Enough, Rach. Whatever is happening between me and Valentina has nothing to do with my medical challenges." The words *or you for that matter* lingered on her tongue.

Funny. While they'd been a couple, half their fights had been about how stubborn and controlling Jenn could be. How she micromanaged, was set in her ways. And yet, sometimes, especially since they'd separated, it was as if Rachel would compulsively hover in the smallest aspects of Jenn's life. When and how she slept, ate, spent her time. Now with whom. Deep down, Jenn understood that it came from a place of genuine care. Rachel loved her. They loved each other. But it was almost as if Rachel had somehow convinced herself that, with Jenn's mom gone, no one else knew how to love Jenn. Including Jenn herself. And sure, the tests, the waiting most of all, had been difficult. She had made a conscious effort the last week not to think too much about it. Thinking about it always led to that all-consuming, panic-inducing tightening of her chest and cycle of nausea that left her paralyzed. No good to herself, the people who loved her, or her restaurant. Jenn wasn't with Valentina because the poison that had stolen her mom could potentially be inside her. She was with Valentina in spite of it.

"Just..."

Rachel stared, waiting, knowing there were things Jenn hadn't said.

Jenn sighed. "Can we just focus on the party?"

The concern in Rachel's eyes didn't waver and her jaw visibly clenched. Then, she said, "Yes. Call Finley about the photos. Otherwise, we'll just end up with a cloud full of Boomerangs and Big City Life filters."

JENN SHUT the door on private dining one and descended the stairs toward the ground floor. She did a quick pass through main dining and the kitchen leaving those lights on, but shutting off those in the bathrooms and offices. She mentally went through her checklist one last time, though she knew it by heart, but after not being at the restaurant for closing for a week, tonight there was something odd about going through the motions. Something bizarre in the stillness, in being alone here, that she used to savor after a long day. Her brain hadn't quite settled on how to process the emotion, hadn't decided why something she'd spent nearly the last decade of her life doing would register as even remotely strange?

The place just seemed changed somehow.

Or maybe it was her.

Traces of her earlier conversation with Rachel lingered in her mind, the weight of her phone palpable in the pocket of her slacks. A taunting reminder she hadn't replied to Valentina's message about seeing each other tonight. These were the moments when her thoughts would settle, after the rush of a fourteen-hour day when she had no choice but to pay attention to them. But Rachel's words had provoked them sooner, prompted Jenn into a premature stint of brooding in her office over budgets and supply lists, and a safety compliance roster Avery was more than capable of managing on her own. She could've been in the kitchen instead—lent herself proximity to Valentina's laugh—heartwarming and melodic—amidst the bustle of the kitchen whenever Landon or Warren said something entirely ridiculous and the wrong side of millennial. And Jenn could do without the debate on why nose hair extensions had cropped up as a beauty trend among Influencers, but she would listen to Valentina's thoughts on anything. Then again...

The quiet, those moments after they'd kissed, after she'd had Valentina all over, under, inside her were probably her favorite. When the race of her pulse and flutter in her chest both alarmed her and put her at ease.

She reached for the handle of the door to exit the building, and her breath caught.

Her heartbeat stuttered then evened with a slow exhale.

Valentina grinned, leaned against the front passenger-side door of Jenn's X6, casually dressed in a Gia-branded shirt. The sleeves stretch beyond her knuckles leaving the tips of her fingers barely visible, nails an indistinguishable shade of blue in the dimness of Gia's side alley. The contrast between the one size-too-big shirt and her skin-tight jeans stirred something deep in the pit of Jenn's stomach, made her mouth water, her heart race. Especially when Valentina pushed away from the car and raked a hand through her hair—tousled and wavy, leaving the right side of her neck free in a taunting display. "This doesn't technically qualify as stalking, does it?"

Jenn's lips drew in a smile she hoped didn't give away the euphoric-like wonder blooming in her chest. "Not technically." She pulled the door shut, locked then tested it before facing Valentina again.

Valentina glanced down the alleyway before stepping forward and taking Jenn's hand, and Jenn instantly tightened her grip. "You never answered my text," she said softly, staring down at their hands.

"I know. I'm sorry." Jenn reached up to stroke her face, drawing her thumb over the constellation of beauty marks until Valentina's gaze met hers. So direct in its sincerity, honest in its desire, devastatingly reflective of feelings Jenn couldn't begin to put into words. Because maybe Rachel was right. Maybe Jenn *was* overwhelmed with the changes in her body and words like "inconclusive" did nothing to prevent that. She loved having Tommy with her—bonding over Netflix and soccer in the tiny concrete tropic that was her backyard only asserted how much she'd missed him—but working *less* hadn't been helping her anxiety, which was something Rachel would never understand. The only thing that did, the only *person* who did—She swallowed against the tightness in her throat.

Valentina's brows knit as she moved to eliminate the space between them. "Hey, is everything okay?" She wrapped her hands around Jenn's neck, fingers stroking gently through her hair.

Jenn's eyes drifted closed. "Everything's fine. I'm just..." She whispered the words onto Valentina's lips. "Thank you. For staying."

"Always." It was said so softly, with so much conviction, that when they kissed, Jenn swore she tasted forever. She circled Valentina's waist, dwelling in the catch of her breath, her fingers scratching at Jenn's scalp as their tongues waltzed. Jenn slipped her hands beneath Valentina's shirt in search of the warm rush of her skin, tracing a lateral pattern to the small jewel glimmering against her navel before moving just beneath the underwire of her bra.

Valentina's teeth grazed Jenn's lips as she pulled away.

Jenn opened her eyes slowly, the chill of the air suddenly more present as she regained consciousness of where they were standing. A poorly lit alleyway just outside her restaurant, well past 1 a.m. *Jesus Christ.* Had she signed away all her self-control with the CRA? "Sorry." Short breaths punctuated her apology. "I'm sorry. I—"

Valentina's lips found hers again. Slow. Lingering. Then gone. "Don't ever apologize for kissing me like that."

"Okay." Half statement, half question.

"Did everything go okay with Rachel at dinner? I'm not trying to pry or anything, I just…"

Jenn found herself wanting to cut her off with a kiss, just like Valentina had mere seconds ago. The night they'd kissed looped in her mind—Valentina's questions about a girlfriend or wife. Jenn would hope by now Valentina knew Rachel was neither, but she also couldn't help thinking it was something they probably should have discussed sooner. Not that this was the time or place. "Dinner was okay. A little tense at points, but okay. We just needed to settle on some details for Tommy's birthday."

Valentina nodded, gaze locked on the hand she had smoothing Jenn's collar. "Okay."

Jenn tilted her head up with a hand under her chin—how could someone so unreservedly confident and sexy also be encased in so much demure? "You never need to be concerned about Rachel, and you never need to worry about asking me anything. I'm private about my personal life, but not secretive. Not with someone I'm—who I—not with you, Valentina."

Glossy, deep brown eyes stared up at her, Valentina's gaze shifting all around her face to her mouth, Jenn's chasing it. Valentina leaned in and slid a hand into Jenn's pocket—the act innocuous yet teasing. Jenn's car came alive with an animated flash of lights and beeps. Then, Valentina was leading her toward it. "Come here."

Jenn never let anyone drive her car, but strangely

enough, the word no hadn't immediately leapt out of her mouth. Even stranger was Valentina opening the back door and sliding onto the pristine black leather. Jenn's heart pounded as she slipped in next to her and mindlessly pulled the door shut behind them—something buried deep deciphering Valentina's intentions, something instinctive. The locks clicked shut. Jenn breathed, "Valentina—"

The gentle brush of lips against her neck sent a tingle straight to her toes. "What time do you have to be home? Is Tommy there alone?"

"Yes. I mean, Maverick is sleeping over."

Hands brushed her breasts over her shirt. "Please tell me they'll be okay for another twenty minutes."

Jenn groaned. "Valentina."

"Fine. Fifteen."

Jenn tapped her watch with an unsteady hand. *1:38 a.m.*. Her breaths quickened. "Seventeen." Not an even number, and not nearly enough, but a middle ground Jenn didn't have the will to reject. Not with Valentina's lips burning a trail toward her chest, fingers undoing the buttons of her shirt with unmatched dexterity. "We have seventeen."

A hand emerged on her outer thigh, the other steady around her waist, leaving her straddling Valentina in a single swift motion. She clutched the hem of Valentina's shirt, tugged it over her head and dropped it on the seat next to them. Through the back windshield, the street loomed beneath beaming lampposts faintly alive with a group of six or so people and a pair of passing cars. Her bra snapped open, fingers tangled in her hair, guiding her mouth to Valentina's whispered, "Stay with me."

"I am." They were in a car with people passing and every nerve in Jenn's body was so alive with Valentina's presence, touch, kiss. She trailed a trembling hand along Valentina's shoulder toward her bra strap, the swells of her breasts, her nipples.

A shiver passed through her. Yet, Jenn registered the faint release of her zipper being undone, the hand sliding into her underwear seconds away from discovering—

"You're so wet."

Jenn's moan melted onto Valentina's lips, lips she could feel arching to a smile.

"Please tell me this is some kind of unattained fantasy. Being fucked in your backseat."

"*Valentina*—"

"God, I love it when you say my name like that."

Fingers circled Jenn's entrance and she shifted her hips to settle onto them. Valentina whispered encouragements—something about Jenn taking what she needed and how she's *so fucking gorgeous like this*. The angle couldn't have been comfortable for her wrist—two fingers deep, her thumb pressed to Jenn's clit—especially with Jenn's pants still on. Maybe Jenn was too high on the pressure building between her thighs and the liquid lust glimmering in Valentina's eyes, but something told her Valentina didn't mind. "I want to feel you." Jenn moved frantic hands to the clasp of Valentina's bra, failing, groaning, moaning Valentina's name again before finally getting it open. She slipped the strap from Valentina's free hand then pressed their bodies flush together, the brush of their nipples pushing her closer to the edge along with traces of Valentina's touch from the base of her spine to her neck.

"I'm going to—Valentina, I can't—"

"Come for me, baby."

Someone must have heard. The zoom of cars—sporadic and faint as they were—stopped. Everything stopped but the force of the orgasm crashing and cresting over and over and over, Jenn's body clenching around Valentina's fingers—claiming and keeping them inside her—and leaving Jenn a breathless, euphoric mess. She came to with the soft strokes against the small of her back, both their skin damp with sweat, something soft and muttered in the space between them.

Something like, "Damn."

Jenn pulled back slightly, staring into Valentina's eyes. Nothing about the moment really made sense. Not where she was or who she was with, or the words that left her lips. "Come home with me."

CHAPTER 22

The jagged angles of the luxury apartment building towering at least twenty floors toward the sky—bay windows overlooking the Pacific—didn't strike Val as all that surprising. Neither did the elaborate pendant lights hung in the pristine lobby, nor the thirty-something year-old concierge standing behind the desk programmed to smile every time the double glass doors swung open to announce someone's presence. If she was being honest, maybe this was why she'd been surprised the first time she'd shown up at Jenn's. Because a lavish condo in a neighborhood Val had only frequented on Zillow was exactly where she'd picture Jenn Coleman living. Now that she'd been getting to know Jenn, had spent more than a handful of nights in the last two weeks sneaking in and out of her Edwardian in the Mission, Val could already say she liked it better.

This place, though striking, lacked the character of toddler-Tommy's key scratch on Jenn's front door and the pictures in her entryway, and Val didn't imagine Rachel's condo being any different.

Val tightened her grip on the strap of the camera bag her mom had knitted just in time for Val's Christmas visit two years ago. There were still traces of her parents' laundry soap on it—a little taste of their home in San Rafael. Val had never been remotely concerned about her humble upbringing, but something about the way the concierge hadn't taken his beady green eyes off her since the second she'd walked in was giving her an inferiority complex. Despite the megawatt smile.

"Can I help you?"

"Um." Val tried not to cringe at the shrillness of his tone, digging into her back pocket for her phone.

The elevator dinged, snapping her head up just in time to catch Jenn exit the lift.

"Chef Coleman."

Jenn bobbed her head in his direction. "Hello, Tishman."

Val wasn't sure whether to focus on the warmth in *Tishman's* greeting—something she assumed to be reserved for residents of the building—or the fact that Jenn seemed annoyed by it. She had a strange inkling that Jenn was here a lot more than she'd given herself time to consider, had probably even lived here once. With Rachel.

"Thank you so much for doing this." Jenn stopped just in front of her—hazel eyes muted shades of gold and green in the natural light filtering into the lobby. "We had a photographer, but they cancelled at the last minute. I mean, they said they were fine. Just a cold. But we can't let a possibly contagious person in a room of twenty teenagers."

Val bit down on a smile—flustered Jenn was a rare sighting, but the faint tinge to her freckled cheeks had Val's mind wandering. Three nights ago. A duvet up to her shoulders, her head between Jenn's twitching thighs, same blush on her face when she emerged from the cover of the pillow she'd pressed to her face to muffle her scream.

Jenn's gaze fell to Val's lips and held. Then, she swallowed, making eye contact with Val again. "Anyway, um, thank you."

"Anytime." Today had been her first Saturday off in the two months since she'd started at Gia. It would probably be months before she got another but there was nowhere else she'd rather be. Well, her first pick probably wouldn't be with Jenn, her ex and a house full of kids, but it wasn't like being and dating a chef would ever leave her swimming in options. The last couple of weeks had been hard enough as it was, and maybe there had been a tiny part of her that had been disappointed Jenn hadn't invited her to Tommy's birthday in the first place. "Just so we're clear, you do remember me saying I only took *one* course. Like, half a century ago."

"The pictures of Golden Gate you showed me were perfect." Jenn squeezed her arm, retracting her hand too soon for Val's liking. "Besides," she turned for the elevator and gestured for Val to follow, "These are for me and Rachel. I'm sure the kids will be taking their own."

"Right."

There *were* smartphones with better camera quality than the $800 Nikon it had taken her months to buy.

The doors to the lift slid open and a hand landed on the small of Val's back, guiding her into the empty elevator. She scanned the inside in quick appraisal. Both their reflections shimmered back at them. Was this thing plated with gold? Fingers brushed hers, inciting her to glance up at Jenn, take a closer look at the light layer of makeup on her face and purposefully wavy hair nestled against her shoulders, her white linen tunic shirt, form-fitting ankle jeans and point toe booties. "You look incredible by the way." Val chuckled softly. "Is that casual for a fourteen-year-old's birthday, because I feel a little underdressed."

Jenn's hand rested on Val's hip over her bubble hem sweatshirt—Zoe had had to talk her out of a crop top and cutoff denims, something about not showing up to her girlfriend's place looking like a teenage boy's wet dream—but she would've welcomed the skin on skin contact now. "You look wonderful." Jenn glanced at the button panel as the elevator climbed floors seven, eight... "There's something I should probably mention."

"Okay?" Val watched her expectantly.

Jenn met her gaze again. "Rachel knows. About us. Which is fine. I was planning on telling her and Tommy soon. It's just that you're about to spend the next few hours with her and there's a possibility she might try to talk to you. She's..." Her face twitched in a grimace. "Protective."

Val's brows crept up. "Of you or your son?"

"Both. I'm establishing boundaries. I've made it clear she's not to mention our relationship, but Rach—"

"Ours or the one you have with her?"

Jenn tilted her head. "Valentina."

Val closed her eyes and drew in a breath. "Sorry. I guess I'm just...not really used to any of this."

"I don't expect you to be, and I know it could get uncomfortable. I would've loved to have this discussion with more time. I—" She shook her head. "I planned to talk to you then invite you to dinner so you could properly meet Tommy, and yes, Rachel too. Probably Luna. So I could introduce you as my—so I could tell them. About us."

Val stared up at her. Girlfriend? Was that what Jenn had been about to say?

"Rachel is difficult, but she's family. I don't have too

much of that with my mom gone and my father..." Jenn sighed, eyes trained downward as she squeezed Val's hand. "What I'm saying is, I would never allow anyone to insult you or...this thing that's been growing between us. Not even family."

Every word, the fierce protectiveness in Jenn's eyes—tiny flecks of green amidst a wildfire—warmed Val straight to her toes. And yet, she couldn't help getting stuck on one thing Jenn had said, something she'd mentioned before but never explained. "Jenn, what happened to your dad?"

Ding.

The doors slid open with a mechanical whir.

Jenn's brows twitched then relaxed, alarm flashing across her features for a second. Less. "He lives in Potrero Hill with his wife."

Potrero Hill, Val considered. "As in here, San Francisco?"

"Yes. He never wanted anything to do with me. I guess you could say the feeling is mutual." The words left her mouth with a detachment so incompatible with the delicacy with which she then leaned forward, pressing a gentle kiss to Val's lips. "I know you're already here, but if it's too much, I understand you not wanting to come in."

Val cradled her face, searching her eyes. So, so many layers. So much unsaid. "I'm with you."

Jenn breathed her in, raising their joined hands to press a kiss to Val's knuckles. "And I'm with you."

VAL WAS STILL PROCESSING the moment Jenn released her hand—just before they entered the condo—when a gleeful squeal drew her attention to Avery, heels in rapid taps against the hardwood floor as she darted over to wrap Val in a hug. "You're here!"

Val's arms circled Avery reflexively, half-indulging the warmth of her welcome, but her gaze followed Jenn across the open floor plan to where Rachel stood by a modern kitchen island candy-stacked like a concession stand. She'd traded her braids for a much shorter style—tapered sides topped with natural raven curls—but it wasn't as if she was the kind of striking Val could ever mistake for anyone else.

Avery pulled away, following Val's line of sight before facing her with a smirk. "Guessing you two have met."

Val shrugged as she redirected her attention to Avery—she preferred to not give too much thought to that day, when she'd just showed up at Jenn's and Rachel had been there looking like she owned the place. "I guess you could say that."

"Rach is harmless. Mostly. And Jenn is so into you it would be embarrassing if it wasn't so fucking cute." Avery laughed, Val joining as her gaze drifted to Jenn, pulse picking up when she found Jenn already looking her way. "Just don't tell her I told you that."

Val turned to Avery and mimicked zipping her lips shut. "Our secret. Besides, today is not the day I unleash my very dormant jealous streak. I'm just here to take pictures." Her brows knit as she surveyed their surroundings. "Speaking of pictures, this doesn't look like the kind of posh that's been in proximity to more than a dozen fourteen-year-olds."

"They're on the roof," Avery explained through a chuckle. "Pool then *A Quiet Place*. Literally."

Val frowned. "Is that even out yet?"

"It is, but Jenn knows a producer who landed her an early copy. Tommy's been wanting to see it, and his best friend is deaf so maybe he'll—"

"Maverick is deaf?"

"Uh huh." Avery nodded slowly.

A bit of panic sparked in Val's chest. It wasn't something she'd exactly needed to know beforehand, but if Tommy and Maverick were as inseparable as every conversation about them suggested, Val would've preferred to be prepared for this. She wanted Tommy to like her, and she didn't see how turning up to his birthday without a gift and — "Shit. I didn't bring a gift." Her eyes widened at Avery as she plucked her phone from her jeans pocket. "How quickly do you think I can make it through a copy of *ASL for Dummies*?"

"Not quickly enough." Avery laughed, resting a hand on the screen of Val's phone. "Besides, Mav is a great lip reader. If you need to say something to him, make eye contact and speak slowly and clearly. If you still want to score extra points with your stepson, I'm sure you'll have other opportunities." She winked.

Stepson. All logic said Avery was merely teasing, and yet, Val found herself mentally repeating the word. If things between her and Jenn continued to progress, she'd have to get used to it.

"By the way, I've been meaning to ask you about your friend from the park. Did you give any more thought to what we talked about? Asking Jenn to help?"

"Asking me to help with what?"

Val spun toward Jenn as she and Rachel came to a stop inches away. She *had* given more thought to asking Jenn for help. She just wasn't sure she wanted to go through with it. Not that she thought Jenn would decline to help. But that was precisely why she'd been hesitant, because things between them were so new and all signs pointed to Jenn being uncommunicative, sometimes stubborn, but so...good. The kind of good she imagined people took for granted. What she had in mind—helping Joey find a job and a more stable place to stay—she could do without Jenn's help. Then again, if Jenn could help get Joey off the street sooner, shouldn't Val be asking anyway? If she could find him. Today made two weeks since she'd last run into him, but it hadn't been the first time they hadn't seen each other for a while.

"Valentina?"

Val blinked at the sound of Jenn's voice, the way she'd stepped closer to rest a hand on Val's arm. "Yeah. Sorry. Um. It's nothing."

Jenn's brows drew together. "Are you sure?"

"I'm sure." She cast a glance at Avery, who seemed just as confused as Jenn did.

"Right." Jenn looked away with evident reluctance, moving her free hand in a sweeping gesture. "Valentina, this is Rachel. Tommy's other mom."

Rachel's handshake was firm. Meant to intimidate. Like the directness of her stare, once she'd completed her hair to Chucks inspection of Val. "We've met," she said.

"Nice to meet you again, Rachel." Val faced Jenn more directly, resting both hands on her hips—maybe Val's jealous streak *was* dormant, but petty was alive and well. "Should you maybe take me to the birthday boy? We're losing daylight for those photos."

"Of course," Jenn answered softly—always so soft whenever Val was this close.

"Jenn, you should probably check on the vegan pizza," Rachel put in. "I'll show Valentina to the roof."

To push me off it?

Avery stepped forward with a diffusing smile. "You two

should do more parent-y stuff. Val and I will hang out with Luna and the kids."

"I don't mind Rachel showing me up." Val shrugged. The longer she stood there, the more she was beginning to think there was only one way to handle Rachel's so-called protectiveness. Zero wilting involved.

For the second time in five minutes, Jenn's gaze narrowed to Val's, lines between her brows as she asked, "Are you sure?"

Val held eye-contact, scrutinizing Jenn's for any sign of alarm as she dared one step closer. When she'd decided there was none, when Jenn's hand came up in its habit of sweeping Val's hair behind her ears, Val stood on her toes and kissed her. "I'm sure."

"Okay," Jenn muttered against her lips.

Val pulled away, redirecting her attention to Rachel. "After you."

There was something of a glint in Rachel's eyes—something Val couldn't adequately decipher as humor, approval or even contempt—until they'd made it to the roof, her words barely audible over the ruckus and some kid's perfectly-timed cannonball Val had grabbed her camera just in time to snap. "Interesting power move."

CHAPTER 23

Jenn took one last look at the large box set in the middle of Tommy's bed before closing the door behind her. The galaxy-print wrapping paper was probably a giveaway but between the living room being darkened to accommodate the screen hung by Jenn's favorite view of the bridge and the movie having at least another hour to go, she'd been able to sneak the gift into his room unseen. For a second, her eyes strained to make him out among the myriad of poor posture silhouettes before clinging to the dyed blonde tips he'd begged to have done for his birthday. Jenn still had her doubts, but she didn't want to "stomp all over his self-expression", which he'd been keen to address in his carefully crafted guilt trip.

She surveyed the rest of the room until her eyes landed on Valentina and Avery both crammed into a chair meant for one, glow from the screen giving away that they were perhaps too invested in the film and more than a little apprehensive from the look of their severe handhold. A smile crept onto Jenn's face as she relived the past couple of hours—Valentina hidden behind her camera at random intervals, snapping anything of interest. Jenn hadn't gotten the chance to formally introduce her to Tommy, but by the time she'd checked on the pizzas and made it to the roof, Valentina already had Tommy smiling her favorite smile. All teeth and bunched cheeks and that ever present glint in his eyes. She still didn't know what they'd been talking about, but the image had laid roots in her mind, and she knew she'd never get it out.

Even so, a niggling sentiment kept cropping up every time she'd found herself more enthralled by Valentina's ability to fit so seamlessly into any situation. However challenging. This was Jenn's life. This moment with her son in a home she used to share with her ex and her best friend here for moral support. This was Jenn's life, and Valentina had fit in without a hitch. The feeling looming in her chest couldn't be trusted. The one that had a demolition ball swinging just beyond her walls in wait for a dramatic crash, that had her thinking it would be nice to go to Valentina's apartment for once and finally put a face to the name Zoe, or talk to Mr. and Mrs. Rosas again. This time in person, in that quaint two-bedroom in San Rafael. The same feeling that had her thinking she had been stupid to even attempt to suppress her feelings for someone who was absolute magic.

Movement to her left drew her attention and she turned to see Rachel approaching with a wine glass clutched between her fingers. "You spoil him, you know?"

"It's his birthday, Rach."

"We agreed we wouldn't get him that telescope. Today, it's astrology, tomorrow who knows?"

"He's a kid. They change their minds."

"A lot." Rachel guffawed, taking a sip of her wine. "Which is why he needs to have less expensive whims."

Jenn smiled. "I suppose that would be nice."

"Speaking of changing minds..." Rachel trailed off.

Jenn's brows crept up in anticipation.

"She's...annoyingly likable." Rachel bobbed her head toward Valentina. "Think she might have even gotten to Luna. Apparently, they're both really into these travel reels on Instagram. Also some lunatic who's always swimming with tigers." She cringed, tilting her head back to gulp down the last of her wine. "Anyway, I think she might be good for you. Strong, but perceptive."

Jenn absorbed the words, thinking them over.

"I know separating was the best thing for us both. It still kind of burns watching you trade me for a younger model."

"Rach, you know that's not true."

"Yeah, yeah, I know. I'm just saying, it's beautiful seeing you like this. This...*light*. Happy." She smiled—something missing in her eyes, even in the poor lighting—and then she took Jenn's face in both hands, confirming her gaze. "You deserve happy, Jenn. So don't fuck this up, yeah?" She patted Jenn's cheek twice before turning away. "I need more wine."

Rachel made her way back to the kitchen, where she refilled her glass with the vintage red Avery had brought then stalked over to Luna. They exchanged a brief kiss before Rachel faced the screen, her back to Luna's chest, Luna's arms loose around her waist. Jenn tried to remember what it had been like hearing Rachel talk about Luna for the first time. Staggering. At first. She didn't really see how it could be any other way after everything they'd been through together. But the blade had dulled over time—whatever Rachel was feeling would fade—and for the first time in as long as Jenn could remember, she felt on the cusp of a change that excited more than terrified her.

Valentina leaned closer to Avery, apparently whispering as she stood and started toward Jenn. There was something so captivating in the simplicity of her beauty—the easy tousle of her hair and subtle radiance of her skin, sweatshirt and jeans, her eyes a million shades of brown.

Jenn held her ground, smiling as Valentina came to a stop in front of her. "Tired of holding Avery's hand?"

Something glinted in her eyes. Fingers intertwined with Jenn's. "Just missing yours. But I um"—a breathy murmur of a laugh left her lips—"I guess I also just wanted to make sure everything is okay."

"Everything's perfect."

"Yeah?"

"Yes. I *am* sorry I called you on your day off, but I can't say I'm sorry you're here."

"I'm glad you called." She rolled her eyes, wincing slightly. "I just hope Tommy forgives me for not bringing him a gift. He invited me to breakfast tomorrow, by the way."

"Oh, did he?"

"Mhm. Says his mom makes the *best* waffles with blueberry compote."

"And lemon ricotta," Jenn added.

"Can't forget the ricotta."

She really shouldn't have—they were standing in a room full of teenagers, including her son—but she found her hand slipping just beneath the hem of Valentina's sweater to the warmth awaiting her touch. No plans to give in to the race of her pulse or the feeling of having Valentina close. Not here. The humor faded, their eye contact steady, as an earlier conversation with Avery resurfaced in Jenn's mind. Usually, Jenn would've let it be—Valentina had said it was nothing—but after Valentina and Rachel had left for the roof, Jenn had probed a bit. "Why didn't you tell me about your friend? Joey."

A visible gulp moved down Valentina's throat as she glanced over her shoulder at Avery.

"I twisted her arm. Also, she will trade most secrets for the sake of matchmaking."

"I may have observed that," Valentina said good-naturedly. She traced the bridge of Jenn's nose with the tips of her fingers. "I guess I was still thinking about it. With all the Gia stuff...me being a stage when this kind of started, you being, well, you. I just...I never want it to feel like I'm with you because of what you could give me. It's weird because it's exactly what you were concerned about, people thinking I got the job because of us. Just—I don't know. I haven't seen him recently. So, there's also that."

Jenn hummed, mulling over the explanation. "Well, first, I would never assume you were with me for any other reason than the tempting dynamic between a charismatic, beautiful, brilliant young chef—that's me, of course."

Valentina giggled then swiftly clamped a hand over her mouth.

"And an anxious, sometimes grumpy misanthrope. That can be you."

She nodded. "Mhm."

"But..." Jenn grew more serious, wanting to make sure nothing got lost in mirth. "Even if we weren't...us, of course, I would help. Provided both you and Joey are okay with that."

"I know you would."

"Good." Jenn nodded. "So, you haven't seen him?"

"No. But I also haven't exactly been running at my usual time, if at all." A blush crept up her neck.

Warmth stirred beneath Jenn's clothes, compounded by a tinge of regret at the idea of why Valentina had probably been missing her usual runs. "What if I join you? Tomorrow."

Valentina's eyes widened. "Join me running?"

"Yes."

"Jenn, you really don't have to"

"But I want to. If you'll have me."

For a moment, Valentina simply stared, leaving Jenn to do the same, to wonder at the thoughts cavorting behind those all-encompassing eyes. "I think I get it now. I mean, I'm sure I always did, but today, especially, I get why Rachel's so..." She trailed off, her exhale a blend of humor and awe? "I believed the word you used was protective."

Jenn frowned, though it must have been obscured by the smile Valentina's own curved lips had drawn from her.

"Don't ask me to explain. Not yet. Just...Yes, Jenn. You can come running with me."

CHAPTER 24

Val slowed her pace, glancing over her shoulder to find Jenn lagging in a valiant effort to keep up. Her hair had attained a curlier appearance since Val had reluctantly kissed her goodbye last night, and a few strands clung to her sweat-dampened skin, slivers of which Val had unhindered access to, thanks to the outfit Jenn had no doubt purposefully selected. The cherry red open back twist tank and matching leggings looked like they'd never been worn, never mind the spotless pair of running shoes on her feet, but the way the smooth fabric melded to her waist, hips and ass had every inch of Val's body humming.

Jenn caught up, breaths somewhere between heaving and controlled.

Val could tell she was struggling, though she'd been reluctant to admit it. And even like this, perhaps especially like this—so out of her element, but insistent in her support—she was unfairly beautiful.

She rested both hands on her hips, glancing around Dolores Park—up and down the concrete trail, the sloped spread of lawn only occupied by clusters of palm trees this early in the day, when the sun had barely begun to peek through the fog. "Is this it?"

"Close but no."

"So why did we stop?"

Val chuckled, taking the hem of Jenn's tank top between her fingers and tugging her closer. "Because you look like a full-course meal in this outfit, but you're not much of a runner."

Jenn's eyes locked in on Val's grip—something she would have questioned if she hadn't grown more sure every day that this side of her drove Jenn just the slightest bit crazy. "I never said I was a runner. I asked to accompany you."

"True." Val grinned. "But I did sort of assume you were perfect at everything."

"That's a high pedestal to sit on."

"It is, but I'm happy to offer my face instead."

Jenn frowned, gears turning in her mind for a second, two...Her eyes widened. "Is that—I mean—"

Val tossed her head back, laughing. "Adorable."

"So that wasn't a serious offer?" Jenn tilted her head.

Val squinted, clenching both fists as she turned to resume her run. "Later. We're definitely coming back to this conversation later." Right now, she needed to make it to her and Joey's bench before eight and sure, she *had* started the teasing—eliciting that look of perplexity turned craving on Jenn's face was her absolute favorite thing of late—but if they kept it up, they'd end up in the opposite direction. Back to Jenn's with Val hoping her headboard was as sturdy as it looked and the walls thick enough to not alert the teenager on the other side of the house.

She looked over her shoulder, just to make sure Jenn was on her tail, ignoring the stutter in her chest at the smile on Jenn's face, her dimpled cheeks. She knew she'd never get used to it. This version of Jenn. Her version of Jenn. Now that she'd built up her endurance and fallen in love with running again, she was pretty sure having Jenn along had ruined it forever in the best possible way.

"HE'S NOT HERE." Val turned on her spot for the fifth time in as many minutes, looking around the park for Joey. The heaviness of her limbs was beginning to set in, her eyes watering a bit from the glare of the emerging sun. Though, she had to acknowledge she was more than a little disappointed. She'd been so sure they'd catch him today. They'd gotten out on time. Jenn was next to her. Everything seemed a little brighter with Jenn next to her. But now she was starting to get worried. A seventeen-year-old trans kid in and out of shelters. Something could've happened to him. She pressed her fingers to her eyes. Why the fuck hadn't she done something sooner?

"Maybe we should wait. He could still be coming, right?"

"He's always here first!" She bit down on her bottom lip, holding up her free hand in an apology as she opened her eyes. "Sorry. I just—I really hope he's okay."

Jenn nodded, watching her intently. "Maybe he's at a shelter or just...roaming around?"

"I mean, yeah." Val shrugged. "He moves around sometimes. But the last time it had been this long since I'd seen him, he'd tried to make it to his aunt's in Albuquerque. She'd moved. No forwarding address. He came back here as soon as he had enough money."

"Right." Jenn surveyed the space before reaching for

Val's hand—both warm and slightly damp from their run. "Sit with me for a while? I've been told I'm not much of a runner."

Val breathed a soft laugh, allowing Jenn to guide her toward the bench. She knew what Jenn was doing. Faint signs of calm had begun to reclaim her anyway.

"Can I see that picture again?"

Val unstrapped her phone and swiped her way to the picture—the one with Joey, long hair dangling into his light brown eyes and an ear-splitting grin on his face. She remembered the out-of-frame foot-long French loaf stuffed with salami and ham, lettuce, tomatoes and about half a jar of mayo almost as well as the bruises on his left knuckles.

"He's a handsome kid."

"Yeah. He knows it too."

"Hmm. Sounds like Tommy."

Val smiled, her mind drifting to the pictures she'd taken at the party yesterday. She'd gone through them all before bed last night, spent well over two hours categorizing and deleting those of subpar quality. One in particular had stood out. She'd gotten to it last, but she was pretty sure it had been the first photo she'd taken—that one kid's cannonball into the pool, right on the hinges of Rachel's comment about Val making a power move by kissing Jenn in front of her. Val had almost missed it. She'd grabbed her camera so fast the shot was slightly out of focus, but in the background, the boy with the blonde tips in his hair making heart eyes at the boy next to him were definitely Tommy and Maverick. And Val could've been wrong, but that was exactly the way she used to look at Sophie Sanders when she was sixteen and questioning. Not that it was her place to mention it one way or another.

She glanced at the time, her eyes constantly wandering

in search of Joey. "Speaking of Tommy, I did promise him we'd be there for breakfast."

"We will." Jenn squeezed her hand. "Let's just give Joey some more time. If he doesn't turn up, we can show a few people his picture on the way back. Maybe someone has seen him."

"Yeah. Maybe." Val interlaced their fingers, shifting closer. Between breakfast and having to be at the restaurant in a few hours, they didn't have much time. She made a silent promise to come back tomorrow and the day after, every day until she knew where Joey had gone. "I just don't know how anyone could do this to their kid."

Jenn twisted just enough to press her lips to the crown of Val's head, her words muffled and her hold on Val's hand marginally tighter when she said, "Parenting isn't for everyone."

Val mulled over the words, trying to decipher the faraway look in Jenn's eyes, the hint of something else in her tone—something beyond this moment. "Like your dad?"

"Yes. And Joey's."

"I didn't want to push you yesterday when you mentioned it. It didn't really seem like the time, but..." Val frowned. "Potrero Hill. Isn't that like an hour from here?"

"Yeah." Jenn scoffed. "That trip to Mexico is only part of the reason I created Gia, San Francisco. I grew up in the Mission. My mom refused to ever live anywhere else. Just like Nonna refuses to leave Florence. They were both so stubborn you'd think *they* were related."

A slow smile spread on Val's face as she listened.

"My mom was his assistant. He was a partner in a pharmaceutical company in the Bay Area. One whirlwind romance later, she's pregnant and he's engaged to his now wife. He wanted an abortion, and she wanted me. So, he blackballed her. She spent nearly half her life in entry level positions because of it."

"Jenn..." So many things made sense now. Even so, Val couldn't think of the *right* thing to say.

Jenn shook her head. "I don't think about him too much. Not anymore. But I do think about the fact that..." She raised a hand to stroke Val's cheek. "She wasn't much younger than you are, Valentina."

"Maybe." Val sat up straighter, turning on the bench to face Jenn directly. "And I don't know your father, but I do know you're not him, Jenn."

"That's what I like to tell myself. Yet here I am. With you." Her gaze wandered, as if she was examining Val's face. "The only difference is I keep finding myself wanting to pull you closer too fast too soon. And maybe I've forgotten how to do this. How to date."

"Is that what we're doing?" Val bit her bottom lip, wrapping both arms around Jenn's neck. "Dating."

"The chefs' version, I suppose. Twelve, sometimes fourteen-hour shifts, basically seven days a week takes a little creativity."

"Sounds like you might need some inspiration."

"Just a bit."

Kissing Jenn brought the kind of content Val couldn't describe. A different feeling each time. Nothing like the tentative desire of their first, or trace of remorse in their second, hunger in their third, or any of the others after. This one hinted of a quiet calm that said everything would be okay. They'd be okay. Joey, too. Even as Jenn slowly pulled away.

"Valentina." It was whispered so softly against her lips, she almost missed it. "Look."

Her first instinct was to spin, look up and down the trail

again then all around them. But when she was met with nothing more than a dog walker being led by a trio of well-groomed Boxers, her shoulders sagged, brows knitting as she turned to find Jenn beaming at her. Dimples and all, which was always nice, but... "What?"

"There." Jenn bobbed her head toward the back of the bench, pointing toward the curved slab of wood Val had been leaned against earlier. Even so, it took her a moment to make out the small carving—a lion with a single rose sticking out either side of its mouth. And she got it—*Rosas de Leon*—but she and Joey had only ever talked about last names once.

The look on his face when he'd hung his head, mumbling, *"It's Joey. Just Joey,"* made her stomach sink, but then she'd smiled and told him she had two so he could borrow Leon, and he'd laughed.

"It makes you sound like a Rockstar," she'd said. *"And my mom wouldn't mind."*

Val tilted her head in a bid to inspect the drawing more clearly, the letters scratched next to it. A social media handle: @joeyl3on. It had to be from him. But... Her eyes locked with Jenn's. "I had no idea he could draw like that."

"He's good." Jenn chuckled. "Let's just hope he didn't get caught defacing public property."

"God, do you think he did? That he could be in jail or something?

She shook her head, brushing her knuckles over Val's cheek again. "Probably not. But"—she picked up Val's phone from the bench and handed it to her—"why don't we find out?"

CHAPTER 25

"So, Val..." Tommy peered up from his plate, both hands busy with a knife and fork as he sliced through a four-waffle tower. As always, he'd overdone the blueberry compote *and* the ricotta, but even still dressed in his favorite Rashford pajamas, the crease between his thick dark brows gave him precisely the air of stern he was aiming for. "What do you think about bacon?"

Jenn smiled, watching Valentina over the rim of her cup as she took a sip of her coffee.

Thomas Taylor-Coleman. Never one to shy away from the real issues.

"Bacon?" Val's gaze shifted to Jenn's almost as if to ask, is this a trick question? Then, she looked at him. "I mean, bacon's great."

"Say you wanted to, like, make a shopping list. For here," Tommy specified. "Does bacon make the list?"

Valentina's lips stretched in a skeptical smile. "It does."

"And what about cheese?"

"Tommy." Jenn shot him a playful glare, before making a sweeping gesture toward the hefty serving of ricotta

Valentina also had on her plate. "I think it's safe to assume she's not vegan."

"Can never be too sure, Mom. And I love you, you know I do, but I gotta say...one vegan girlfriend is my limit, and Mama had Luna first so—"

"Are you listening to this?" Jenn asked through a laugh.

"I am." Valentina reached for her glass of apple juice, everything from her eyes to her smile alight with interest. "Please continue."

"You are just as bad." Jenn shook her head, redirecting her attention to her son. "Well, I think we've all established your concerns are unwarranted. And Valentina is not my..." She trailed off, reluctant to finish the statement, unsure what would be better one way or another. Valentina hadn't seemed to mind Tommy's suggestion she was already Jenn's girlfriend, but she had also seemed content with their lack of a label. Not that Jenn had brought it up either. She didn't know how to bring it up, but the more involved Valentina became in her life, the more it occurred to her that she wanted to discuss it. Explicitly. Exclusively.

Tommy regarded them both. "But you invited her to my party."

"Just to take pictures," Valentina chimed in. She exchanged a knowing look with Jenn then turned to Tommy. "I got some really cool shots, too. I can show you later if you're up to it. In case you wanted to keep any of them in particular."

"Okay." Tommy nodded. "Yeah, that sounds cool."

"Perfect. We'll try before I leave but—" Her phone buzzed, sending a light tremor across the cherrywood table and she reached up to silence it. "Sorry."

Jenn finished the bite in her mouth, casting an instinctive glance at her watch before saying, "You should take it. You know they're just going to call back."

Valentina rolled her eyes. "They need to get used to the idea that one unanswered call doesn't mean I'm lying in a ditch somewhere."

"Dark," Tommy mumbled, his eyes wide.

Valentina laughed, shaking her head. "It's just my parents. They like to check in every other day. I finally got them down from once a day, but your mom encourages them. At least not so they can hear."

"What? She never calls me that much."

"Yeah, well, wait 'til you go off to college," Jenn joked. Still, his comment, however lighthearted, nudged at something buried deep, that typically only Rachel had the ability to unearth. But she was looking forward to more moments like this—breakfast made by the two of them. Though, with the way their first meal together had been going, she'd happily extend her kitchen to Valentina whenever the opportunity arose.

"Whatever, you're just kidding." Tommy looked down at his plate, forked up another bite then paused. "Mom, you are just kidding, right?"

Valentina chuckled. "Don't worry. It can be a bit much, but it's also kind of nice. Especially if you go to school far away and you don't get to see her that much anymore."

Tommy put down his utensils, folding both arms on the table in front of him as he leaned forward. "You don't get to see your parents?"

"Well, I do. But they had to move back to Mexico, so I only see them when I get to visit."

"Why did they move back to Mexico?"

"Tommy," Jenn scolded. "Some things are personal."

Valentina waved away the implication. "No, it's fine.

Their whole lives were here. Their jobs, the home I grew up in. Well, *here* in New York. But they'd overstayed their visas, and…after a while, I guess, it just seemed less complicated to leave."

Jenn lowered one hand beneath the table to rest on Valentina's knee. For some reason, that version seemed simplified—devoid of fear of persecution, being detained, things Jenn couldn't even imagine.

"That sucks." Tommy frowned. "Didn't you ever want to go with them?"

Valentina's hand joined Jenn's, resting lightly over it before squeezing. "I did go, for a while, but I could always come back because I was born here. Plus, I'd just gotten into the Culinary Institute." She smiled wistfully. "Let's just say they might have given up on their dream, but they were never willing to let me give up on mine."

Tommy bobbed his head in understanding. "That's really cool of them."

"Yep, and now I get to work with your mom."

He tsked, grinning. "Yeah, I guess she's sort of cool, too."

IT WAS another ten minutes before they'd had to cut their meal short so Valentina wouldn't be late for her shift at Gia. Still, she'd insisted on staying a while longer, arguing it was only a five-minute drive from Jenn's and she just really needed to show Tommy some of the pictures she'd taken the day before. The urgency was still lost on Jenn, especially because she was secretly hoping Valentina would come back once her shift had ended. There was little point in hiding their 'sleep overs' after Tommy had literally invited her to breakfast. But as Jenn cleared the table of dishes, she found herself too enamored with the sight of the two of them, both hunched over Valentina's camera muttering and laughing as if they hadn't only just met. She figured it had more to do with their charismatic natures—how they both seemed to be able to get along with just about anyone. Yet, apprehension lingered beneath the surface—a probing reminder that Jenn needed to pace herself. Her connection with Valentina was still so new, though not entirely untested, and things between them couldn't always be easy. And maybe, just maybe, she had been a little hasty in introducing Valentina to Tommy, because who knew what coming weeks, months, would hold.

The distinct vibration of a ringing phone drew her attention, and she noticed that Valentina and Tommy too had looked up.

Valentina's brows rose, her eyes the same shade of the hazelnut blend lingering on Jenn's tongue. "I think that one's for you."

"You actually noticed?" Jenn questioned playfully, wiping her hand on a towel as she started toward the table for her phone. "You and Tommy seemed so perfectly okay with letting me clear the dishes alone, I thought you were in a whole other dimension."

"Aww, babe."

Jenn's stomach flipped unexpectedly.

Valentina pouted, her gaze drifting to the nearly empty table, sweeping from one end to the other before meeting Jenn's again. "I promise I'll make up for it. I just—"

Tommy tugged on her Gia-branded shirt. "Oh, you caught this?" Apparently, he *was* in another dimension.

Jenn blindly reached for her phone, assessing Valentina's face for any sign her use of an endearment had been unintentional, but she simply smiled, tucking a strand of hair behind her ear before assuring Tommy she had in fact caught whatever photograph he'd found so intriguing.

The buzzing stopped the second Jenn locked in on her phone. Missed call. D*r. O'Connell's Office.*

Her gaze narrowed to the date and time. *Sunday, July 23. 10:39 a.m.* Between planning Tommy's birthday party, spending more time with Valentina and being back at Gia almost full time, she'd had plenty of distractions, all of which she'd fully embraced. But she was sure she'd had another day at least. Dr. O'Connell's office had been open for nearly an hour already, but they never called on Sundays. Unless…

Her stomach churned, a familiar tingling welling in her arms and legs, tightening in her chest.

Unless the results were unfavorable. Unless, unlike the first, these results *were* conclusive, and her status had suddenly gone from 'nothing to be concerned about' to critical. Wouldn't they have to act immediately then? Sundays be damned.

When her screen lit up, the buzzing struck like a jolt of electricity, enough to draw Valentina's attention.

Her forehead creased. "Everything okay?"

"Yes," Jenn answered too quickly. She cleared her throat, straightening her posture a bit. "Yes. I just need to—" She hooked a thumb over her shoulder. "I have to take this." Her feet were headed across the kitchen, toward the door leading to the backyard before she'd even given them permission. She pushed the door open and hit the answer button, bringing the phone to her ear. "Dr. O'Connell?"

"Jennifer." Still the only person who called her by her full name. "I know this is unexpected, but I was hoping to get through to you as soon as possible. Your results are in."

Jenn's heartbeat slowed as she waited for him to

continue. She brought a hand to her necklace and took the pendant between her thumb and forefinger.

"Jennifer?"

"I'm listening."

A dry chuckle reverberated in her ear. "You're all clear. No sign of cancer."

The breath she released left her so light, she could almost float away. And yet, a hint of indignance had slipped into her "Thank you, Dr. O'Connell." He'd come highly recommended by her GP—she trusted him, mostly—but she was not a fan of his delivery. Suspense was for movies, not medical results damn it!

"Now..." She imagined his pointed stare and raised index finger. "We still want to monitor the FBD so I will refer you for another ultrasound in six months, and one more after that. Then, based on those results, we can see about reducing the frequency. Until then, keep doing your self-exams and if anything seems out of the ordinary, we'll set up an appointment right away."

"Yes. Of course."

"Good. Bye-bye now."

Jenn withdrew the phone from her ear with a bizarre blend of muted elation and detachment. It was almost as if her brain was still processing all Dr. O'Connell had said. She was *okay*. At least for now. Two tests a year would require some adjustment, especially to the constant anxiety surrounding every appointment, every call, but Jenn was more than ready for it all. She hadn't sat through two years of prognoses, chemo, spent hours in waiting rooms with her mom in surgery only to not be more proactive about this. Nothing would dishonor her mother's memory more. Besides, she had Tommy and Rachel, Avery and—

"Jenn?" Valentina exited the house, brows furrowed as she cautiously stepped forward. "Is everything okay?"

Jenn's chest warmed at the sight of her. God, everything was so okay. Especially with her here. "Yes." Jenn smiled, meeting her halfway. "Are you and Tommy done conspiring over those pictures?"

Valentina laughed. "I did fortuitously capture a moment that might mean a lot to him, but that's it. Very little conspiring was done, I promise."

"Should I be concerned?"

"Not at all." She shook her head, lightly taking Jenn's hand. "You looked a little...panicked over that call. I just wanted to check on you before I leave."

"Because checking on me after a panic turned out so well last time."

"I mean—" Valentina bobbed her head from left to right. "It did. At least, the talking." Her gaze fell to Jenn's lips. "I guess the kissing was okay, too."

"I seem to remember it being more than a little okay."

"Oh, do you?"

"Absolutely." Jenn nodded. This was one of countless things she loved about Valentina—her ability to saunter into any moment and completely alter the atmosphere, to inspire lighter but never less meaningful sentiments in Jenn. A Jenn who could joke about having a panic attack, when she'd typically prefer to force it to the furthest depths of her mind, put on an ironclad shield and step into her kitchen. And this was what made her want to share everything with Valentina—including the details of her latest call—and hope against all hope that Valentina wanted to share everything with her too.

"Well..." Valentina surveyed the backyard briefly before

locking eyes with Jenn. "I think both our memories of being here last time are a little less fond."

The memory flashed in Jenn's mind. Valentina showing up unannounced the morning after their first kiss. Jenn denouncing Valentina's feelings as infatuation. Telling her not to risk everything for someone unwilling to do the same for her. A month later and Jenn was ready to risk it all.

"Maybe we should make new ones," she said softly.

Valentina leaned in, smiling as she brushed her lips against Jenn's. "You read my mind."

Jenn took her face in both hands and deepened their kiss, briefly losing herself in Valentina's hands on her hips before pulling away. "Let me know if Joey messages back?"

"I will." Valentina nodded. "Going to miss you in the kitchen today."

"And I'll miss being there." Jenn paused. She still wasn't quite used to not being at Gia every day, not being there to ensure that everything was as it should be. "But Tommy's going to be back in school in a few weeks, and there'll be football and soccer and…I think we needed this time."

"You're a good mom."

Her lips curved in a warm smile. She had a good example, but they could always get into that later. "Message me at close? I think I'd like to show you something."

"Yes," Valentina agreed, her eyes gleaming.

Jenn's brows inched up. "You're not even remotely curious as to what it is?"

"Nope." Valentina shook her head, pressing her lips to Jenn's one last time before backing away. "Whatever it is, yes."

CHAPTER 26

"A taco spaghetti and four pizza quesadillas all day!" The POS whirred as it fired out another batch of chits. Utensils clanged in the dish pit matched by the untimely whoosh of a flash of flames by the fry station.

Val gave herself a mental pat on the back for not flinching, instead keeping her gaze locked on the pot in front of her. She gave the contents one last stir before scooping up a full ladle and pouring it back in with a possibly overly critical eye. Gia's enchilada sauce was precise not only in taste and consistency but a very distinct shade of red. Since Kent had been running the pass all night, she had been left alone on saucier duty for the first time with the sole responsibility of not fucking it up.

So far, so good.

"Where is my damn calzone?" Mel screamed. "I needed it yesterday!"

"Here, Chef!"

Val glanced up in time to see Landon slide the dish onto the expo stand then rush back to his station. Something seemed off about him tonight—he was lagging, quiet—

despite the fact that half the Mission had apparently decided to eat out. And Mel was a pro, having been appointed as Head Chef nearly three years now, but there was a different directive to the madness in Jenn's absence. An ordered chaos. Except, more chaos. Then again, it was sort of the way Val imagined most restaurant kitchens. And, well, there was only one Jenn Coleman—someone who embodied a rare kind of precision, perhaps even genius, and inspired if not demanded the best from everyone in her kitchen through her mere presence.

For the first time almost since she'd started at Gia, she realized it had been a while since she'd thought of Jenn like this—with near fangirl-like admiration. She had so much respect for the renowned chef who sometimes ran on five hours of sleep for monthly food drives and organized nightly deliveries to shelters. But the woman who had kept her talking through her phobia of blood and had had a full in-Spanish conversation with her parents, was as shy about being stared at as she was about admitting what she wanted in bed, and shared her concerns for a boy with whom neither of them had any tangible connection...That was the person she'd fallen for. Head over her homely Birkenstock Londons.

"I'm going to need someone to run this out to table 9!" Mel yelled. "Where are all the servers?"

Warren speed walked by Val, muttering, "It's going to be a long ass shift," before disappearing to the walk-ins.

Val breathed a laugh, shaking her head as she brought a taste of the sauce to her lips.

It *would* be a long shift.

She couldn't wait for a thousand more.

Dinner service was nearly halfway through by the time Val had gotten a response to the direct message she'd sent to Joey on Twitter: *I can't believe you actually made out that chicken scratch drawing.*

Val had been so excited, she'd let out a squeal that had drawn the attention of half the kitchen staff, including Mel who'd shot her a death glare transmitting something between 'Are you fucking kidding me?' and 'Put that shit away before I shove it down the garbage disposal.' It was probably safe to say Val had a few extra closing duties in her future if she wanted to get back into Mel's good graces, but it was more than worth it to hear that Joey was okay, that he'd been okay all this time and was on his way to explain everything. He'd asked if Val could meet at their bench in Dolores, but it wasn't as if she could just leave in the middle of her shift, so here she was five minutes into her fifteen-minute break, obsessively scanning the street for any sign of him.

"So, how come you didn't tell me you were a big shot chef?"

Val startled, spinning in the opposite direction to find Joey grinning back at her. He'd gotten a haircut, his bangs now brushing his brows instead of dangling before his eyes, and his cheeks seemed rounder somehow, like he'd gained a pound or two since the last time they'd seen each other. He looked good. Better.

Val let out a content sigh, lips parted as she shook her head then broke out into a laugh. "Chef, yes. Big shot, not yet."

"Really?" He peered up at the sign hanging by the entrance of Gia. "My friend's dad said he's been trying to get a reservation here for three months."

"Is that where you've been? With your friend?"

"Yeah." Joey scoffed. "I was down on Panhandle. I guess they were driving by and she recognized me. We hadn't seen each other since before school let out for the summer. Once she started asking me where I'd been and stuff, I don't know. I just kind of cracked and told her everything. Her parents took me in the same day."

"But—" Val shook her head, taking a step closer. "I don't —Why hadn't you told her before? Maybe they could've..." she trailed off, frowning. Maybe he would've never had to be on the street to begin with. Maybe he could've had a safe place to stay all this time. Then again, there was no actual way of knowing that. It's not like she had readily opened her door.

"I guess..." Joey winced. "It's kind of embarrassing, you know? To have to explain to my friends that my dad is an ignorant dick, that he hates the sight of me so much he doesn't even care where I sleep at night."

Val wrinkled her nose in disgust. She had a few choice words for whoever this guy was, but something told her those weren't the ones Joey needed to hear. She took a step closer and rested a hand on his shoulder. "You know what though, Jo? He's the one who should be embarrassed. I kind of feel sorry for him because he might never get to know the incredible person you're becoming. That you already are. But I'm really happy your friend and her parents will."

His jaw visibly clenched, his eyes glimmering as he looked down at his feet.

Val sniffled, feeling a little choked up herself. Then, a laugh bloomed in her chest—she wasn't sure what their boundaries were—but she found herself lunging toward him, both arms tight around his neck as he hugged her back. "Just don't fucking disappear on me again."

"Don't plan on it." His laugh resonated close to her ear.

Full-bodied and bright. She wasn't sure she'd ever heard him laugh this freely, but she willed herself to commit it to memory. This was how she always wanted to remember him —just a happy seventeen-year-old boy whose biggest worry wasn't that he didn't have a bed, or money for food, or a single person who cared about him.

Joey pulled back, swiftly wiping at his eyes. "The Petersons said I could use their address, so now I just have to find someone willing to hire me before the summer's out." He sunk both hands into the pockets of his worn jeans. "They're helping me out, but I don't want to be a burden, you know?"

Val smiled. As someone who'd gotten her first summer job at sixteen, she could appreciate that. "Let me see if I can help with that?"

His eyes widened. "Really? I mean, yeah. Of course—"

"Val!"

Val glanced down Gia's side alley to find Landon's torso sticking out the door. One hand went in search of her phone, her appraisal of the time confirming her assumption, based on Landon's emergence. "My break's over." She grimaced, starting toward Landon in backward steps. "But I'll message you, okay?"

Joey nodded. "Okay."

She pointed a mock-stern finger at him. "Be careful getting back."

"Will do!"

When she'd made it to the door, Landon was still there, leaned against the frame with both arms crossed over his chest. "Who was that?" he asked, bobbing his head in the direction Val had just come.

Val shrugged, glancing over her shoulder. "A friend."

"Hmm." Landon's expression turned considering. "The kind you are with me, or like you are with Coleman?"

"Excuse me?"

Landon scoffed. "I saw you. At her kid's party on Avery's Insta story. Funny. I've worked here three years. Many of us longer than that. We've never gotten invites to her house, but I guess there are perks to screwing the boss. Aren't there, Val?" He pushed off the door with his shoulders and started past her. "Mel's waiting for us."

The intensity of the dinner service rush had only lasted until around ten, and what had been building up to be a long day for most of Val's shift was starting to feel like an early night. At this rate, they'd have everything checked and ready for close by midnight. Given the way her day had begun, Val would've welcomed the idea to rush home and find out exactly what Jenn had been meaning to show her, but she'd also spent the last few hours with Landon's comment ricocheting around her brain. Not that it should have come as a surprise. Someone was bound to find out at some point, especially if she'd been hanging in Jenn's extremely small circle of friends and family. And wasn't this exactly what Jenn had warned about anyway?

Val scoffed. At least Landon hadn't suggested sleeping with Jenn was the reason she'd been hired at Gia. Or was it implied?

She huffed, shoving the dumpster open with unnecessary force and hoisting in one of the bags she'd dragged into the alley. The second followed with a bang, and she paused, struggling to remember if she'd somehow grabbed one of the bags of recyclables. She did not have the will to double-check one way or another. Tossing in her last bag, she shut the lid and turned for the door.

A shadow crossed her line of sight before she could adequately process the face of the person standing a few feet away, and she yelped, jerking back.

"Shit, sorry. I thought you heard me coming."

"What the fuck, Landon?" Val closed her eyes, bringing a hand to her chest in an attempt to soothe her racing heart, the burst of adrenaline in her bloodstream.

He hooked a thumb over his shoulder. "The door banged and everything, I swear."

Val's brows knit as she regarded the heavy metal door—it did make an obnoxious amount of noise when it opened. Had she been that deep in her thoughts? In any case... She shook her head impatiently, starting past him. "Dumpster's all yours."

"Val—"

"Let me guess." She rounded on him, her pulse elevated for entirely different reasons. "You're skulking around in the dark because you said a really shitty thing and you've come to take it back?"

"I did." He visibly swallowed, glancing at his feet. "Say a shitty thing."

"Yeah, that's kind of starting to feel like your MO." The night they'd all hung out at Fisherman's Wharf felt like an eternity ago and yesterday all at once—Landon and his comments about Val being one of those 'bright-eyed interns who think Jenn Coleman walks on water' then attempting to take it back almost immediately.

"Is that why you wouldn't go out with me?" He glanced around as if he expected the answer to emerge right there in the dimly lit alley.

And Val didn't owe him any explanations—not really—but something about the rejected look on his face tugged at the soft spot she had for the Landon who joked about everything because it was simpler that way. Because sometimes feelings were hard fucking work. "Lan, it just wasn't a good idea."

"Because we work together?" His lips twisted in a grimace. "I would have a lot less trouble wrapping my head around that if Coleman didn't own and run the place. And I know what I said earlier was fucked up. I am sorry, Val. Truly. I just...I thought we could've had something good, you know?"

"Landon, I didn't plan what happened with Jenn. But I'm also not going to apologize or try to explain it, because that thing we have...No one needs to get it but me and her." Val sighed. "You're a good guy. One with a stupidly short fuse, but a good guy."

Landon laughed.

"And if I felt the way about you that I do about her then we'd already be together. But anything less isn't worth jeopardizing my dream. And that's what Gia is for me, Landon. A place I dreamed about, created by someone who looks like me, even figuratively, and built on values I respect."

His brows furrowed, his gaze trailing toward the asphalt beneath their feet before he nodded his understanding. "And Coleman really makes you happy? I know she has a kid and everything, but I seriously can't imagine her in a relationship."

"She does make me happy. You'd have to know her to understand how much."

"Guess that's part of the problem. She's been in a kitchen with us nearly seven days a week for years, but we don't know her."

Val frowned. That made more sense than she wanted to admit. Not every acquaintance had to turn into a friendship or more, but she understood how Jenn's reservation could be taken as indifference.

"Anyway, I'll make my peace with the friend zone. If it's still open, that is."

Val smiled, shaking her head as she headed for the kitchen. "I'll get back to you on that. I might keep Avery instead. She's still the less problematic Dimaano twin, even if she did accidentally out me on her Instagram."

CHAPTER 27

Jenn shut the door once Valentina had comfortably settled into the front passenger seat of her SUV. The glow of the sign hung above the main doors of Gia reflected in her windshield—her pride, glory and affection for her grandmother forever tied to those three letters, her home away from home. A part of her itched to pop inside and glance around, make sure everything had been done according to protocol, but after her talk with Nonna earlier today, she was committed to loosening her grip on operations somewhat. Mel and Avery had always done fine in her absence. Someday, she'd probably have to take the therapy leap to explore what it was about control that made her feel safer. Tonight, there was only one place she wanted to be and one person she wanted to be with.

She slipped into the driver's seat and clicked her seatbelt into place as she glanced over at Valentina.

"You do remember I drove here this morning, right?" Valentina asked.

"I do." Jenn took both her hands, pressing a kiss to the

knuckles of one then the other. "But I convinced myself you had an exceptionally long day and it would be nice if I picked you up. I hope that's okay."

Valentina smiled, squinting. "You hope that's okay?"

"Mhm." Jenn nodded, freeing one hand in favor of tending to the actual driving as she made sure the road was clear.

"I'm beginning to think you're a lot better at this than you pretend to be."

"A lot better at what?"

"Romance?"

"Oh, I don't know." Jenn scoffed. "Romance seems a little more intricate than a five-minute drive home."

Home. The word echoed in her mind. She should probably stop saying it like that, like it was Valentina's too, especially this soon.

"I don't think it's all that intricate." Valentina interlocked her fingers with Jenn's. "I think romance is all about the simple things. Lingering touches, the way you brush your nose against mine after we kiss, being there for each other in all the right moments. I mean, it can't be all roses and chocolates, right?"

"Right." Jenn nodded slowly, latching onto the words. "But just so nothing gets lost in translation, do you like roses and chocolates?"

Valentina chuckled. "I do. But that wasn't a hint."

"No. Hints, please. I like hints. And detailed explanations. Definitely wouldn't say no to an annotated diagram."

"Uh huh."

Jenn gave in to the urge to look at her directly—just for a second, just for the inexplicable flutter in her chest when Valentina smiled like that. Her brand of awkward humor wasn't for everyone, but if she could only make one woman laugh for the rest of her life, she would be okay with that. She squeezed Valentina's hand a little tighter, increasing her pressure on the steering wheel to balance it out. "How was your day?"

The heavy sigh that followed was enough to draw Jenn's attention to Valentina's widened eyes and slightly parted lips. "Busy. But the kind that makes you remember why you love the kitchen, you know?"

Jenn smiled, nodding as she pulled up to a red light.

"And Joey dropped by, which you already know."

"Yes. Thank you for the text."

"God, he looked so good, babe. So happy. Healthy. I wish you could've been there to meet him." She shifted more toward Jenn, bending one leg at the knee and pulling it up onto the seat.

Jenn's eyes followed the motion with mechanical scrutiny, but she didn't have the heart to tell Valentina she didn't like shoes on her furniture, car seats by extension. Not right now. Not when her eyes shone like that, and she made cute, arbitrary gestures with her hands while she talked.

"It seems like he has a pretty stable place to stay with the Petersons, but he mentioned wanting a job, so I'm thinking I could help him with a resume and a list of possible places."

The light turned green, and Jenn redirected her attention to the road. "I hope Gia is on that list."

"I mean, yeah." Valentina dropped her hands. "But I also didn't want to assume anything."

Jenn took a quick mental inventory of the staff on the younger side at Gia. "I think three of the servers are seniors in high school. I'm sure we could find something for him."

"Jenn, I *can* help him find a job somewhere else. The Mission is crawling with *Help Wanted* signs, especially during the summer. Signs at less...*established* places."

"Okay." Jenn frowned. "Does he want somewhere less established?"

"No, I just—I know how hard you work to keep everything running perfectly at Gia. I can't guarantee he'll be any good at...well, anything, and I don't want you to feel like you have to say yes because I'm asking."

Jenn turned into her driveway and reached for the remote to the garage. "Everyone is good at something. And you didn't ask. I offered." When the doors whirred open and she drove into the garage, she was more than happy to shift into park and face Valentina fully. Driving and talking was a delicate science.

Valentina cradled her face and leaned in to join their lips in a brief kiss. "Sometimes I wish everyone got to see this side of you, but I can't say there also isn't a part of me that just wants to keep you all mine."

"Does that make you all mine too?"

Jenn felt more than saw her smile. "Are we really pretending this wasn't official the second I got on my knees for you?"

"I haven't dated in a decade. My brain was still dawdling between 'wanna go steady' and 'will you be my girlfriend?' I guess your way was a bit more..." Jenn brushed her lips against Valentina's, despite the sensation building low in her stomach. "Imaginative."

"That husk in your voice is making me imagine all kinds of things right now, but I would prefer to shower off that shift before I get you naked. Besides," Valentina pulled away enough to make eye contact, "You said you had something to show me?"

"I still do." It had taken Jenn hours to get everything set up once she'd taken Tommy back to Rachel's for the night, but she would've spent days at it if necessary. "But it will still be there after your shower."

"Good." Valentina pecked Jenn on the lips before opening her door to get out of the car.

"Are you sure Zoe doesn't mind you leaving her alone in the apartment all these nights?"

"She is refusing to 'fully acknowledge' our relationship until you've been officially introduced, and a few friendly threats have been exchanged, but she and Warren have been making good use of the privacy, trust me."

Jenn's mind got stuck on the words 'friendly threats', and then another thing registered. "Warren? As in Warren who—"

"Yup."

Her brows crept up. "Oh. Well, good for them."

"Better for us." Valentina turned on her heels and hooked two fingers into the hem of Jenn's jeans, pulling her closer.

Jenn's eyes fell shut, her stomach tensing. "You know that drives me crazy."

"Which is exactly why I do it." A kiss landed just beneath the lobe of her left ear. "Where do you want me?"

Jenn gulped. "Um..."

Valentina breathed a laugh. "After my shower, baby. Where's show and tell?"

"Right." Jenn blinked. "Backyard. Dress comfy, or in—" She shook her head. "Whatever you brought for the night."

"Kind of assumed I'd be sleeping naked, but in the interest of not flashing your neighbors, I'll borrow a hoodie." Valentina unhooked her fingers, releasing Jenn's jeans with a snap that went straight to her core, leaving her powerless to do anything but stare and yearn as Valentina disappeared into the house.

JENN EXAMINED the backyard setup for the third time since Valentina had gone upstairs. According to her watch, it had already been twenty minutes and she was pretty sure she'd found at least half as many things that had needed adjusting. At least two of the fairy lights had gone rogue and decided on some unsettling flickering pattern, and the fact that some of the throw pillows looked better askew—aesthetically, anyway—was still giving her pause. She narrowed in on the tent door, tilting her head slightly. *Open or closed?* The flap did look a little dangly with it open.

She started toward it then stopped. *No.* She'd tried it closed, and that looked fine, but it *felt* weird. Why would it be closed if no one was inside?

She tightened the grip on the bottle of Pol Roger champagne she'd picked out, the cold growing more numbing by the second, especially paired with the light breeze.

Maybe she should've gotten more blanket options? Actually, options could be stressful sometimes. *For her,* she reminded herself. Maybe Valentina would like a pick of more than heavy knit or—

"Oh my God."

Jenn turned at the sound of Valentina's voice, the bottle slipping though she recovered quickly. Her lips parted as Valentina descended the brief flight of stairs, indeed dressed in only Jenn's white Le Cordon Bleu hoody and her own favorite pair of fuzzy slippers, hair in damp waves down to her shoulders, eyes constantly wandering. By the time she'd come to a stop in front of Jenn, Jenn had almost forgotten she was supposed to be nervous about the damn blankets, because surely...

Jenn's gaze trailed all the way to Valentina's feet and back up. "You must be cold in just that."

Valentina's mouth opened then closed. "You did all this?"

"Yes?" Jenn gulped, holding the bottle tighter. "This morning you mentioned how we didn't have good memories here. And I didn't exactly mean—" She gave the surroundings another skeptical pass. A lizard darted up one wall and disappeared into a palm tree. "I forgot the lizards."

Valentina giggled. "What?"

Jenn shook her head. "Nothing. I just...After you left for work, I thought we *should* have good memories, wonderful memories here. I actually considered doing it on the roof of Gia, but there were too many logistics and not enough time and—"

"I love you."

Jenn blinked. "You..."

"I. Love. You, Jenn Coleman." Valentina grinned, slipping her arms around Jenn's neck. "And it doesn't matter that Landon knows, or whoever else may have figured it out. Right now, I kind of want the whole fucking world to know."

Jenn shifted the champagne to one hand, wrapping the other around the small of Valentina's back to pull her closer. She brought her forehead to Valentina's, and she replayed the declaration in her mind. Valentina loved her. She loved her, she loved her— "Wait, did you just say Landon knows?"

"Yeah. Something about Tommy's party and Avery's Instagram. He figured it out, I guess." She adjusted her hold on Jenn, pulling away an inch. "Are you okay with that?"

Jenn took a moment to think about it. Realistically, they both knew this moment would come sooner or later. And yet, after everything they'd been through to get here—all her failed attempts to suppress her feelings, to push

Valentina away—hearing that Landon knew had little to no effect. Because she'd thought about this long and hard, and she knew the moment she had signed that consensual relationship agreement that she was in this with Valentina for the full ride. It didn't matter who knew. Her primary concern was for Valentina's professional future, and she would do everything in her control to ensure their relationship had little impact where that was concerned. And she knew it wasn't the question Valentina had asked, but the words that left her lips were, "I love you, too, Valentina."

A hand shifted to her face, the touch as warm as the whispered, "Jenn..." on her lips.

"So, I guess my answer is, yes. I am okay with that," Jenn amended. "And if you ever really are ready for all of Gia, or the world to know, then I'm with you." She tightened her hold around Valentina's waist, breathing in the traces of shea on her skin as she let the calm of Valentina's presence wash over her.

And it finally occurred to her why something had seemed out of place in a setup she'd devoted hours to perfecting, why everything felt not quite right until now.

"I'm with you."

EPILOGUE

Val tightened her grip on the headboard, her knuckles turning a ghostly white. Not that she could even feel her fingers anymore. The tell-tale tremor of her thighs said the sensation in her legs were soon to follow. Her legs always went numb that single second just before—

"Jenn, baby—Don't—*Fuck*." One hand fell from the headboard in a clumsy search for the sensation of Jenn's hair between her fingers. She hadn't meant to thread them as deeply, to tug on the strands in that particular way that made Jenn moan around her clit.

Jenn's eyes shot open—all fire this early in the morning, like meadows beneath the glow of first light—and she tightened her grasp on Val's ass, her blunt nails undoubtedly leaving traces. At least, temporarily. Val's chest heaved. To her pleasure, the marks on her breasts and inner thighs would take a bit longer to fade. Long enough for her to relive the last hour for days—when she undressed for showers, had to pick her clothes with a bit more consideration, when she likely had to make up some practical explanation for why she didn't want to go to the beach with her parents after visiting for the first time in a year.

There are no beaches in Mexico City.
She lived close enough to the beach in San Francisco...

A shiver went through her as one of Jenn's hands trailed up her abdomen to settle on her breast.

Jenn mumbled something unintelligible then flattened her tongue, and Val didn't know if it was the twist of her nipple or the spank that followed, but her body tensed in that inexplicably delicious way it always did right before she crashed into an orgasm. She'd never been much of a screamer, but she crumpled toward the headboard, biting down on her arm just to suppress the sound clawing free of her lungs.

She came to with Jenn kissing her way up the faint stretch marks on her outer thighs, along her spine, sweeping hair away from her shoulders to nuzzle against the back of her neck. Humming, she took a moment to appreciate how perfectly the curves of Jenn's body melded with hers—how they fit for reasons that didn't always make sense to others, but ones neither of them cared to explain. Then, she twisted to face Jenn directly, always so taken by the beauty of her, especially in the rare moments of remembering Jenn's story about her dad—moments that always left her wondering how anyone could ever have found the existence of this person inconvenient or unwanted.

Jenn pulled her closer and entangled their legs. "That's one way to say good morning."

"Bueñas dias, mi amor." Val's lips stretched in a smile as she trailed two fingers over Jenn's cheeks, her own body still on edge with having Jenn's lips, tongue and hands all over her mere minutes ago. "So, when my parents inevitably, embarrassingly"—she winced, smiling—"start talking about grandchildren, do we tell them they'll have freckles like these, or battle the genetic lottery for the de Leon nose?"

Jenn breathed a laugh, leaning in to brush her nose against Val's. "Your nose is perfect. And I'm guessing from the pictures you've seen, you know these freckles are my father's, so I think they could do without them."

"Your freckles are yours, baby. And if our very cute, very hypothetical child happens to have them, that's what they'll see. That, and what's in here." Val placed a hand on Jenn's chest, her gaze reflexively falling to the spot where she'd watched Dr. O'Connell insert a needle to aspirate another cyst. Something she only knew had happened before because little more than a year ago Jenn had told her all about it—both snuggled beneath a tent in Jenn's backyard, the stars faint but discernible. Sometimes new ones emerged or old ones enlarged, moved from one point to another. There was nothing to do but monitor them.

"Hey." Jenn tilted Val's head up with a hand beneath her chin. "I'm okay, remember?"

"I know. I just..." Val nodded. "I know." It helped to remind herself that FBD was pretty common among women.

"And we're doing everything to make sure I stay okay."

"We are." Val lolled her head back as Jenn pressed an open-mouthed kiss to her pulse point, effectively redirecting her train of thought.

"Are we still bequeathing physical traits to our future child, or should we test just how sound of sleepers your parents are?"

Val closed her eyes at the brush of Jenn's lips against the shell of her ear, though her hand slipped just a bit lower to caress Jenn's breasts. She couldn't help but be a bit gentler whenever she thought about holding Jenn's hand through her last appointment, but she also couldn't help the feeling stirring between her thighs all over again. "Well, since they do sleep like the dead..." Her eyes locked with Jenn's before moving toward her exposed neck and chest, the curve of her hips straight down to her feet. Moments like this Val couldn't seem to decide where or how she wanted to have her, moments when she wanted every inch of her body on every inch of Jenn's, to stimulate every erogenous zone so fully that Jenn would melt right into her. "Come here." Val sat upright against the headboard, opening her legs as she guided Jenn into place.

Jenn settled in front of her, her back against Val's chest, ass pressed to her center.

Val trailed her lips over Jenn's shoulder, deliberately hooking both legs over Jenn's thighs to keep them apart. "You should've let me bring it."

Jenn's breath caught, her chest in a steady rise and fall as she reached one arm behind her to wrap around Val's neck. "Were you looking forward to explaining to the TSA agent?"

"TSA agents are fully briefed on what a strap on looks like, babe. I think you're just...a little shy." Val licked her lips, fully aware of the irony of the moment, of how unreservedly open Jenn was for her—glistening and ready. She trailed one hand between her breasts along her stomach to her clit.

Nails gently clawed at the back of her neck. "Valentina."

"Yes, baby?"

"No teasing."

Val circled her center before drawing her fingers back up, reveling in just how wet she was. "But you come so much harder when I make you wait for it."

"You don't think having you on my face then a full intermission's worth of talking is enough waiting?"

Val chuckled. "Is that what that was? An intermission?"

"An impromptu one, yes." Jenn fisted a handful of the sheets in her free hand, shifting slightly to angle her face toward Val's. "Kiss me."

"Hmm." Val hummed at the taste of herself on Jenn's lips as she slipped two fingers inside her at an achingly slow pace.

Jenn's hips canted, a whimper of Val's name slipping from her mouth as she broke their kiss to drop her head back against Val's shoulder.

"I love you." Val breathed the words into the crook of Jenn's neck, keeping her pace steady as she drove her fingers deeper. "I love you. I love you. I—"

"Hijas!"

Jenn startled and Val's hand went still at the call from the other side of her bedroom door.

"El desayuno está listo!"

Her eyes fell shut. This was why hotels and AirBnB had been invented—both of which Jenn had suggested six months ago when they'd begun planning this trip. Suddenly, Val couldn't remember why she'd been against the idea. Words like bonding and family and perfect popped into her head.

A series of raps echoed through the door. "Vale? Jenn?"

Jenn squirmed, moaning softly, "Valentina."

A shiver crept through Val as she looked down at Jenn— her glossy eyes, flushed face and slightly parted lips, the way she looked exactly the kind of disheveled that left Val aching and desperate, even with the hint of panic in her eyes. And Val shouldn't have even been considering it, not with her father just outside the door, not knowing her parents had probably been up for a while, that she and Jenn could've been heard... Then again, they'd been quiet—mostly—and as long as they kept it that way, her parents had no reason to believe she and Jenn weren't still asleep. Couples on vacation slept in, didn't they?

She brought her lips to Jenn's ear as she resumed the gentle thrust of her fingers. "Tell me to stop."

Jenn squeezed her eyes shut, digging her nails into Val's skin. "Valentina, please."

"I'm going to need a *stop*, baby."

"I don't think—*God*—" She bit down on her bottom lip, breathing out through her nose. "Don't." She shook her head, opening her eyes again. "Don't stop."

Goosebumps rose on Val's skin, her entire body on edge at the sight of Jenn like this. So out of control. A slight shuffle sounded from beyond her door, briefly drawing her gaze toward it before she locked eyes with Jenn again. "Okay, but you're going to have to be quiet for me."

THEY EMERGED from their bedroom an inconspicuous half an hour later, both dressed in respectable looking pajamas, Val feigning a yawn for good measure and Jenn disappearing to the bathroom with a shy smile and a mumbled good morning.

Val's mom glanced up from her phone, glasses perched on her nose as she trailed Jenn's path to the bathroom until the door clicked shut behind her. "¿No es una persona mañanera?"

And Jenn was definitely a morning person, if Val had ever met one, but she nodded, wincing slightly when she said, "Si, Mami. Restless sleeper." The last bit at least was true.

"Ay, no." Her father turned on his spot by the stove, his

eyes wide with alarm, a taquito in one hand. "¿Las desperté? Lo siento, cariño. Me emociono demasiado."

"Esta bien, Papa." Val chuckled, shaking her head. "Ya vuelvo." She turned, crossing their modest open plan toward the bathroom, only to find it locked. "Baby?" She knocked, shifting from one foot to the other. Her bladder did not have the capacity for sex after a full night's sleep *and* waiting until her girlfriend had deemed it safe to come out and greet the parents.

Val smiled at the thought, glancing across the room to where her parents were now both seated by the small dining table debating over whether the trajinera in which they'd planned to have dinner later should have Val's name or Jenn's. Details, details...

Her mom's brows rose as she looked at her dad. "¿Y si a Jenn no le gusta el maricahi?"

"Mi vida, a todo el mundo le gusta el mariachi."

Val chortled. *Right.*

The knob rattled and the bathroom door swung open, revealing Jenn wrapped in a towel tucked in at her chest. "You can't come in."

Val's lips curved upward as she narrowed her gaze to Jenn's. "And why is that?"

"Because clearly..." Jenn leaned forward, chancing a glance toward the small dining area Val's parents currently occupied only to be met by beaming faces and a simultaneous wave. She jerked her head back.

Val sputtered a laugh, moving forward only for Jenn to remain in her path. "Baby, you're being ridiculous."

"I'm acknowledging my limits. I have poor impulse control around you, and you have wandering hands."

"Well, these wandering hands haven't been washed and

my dad made taquitos. I also can't kiss my mom with the taste of you on my tongue."

Jenn frowned as if considering Val's points. "That is extremely sound logic."

"Uh huh." Val pressed a quick kiss to her lips before making her way to the sink.

Jenn hesitantly closed the door behind them. "Do they know? They know, don't they?"

"Do they know that I just covered your mouth while you came all over my—"

"Valentina..."

Val laughed, reaching for her toothbrush. "No, they don't know. So please..." She tugged on Jenn's towel to pull her closer. "Tranquila, baby. They've known about us for a year. You talk to them once a week. They're completely in love with you. I'm pretty sure my mom has already told Tia Maria, and Papa has told Tio Jorge who can't keep a secret to save his life, so half the family also knows how great you are."

Jenn's chuckle was the soft kind of content Val never got tired of hearing, the indentation of her dimples subtle but there.

Val rolled her eyes. "By tomorrow, they'll all start spontaneously showing up, pretending they didn't even know we were visiting, or my dad will plan a party and invite them all. If he hasn't already invited them to the trajinera later."

"He does love a party," Jenn agreed, having been privy to all the excuses her dad had used for a gathering in the last year. Val's stage, Val being appointed as commis chef, Val's birthday, Jenn's birthday—all while they'd been in different countries.

"Speaking of parties, have you been practicing your dancing?"

"No. I thought mental preparation for a week of being social and brushing up on my Spanish should take precedence."

Val tilted her head to one side. "Sounds about right."

Jenn sighed, her smile brightening as she tucked a strand of hair behind Val's ear. "Really, though, thank you for inviting me here, for wanting to share this part of your life with me."

Val leaned closer, brushing her nose against Jenn's. "Always."

Her home, her family, her life... There wasn't a single thing she wouldn't share with Jenn, and for the first time, she felt she'd found someone willing to share everything with her too. She'd never been the kind of person who had spent her life chasing love. Careers, goals, dreams... Absolutely. She'd always been content for the rest to find her. Maybe it had taken a few extra years and an MBA she'd barely used to get here. Maybe it would take a few more years still—climbing the ranks in a restaurant like Gia wouldn't be easy. And she didn't know if she would ever live in the same country with her parents again, but she'd never been more content. Here, with the woman she loved, and her lovable, ridiculous parents who had given their all so she could have the life they couldn't.

She had everything, and so much more.

Thank you for reading *Chef's Kiss*!

If you enjoyed Val and Jenn's story, please consider leaving a review by clicking the links below!

Amazon
Goodreads

For updates on upcoming projects, sneak peeks and giveaways, subscribe to my newsletter or follow me on Twitter, Instagram or Facebook.

Remember to take breaks and be kind to yourselves.

— STEPH

ACKNOWLEDGMENTS

Say, thank you for always being by my side, even when we're miles apart. I can never say how much it means that you've embraced this crazy vulnerable journey with me. I love you.

L, thank you for always being my beta but even more for being my friend—thank you for the talks, light and dark alike, and the hysterical Twitter threads.

B and Dreamy, your support is always so uplifting, and I probably wouldn't have gotten through the middle of this book without Tappy Hour.

Amanda, thank you for teaming up with me and for always committing to understanding this story and these characters. Oh, and for the skittles bunny ad!

Noel, I'm so glad to have met you. Thank you for the beta notes and our two-person book club.

Ivy and Jess, thank you for being friends and fans. Jess, please finish your book. Ivy, just pick a plot, love.

And the biggest thank you to all my readers. Thank you for taking the time to read my words. You've allowed a dreamer to keep dreaming.

KEEP READING

If you enjoyed *Chef's Kiss*, keep reading for the first three chapters of Missed Connection, the second novel in the Gia, San Francisco Romance series.

MISSED CONNECTION

PREVIEW

PROLOGUE

Christmas at the heart of summer was a bizarre concept.

Then again, so were fourteen-hour flights. How had no one already figured out a way to make teleportation a thing?

"Your paloma, Ms. Dimaano."

A tall glass emerged on the bar top, and Avery glanced up at the bartender—his gruff tenor in perfect alignment with his bulky frame, bearded face, and the shades of gray streaking his blonde hair. He said her name with the same Aussie inflection that had grown on her in the last week. The last year, if anything. Although, she could count on one hand the number of times in their attempt at a relationship that Oli, her ex, had called her by her last name. She pushed the thought away—that was over and done with now—and she looked down at her drink.

Her mouth watered at the vibrant pink-orange of the grapefruit and mint leaves submerged among the ice cubes, the colors muted by the heavy tint of her sunglasses. The whiff of tequila turned her stomach. Memories of yesterday pulsed behind her eyes—Bronte Beach, some guy's... Some woman's yacht party? Way too many shots.

As if on cue, a machine hissed, drawing her gaze over her shoulder and across the room. She shook her head at herself.

The AirNZ lounge in Sydney International had its own barista stand, and her go-to remedy for this beast of a hangover had been hair of the fucking dog?

Go figure.

A sigh escaped her lips as she closed her eyes. Between running on fumes and the relentless jackhammer inside her head, she'd no doubt drift off to sleep the second she got on the plane back to San Francisco. The prescription Valium in her purse was a safe back up, but it also reminded her that alcohol and pills were a no-go.

She raised the glass in mock cheers, then replaced it on the counter. "Here's to making better choices," she mumbled to herself. Standing, she gripped the handle of her carry-on as her heels gained purchase against the floor. It shone like marble—tasteful, though an honest to God lawsuit waiting to happen in an airport lounge—but as she crossed the open plan toward the barista stand, the muted tap of her pumps suggested something closer to linoleum. Tasteful linoleum. Who knew?

The quiet hum of the lounge taunted her gaze into roaming the room. At least a dozen people occupied charcoal armchairs, including an Asian couple with a babbling toddler whose new favorite word Avery deciphered as "*chair*." Or was it *shit*? She frowned, staring at the baby—hair in short pigtails, eyes bright and brown, sporting the biggest one-tooth smile. Avery's Mandarin was a little rusty, but this kid was way too cute to be swearing already. Then again, her limited experience with kids dictated that an endearing smile could twist into wailing sirens in a second. In which case, she was fully on board with some early self-expression, especially with the headache pounding at her temples.

She faced forward as she got to the coffee stand, just in time for the barista's beaming smile and energetic, "What can I get you?"

Where the bartender was brusque and rugged, this man —boy, person?—bore the fresh-faced innocence of someone still grappling with puberty.

Avery brought one hand to her oversized sunglasses, if only to reassure herself she was still wearing them. She wasn't sure what her face was doing half the time, but between a hangover and a breakup, her expressions were just south of gracious. Even working in the food service industry herself, knowing none of the staff at Gia would ever be anything but professional, she'd heard some horror stories. She could do without the healthy dose of spit that might wind up in her coffee if she unconsciously offended this person. And for what? Being happy while she suffered the ill effects of her own poor decisions?

"Um." Her brows drew together as she peered up at the blank white wall behind them. No menu. *Of course.* She shook her head, raising one hand before dropping it to the counter. "Surprise me."

"Ooo. That's risky."

It took a second for Avery to process that the words hadn't come from the barista—that the voice of the person lacked the blatant enthusiasm of someone paid to overcompensate—but when she turned she needed a moment to replay the simple intrusion in her mind. To match the subtle confidence in tenor with the woman standing next to her.

The woman didn't look up from her phone, but Avery's

eyes trailed her from the loose waves of her dark shoulder-length hair, designer sunglasses and glimmering nose piercing to the eclectic, navy shirt and pants combo she'd paired with... Sneakers? It shouldn't work—any of it—but the burning in Avery's chest was reminiscent of the kind of flustered and jealous she only got on the rare occasion she was, well, intimidated.

The woman looked up with a crooked, if bashful, smile. "Sorry." Even beneath the soft rays of the inlet lighting fixed to the ceiling, her skin had the subtle radiance of liquid caramel. She chuckled. "I didn't mean to intrude. I just didn't realize people go around letting baristas experiment with their coffee."

Avery pushed her own sunglasses into her hair. Her eyes protested with a squint that made her reconsider exactly how soft the lighting was. She couldn't think of any reason she was denying herself the simple comfort of tinted lenses, but the woman removed her glasses too, extending a hand, and Avery's impulse suddenly made sense.

"Ky Logan." It left her lips like she was used to presenting herself this way—all casual yet formal about stating her full name. "You should have a regular iced coffee with coconut milk."

Avery smiled, accepting the handshake. "Avery. That's a weirdly specific order."

Ky shrugged. "Caffeine isn't actually great for a hangover, but since you're clearly not too invested. Iced Coffee. Coconut milk. Trust me."

"Is it that obvious? The hangover."

"No. I just have a little practice with the signs." Ky's smile held, revealing a near imperceptible chip in her top right canine and teeth that gleamed with professional care.

"Although, full disclosure, I did also watch you rethink all your life choices with a single glance at that drink by the bar."

Avery's amusement bloomed to a full-on laugh. The pounding in her head intensified, and she winced. "Shit."

Ky scrunched her face in solidarity, though the glimmer in her brown—more cognac-colored—eyes lingered, her gaze unrelenting, engrossed.

Warmth prickled beneath Avery's skin. Her gaze dropped to the site of the kindling, to her hand still joined with Ky's. She startled into a backward step, licked her lips, and ran her reclaimed hand through her hair, only for it to get caught on her sunglasses.

Ky's brows inched up as she bit down on a smile. "Need some help?"

"I'm good, thanks." It took a second too long, but Avery untangled her eyewear, slipped them back onto her face and successfully raked a hand through her hair. She tried not to think about how the waves fell—if she looked a hot fucking mess right now—or how Ky seemed much too amused by it.

The barista, too, had done a poor job of hiding how entertained they were by the entire exchange. "An iced coffee with coconut milk, then?"

"Yes, please."

"Make that two," Ky chimed in.

Avery didn't look at her. Not when her own skin was flushed and her cheeks were on fire, and she had no idea what the hell was happening right now. Her mind went back to the week she'd had—nothing like the seven-day bedroom marathon she'd planned, though she didn't begrudge those eighty-degree afternoons on the beach, even if they had involved too much tequila. Tomorrow she'd be home where it wouldn't merely look like Christmas decorations had exploded on every street. It would have temperatures in the sixties and all the family dysfunction of Christmas, too.

Seriously, Australia was like a whole other dimension—one where Avery had been dumped by Oli before her plane had even landed in Sydney and she now had what her adept knowledge of rom-coms dictated was a meet-cute with women. One woman. The derailed train that was her thought process paused with a startling realization.

Ky's eyes were still on her. Avery felt more than saw it, because she was absolutely *not* looking, and she wished what's-their-name would hurry it up just a little.

"Two iced coffees with coconut milk!"

And three shots of sunshine, apparently. Avery resisted the urge to roll her eyes but scolded herself for it anyway. Bitchy Avery was no one's friend, including her own, and she was absolutely done with drinking. Forever.

"Thank you." She reached for her phone, retrieved a card from the back of her case to pay, then gestured to Ky. "Hers too, please."

"No." Ky's hand landed on Avery's wrist with surprising intimacy. "I got it."

Their eyes met again—the warmth of Ky's touch and eyes equally beguiling. One corner of her lips quirked up, and she squinted as if trying to decipher something in Avery's expression. As if she already had.

The buzz of Avery's watch alerted her to the notification that boarding was about to start for her flight. She glanced at Ky's hand on her arm; Ky's nails polished an eye-catching shade of mauve, mismatched rings adorning her fingers. This time, Avery didn't startle—she was not going to give *anyone* the satisfaction of witnessing that twice—and she licked her lips, taking a step back. "Thank you for the coffee suggestion. But my flight's about to board, so I do have to excuse myself from this super polite standoff." She offered her card to the barista without looking away from the smile budding on Ky's face.

Ky nodded. "When you put it that way..."

There was something in her tone Avery wished she could grab and run through a 3D printer. Sit and analyze it. Even if she'd always prided herself on being the type of person who never had to overthink anything. It wasn't friendly—Avery had had women hit on her before.

Wait...

Her eyes widened. Ky grinned like she could see it, even behind the shield of Avery's too large sunglasses.

"Your card, Ms. Dimaano."

She turned to the barista and mumbled, "Thank you," then started toward the door. The unfinished thought in her mind lingered with quiet insistence. Ky *was* hitting on her, wasn't she? The constant quirk of her lips, steadiness of her gaze, the way her hand stayed with Avery's too long...

Avery paused for a glance over her shoulder and their eyes locked, Ky's coffee halfway to her lips. Avery's gaze followed the motion as Ky took a sip, the peek of her tongue as it glided across her top lip to lick away a glimpse of foam.

"Forget something?"

"No. Nice to meet you, Ky." Avery shook her head and turned for the exit, determined to not give a second thought to someone she'd never see again.

Twenty minutes later, when she'd settled into her cabin seat, relaxed and ready to sleep away at least the next three hours, she was sure the words, "And so we meet again," uttered in a silky voice identical to Ky's had only resonated in her head. But as the shuffles of someone settling into the seat next to hers wrestled her eyes open, it hit with startling clarity that she hadn't imagined it at all.

The curve of Ky's lips drew Avery's gaze, and something fluttered in her chest. "Hi, Avery."

CHAPTER 1

Bad ideas disguised as beautiful women were a thing of Kyla's past.

At least, that's what she'd told herself six months ago as she'd paced the living room of her Malibu high-rise, at three-something in the morning no less, and booked an afternoon reservation at Gia, San Francisco. Now that she stood on the curb outside, scrutinizing the building's taupe siding and modest casement windows, she tried to remind herself of that—remind herself she was here because everything she'd read online echoed that this was *the* Mexican-Italian restaurant to know on the West Coast. Not that the four-month wait for a reservation hadn't been a dead giveaway.

She could've been here two months sooner, seen Avery sooner, but Kyla had had plans for Rio that would've been costly to cancel, and anyway, she wasn't in San Francisco for *her*. After a year of international travel, it was time to add more local experiences to her socials. San Francisco *was* Malibu's backyard. Well, not exactly. But close enough. And the Mission district seemed like the place to start—the streets constantly alive with art, music, and culture, not to mention the gorgeous weather.

Behind her, a car door slammed shut, and an image of Stassi climbing out of Ky's Jeep after finally ending her fifteen-minute argument with her boyfriend cropped up in Kyla's mind. Her body hummed with something undefined —a restless energy she hadn't experienced since before she'd taken her first trip almost eight years ago. Her skin prickled with sweat. One hand tugged at the collar of her palm-print button up as she peered up at the sun, her eyes secure behind the shield of her sunglasses.

"You okay?"

The sound of Stassi's voice drew Kyla's attention. "Yeah." Her lips quirked into a grimace. "It's just...It's hot, isn't it?"

"No hotter than LA." Stassi shrugged. "Besides, you're the one who rushed out of an air-conditioned car to stand around on the sidewalk."

"Yeah, well, the environment was becoming a little hostile."

"What? On a scale of tame to our worst arguments, that doesn't even rank."

"I still don't get why you're with him when you two can't go a week without wanting to kill each other."

"Because, Baby Sister..." Stassi chuckled, bopping Kyla on the cheek with an index finger Kyla swatted away. "After we fight, the sex is fire."

Kyla laughed, rolling her eyes—Stassi calling her "baby sister" had always frustrated as much as endeared her. "Remind me how you're considered the more wholesome daughter."

"That's an answer neither of us wants to dissect, so how

about we go have some lunch? Unless you want to spend the next hour and a half wrangling a hangry Brady." Stassi reached for the door.

Kyla's tongue itched with a comeback. Something about how Stassi had been the one who had kept their friend waiting, and if there was any wrangling to be done, it would be on her. Yet, she found her lips pursing as her eyes drifted to the building again, her feet grounded with apprehension. Regret? Because Gia may well be one of the premier restaurants this side of the country, but how does one simply show up at the workplace of a woman she'd kissed in an airport, thinking they'd never see each other again?

A memory of the look on Avery's face right before their lips touched pulsed in Kyla's mind. The questions in her eyes—their walnut shade deepened to something more spellbinding. The strands of copper brown hair—her gorgeous, tousled, fourteen-hour flight hair—beckoning for Kyla to reach up and brush them out of her face. Traces of strawberry ice cream on her lips. It was the gasp, though. The fucking gasp when Kyla had finally kissed her. An absurd, immaterial catch of breath. That's what had kept Kyla up at night. That, and the way Avery's velvet smooth lips had moved beneath hers. *With* hers.

But Avery had found her on Instagram, and they'd talked. No mention of the kiss. They were... friendly, if not friends. And decidedly not something more.

"Ky?" Stassi's brows inched up with impatience, her hand still on the golden handle of Gia's main entrance. "Are you coming or what?"

Kyla clenched her molars, nodding as she followed. "Yeah. Right behind you."

The Italian hit first. Cheese, garlic, and bread.

Stassi approached the hostess—a woman who looked around Kyla's twenty-nine years with a dimpled chin and braids wrapped in an intricate updo.

Kyla's eyes roamed the entryway, as if to identify where each scent had originated with pinpoint accuracy. Two pairs of people lingered beyond the hostess stand, seated opposite each other on padded wooden benches, one set entertained by their phones while the other kept up a whispered conversation—something akin to the general atmosphere of quiet exchanges and clinking utensils, that unspoken decibel rule of a "classy" restaurant.

"One of your party has already arrived so I'm going to have Summer seat you now."

A beaming stereotype of an Alpha Phi sorority girl swept into the entryway, a red bowtie the only pop of color against her pristine all-black server's uniform. "Welcome to Gia, San Francisco. I'm Summer and I'll be your server this afternoon. If you'll follow me, I'll have you with Brady in a second."

Stassi's eyes widened, the corners of her lips curled downward to telegraph her approval.

Kyla rolled her eyes. Of course, Brady had beaten them here by a mere ten minutes and had already befriended their waiter. Even in anticipation of all the drama to come about how he'd been waiting for hours, Kyla struggled to relinquish her intense scrutiny of her surroundings. It was midafternoon, but the bartender had his hands full with almost every stool occupied. Never mind the array of tables arranged throughout the dining room. A server brushed by her with two handfuls of steaming plates. Spaghetti tacos, enchiladas, and a gooey, gourmet take on mac and cheese. Not that she'd been reading the menu like it was a gossip site or something.

Her stomach grumbled its eagerness.

Her eyes caught on a *staff only* door a few feet away. If she'd sent Avery a message that she'd be in the Mission, she wouldn't have to wonder if Avery was back there now doing whatever it was HR slash Admin did. A memory of Avery seated next to her on the plane cropped up in her mind, the glimmer in Avery's eyes when she'd laughed and said, *"Think of me as the person who keeps everyone on their toes."*

"Here we are," Summer announced.

Kyla snapped back right in time to stop herself from crashing into Stassi's back, Brady's head jerk a clear sign he hadn't missed her stumble.

His moss green eyes narrowed at Kyla before shifting to Stassi as he slid his chair back and stood. "If I didn't know better, I would think you two pregamed before you got here."

Stassi planted a kiss on his cheek. "But you do know better."

"And no one pregames before lunch, B." Kyla's gaze darted back to the *staff only* door as they took their seats.

"An hour late and you can't even be bothered to make eye-contact with your favorite bestie? Wow, Ky. International travel has changed you."

Kyla laughed. "You are my only bestie." Brady was all theater and hyperbole, and if anyone could pull her out of this wonder haze of panic over a woman she probably shouldn't want to know better, it was him. But then, she would have to tell him about Avery first—she would have to tell literally anyone—and she already knew what he would say. "As for why we were late, take it up with Stassi," she remarked, noting their server loitering an unintrusive distance from their table with gleaming blue eyes and hands behind her back. "Preferably not with our waiter politely trying to get our attention."

Brady's head snapped in her direction. "Summer, hon, so sorry. These two *were* raised better than this."

Summer stepped forward, smiling. "No worries, Brades."

Stassi's brows drew together, eyes locked with Kyla's as she mouthed, "Brades?"

"Our menus are contactless, so you can access those by scanning"—Summer pointed to a QR code on a tiny postcard at the center of the table—"this code here, and that will show everything you need. In the meantime, can I get you started with drinks? Maybe some bread?"

"Just water for me, please." Kyla reached for her phone to pull up the menu as Stassi and Brady rattled off their respective orders. As usual, her notifications center had been too active in the last hour, but she'd taken that as a good sign. Likes and follows were fickle, fragile notions she still hadn't gotten used to, but their significance had never escaped her. She grappled with the urge to tap the Instagram icon on the off chance that Avery had messaged her today.

Unlikely.

Three times a week had become their unspoken rule, and they'd already messaged five times this week. Last night included. Quarter to midnight. Two words: *You up?*

If they weren't a six-hour drive apart, Kyla would be sure it was a booty call. And well, Avery was straight.

Apparently.

"So, *Brades*..." Stassi teased. "How's Justin?"

"Ugh." Brady ran a hand through his ash gray blowback. "Up to his ass in litigation. Divorce law is messy shit. It's a wonder he agreed to marry me."

"It *is* a wonder he agreed to marry you."

"Okay, is this my repayment for more than a decade of love and loyalty? And excuse me..." A bulky, manicured hand emerged over Kyla's screen, Brady's thumb and middle finger poised in a snap. "Seriously, did something happen? You're, like, halfway to space right now."

Kyla blinked. "I was paying attention. Justin's ass. Litigation. Marriage."

"Yeah, she's been like this since we left the loft," Stassi put in.

Brady's eyes narrowed to slits as he leaned forward on both elbows.

Kyla set her phone down. No messages. Not from Avery, anyway. "So, how's the wedding planning coming?"

"Justin cannot be trusted to show up to anything on time, our planner doesn't know the difference between eggshell and mascarpone white, I've gained five pounds since I last fitted my tux, and the tailor called me Bridezilla, so obviously I can no longer work with him." Brady closed his eyes, huffing an exaggerated exhale before leveling Ky with a stare that said she'd asked, and he'd been desperate to get that out of his system. "Now, would you mind telling us what the fuck is going on with you?"

A plate emerged at the center of their table, the fresh baked scent of ciabatta drawing Kyla's attention to the three slices of bread topped with melted brie. Brady and Stassi's wine followed. "Two glasses of chardonnay and one water. Bottled not tap." Summer grinned, tucking a silver tray to her side. "Are we any closer to starters, maybe entrees, or do you need a bit more time?"

"Just a few more—"

"I'll have the—"

Kyla and Stassi's eyes locked as they both cut off, but it was Brady who said, "You haven't even looked at the menu."

Kyla *had* looked. A few too many times since she'd made the reservation. Even so, she knew what she'd be ordering the second she had asked Avery her favorite dish on the menu, and Avery had replied, *"Easily the white chicken enchilada."*

Kyla bit down on the words, flashing Summer a smile. "A few more minutes, please."

"Of course. Take your time."

"I thought you said you've never been here," said Brady.

"I haven't been here. I just...may have done a little research."

"Did research bump you up the four-month wait list, too?"

"Influencer perks." Ky shrugged. "I eat here, make a few posts. It's quid pro quo for places like this. You know that." The lie rolled off her tongue with surprising ease, but when she inevitably told Brady the truth about why she'd come to San Francisco early—apart from to see him—she did not want to do it in front of her protective, if somewhat judgmental, older sister.

Brady scoffed, reaching for his phone to scan the menu code. "Okay, settle down before I have to leak your geeky photos from high school. Bet your Insta stalkers would love that."

Kyla chuckled, half-attentive as she scrutinized her surroundings. She didn't have any Insta-stalkers, but she couldn't help but wonder what one particular follower would think of all her high school phases. The baggy clothing. Forcing herself to outgrow them, if only to fit in more with the girly-girls. All the pink. God, the pink.

The black font on the door across the dining floor beckoned her gaze like a taunting restriction.

Staff only.

Staff. Only.

"I get it," she replied. "You have receipts for the blackmail you keep planning but never follow through on."

"That's because you have nothing I want," Brady countered.

"Yet," Stassi chimed in.

"Exactly."

Right on time, Stassi's phone vibrated against the table, the buzzing insistent enough to draw all three sets of eyes toward it. *Dempsey Financial*. A sigh escaped her lips as she slid her chair back. "I have to take this, and don't—" She held up a hand as if she knew the words loitering in the back of Kyla's mind.

Kyla shook her head. "I didn't say anything."

"But you were thinking it." Stassi pressed the phone to her ear. "This is Nastassia."

Brady's eyes trailed as she crossed the wooden floors toward the restrooms. "She's only here for the weekend, right?"

"Yup. But one vacation day without a work call is too many."

"Thank God for freelance writing."

"Thank God for literally anything but *that*." Kyla had never understood how it was more respectable to be constantly at someone's beck and call, but there were "real" jobs, then there was what she did. And being a travel influencer had never been quite *real* enough for her family, even if it paid half their bills.

"So, what's the itinerary for the trip?" Brady asked, reaching for his wine.

Kyla picked up her phone, if only to give the illusion that she was looking at the menu, that she was thinking about anything but what Avery might be up to right now or if she should just fucking message already. "Making it up as I go, B."

CHAPTER 2

The impending freedom of Friday afternoons was unparalleled. Even for Avery, who loved her job at Gia more days than she didn't, and even if she still had no idea what her weekend plans were. Two full days in her apartment—no errands, no brunch dates or date-dates—had never sat right with her. And maybe there was some stuff to unpack there, but she enjoyed being alone about as much as she liked the ominous sense of loneliness she'd sometimes feel skulking around her chest cavity. It could've been that she'd been brought into the world with another person at her side, being a twin, but there was also something unsettling in the possibility that she needed more friends.

Single friends.

Not Jenn and Val, who worked seventy-hour weeks and co-parented a teenager with Rachel, and Mel, who—

The door to their office swung open, banging against the stopper as Mel emerged in a rush of ginger curls, chef's whites and signature odors of garlic and cheese. "Never get divorced." She shoved the door shut, then started toward her desk. "Actually, never get married. Then the whole divorce bit is null and void."

Avery parted her lips, cringing. "Take it the call didn't go well?"

Mel's laugh rang humorless, maniacal, as she plopped down onto her chair. "He wants the house. I mean, he wants *everything*, including my grandfather's watch. What kind of person would try to claim someone else's family heirloom in a divorce? You have to be a special kind of entitled prick to pull a stunt like that."

A muscle twitched in Avery's face. She loved Mel. Six years of sharing an office had cultivated a friendship built more on proximity than commonalities, but she'd be there for all of, well, *this*, whenever Mel needed her. Still, an ugly divorce hit close to home, and if Avery felt bad for anyone in all of it, it was the kid. Her parents' divorce had been brutal, even if she and her brother Landon had been adults when they split. She rolled her chair back, heels of her stilettos clacking against the hardwood as she crossed the room to sit on the edge of Mel's desk. "Justin is good, Mel. He'll take care of you. Mike and his lawyers can't just throw a tantrum and get everything they want."

"Can't they?" Mel scoffed. Her jade green eyes shimmered, the creased skin around them a blend of restless-dark fading into the pasty sallow of apprehension.

Avery would've pulled out her phone and set a spa date that second, but she didn't. Massages and facials could fix anything.

Except this.

"I think—" Mel's voice cracked. "I think he's going to try to take Quentin."

Avery put a hand on top of Mel's. "That's not going to

happen. You're a great mom. The *best* mom. Even Mike knows that."

"Ave, I—You don't..." Mel trailed off. Her lips stretched in a closed smile, gaze dropping to the desk before she shook her head and looked up again. "Thank you. I know I've been a nightmare to work with this last month. I don't know how I'd keep it together here without you."

Avery's brows furrowed. Something about the way Mel had said the words resonated like a last-minute glaze of a sentiment, and a part of Avery couldn't help but wonder what had been buried underneath. Avery didn't what? Instead of probing for an answer she was almost certain Mel wasn't ready to share, she shrugged, flipping a few strands of hair over her shoulder with her free hand. "I'm good in a crisis."

A laugh crackled from Mel's throat. "No shit. It's not like you keep this place running or anything."

"I mean, you and Jenn help here and there."

"Cooking *is* the bare minimum in a restaurant," Mel played along.

Avery breathed a chuckle, shaking her head before sobering. "Seriously, though, it's going to be okay. I promise."

Promises like those could be reckless—promises to someone whose life was essentially ripping at the seams. And yet, Avery had never been the type of person who was capable of not making them, of sitting around while her friends' lives fell apart without lending a hand or a kick in the ass—whichever got the job done. Besides, Justin was a shark. Dimaano Law only hired sharks, or so her father claimed.

"So..." She stood, tugging at the hem of her pencil skirt with one hand. "Since I have it on good authority that you never made it to lunch after that call, I'm going to go make a kitchen run. The look on your face is breaking my heart right now, and I know avocado caprese quesadillas make you happy."

"You have it on good authority?" Mel arched her brows. "Do you mean yourself?"

"You keep forgetting, Mel." Avery headed toward the door, stopping at her desk to swipe her phone. "There's no one more reliable."

The short hallway hummed with the sound of soft music, muted conversations and clinking utensils streaming in from main dining, the air weighted with the day's lunch orders. Her mind never failed to process the atmospheric shift—everything in her and Mel's office seemed so still by comparison, perfumed with the vanilla-lemon candle she'd taken to burning at least an hour a day. She wouldn't trade her little corner of this well-oiled machine for anything, but there was a magic in how constantly alive Gia was, in having a front-row seat to the smiles on people's faces on a first date, soft gestures shared on an anniversary...

A magic unbroken by the revolving door that was dating.

Then again, if she hadn't turned down her last six offers, she wouldn't be thinking about why she didn't want to sit alone on her couch tonight, watching another guilty pleasure rom-com. Her mind drifted to the night before, well after midnight, *Coyote Ugly* serving as background noise as she found herself rewatching Instagram reels.

Kyla's reels.

Avery hadn't expected her to be up—despite her doubts Kyla wasn't a party girl—but talking to her had been... Nice.

Kyla might've been Avery's single friend if she didn't live six hours away in LA. And if they hadn't kissed. Then again, things had been strictly platonic since then. Neither of them had mentioned it, so had it even happened? And it's not like Avery had thought about it. Much.

She fixed her attention on the *staff only* door that led to the kitchen, reminding herself that she would not be the type of straight woman to obsess over a kiss with—

"Avery."

Avery's head snapped up at the sound of her name, though it had come with a breath of surprise that faintly carried over the buzz in the room. Her mouth fell open. Something moved—fluttered? No, definitely moved—in her stomach. She took a moment to question whether her powers had finally manifested and she'd willed this moment into being. Kyla stood in front of her, black shoulder-length hair swept into a half ponytail that left strands curling along her hairline and down her cheeks, dressed in someone's dad's vacation shirt—palm trees and all—skintight distressed jeans and sneakers.

But she hadn't wished for Kyla. Had she?

Kyla's bottom lip disappeared between her teeth in a dimpled smile, the tiny stud adorning her nose glinting that much brighter.

It took until right that second for the hammering in Avery's chest to register, for the words, "I was just thinking about you," to leave her lips. Her eyes fell shut, and she breathed a laugh. "I mean, in a completely *not* weird way."

Kyla brought her thumb and forefinger within an inch of each other. "I'm going to need *a bit* more than that."

"Oh my gosh." Avery pulled her in for a hug Kyla didn't have time to reciprocate before Avery stepped back, both hands on Ky's shoulders. "What are you doing here?"

"If I knew you would've been this excited to see me, I would've told you the second I got here."

"Why wouldn't I be excited to see you? How are you even here? *Why* are you even here? So many questions."

Kyla stared, lips curling as something like wonder with a hint of mischief filtered up to her eyes. The wordless exchange weighted the moment with a reminiscence that sent Avery back six months—Sydney International, a lingering handshake, too much eye contact. This time, Avery didn't startle, but she found herself grateful that Ky still hadn't answered any of her questions, grateful for a moment to pause, temper an excitement that made little sense the more she thought about it. She'd greeted Kyla like an old friend, like someone she missed. Could she miss someone she'd spent one flight with? Even if they had been messaging on Instagram for the last three months.

Ky's expression shifted, the faintest furrow of her thick brows, almost as if she sensed Avery's mind at work. "I'm on vacation. Sort of."

"What *does* vacation look like for a travel influencer?"

"Less camera time?"

"Okay." Avery tilted her head in consideration. "And you just happened to be in the Mission? In the restaurant where I work?"

"Rumor is, it's the best on the west coast."

"Well, all the rumors *are* true."

Humor laced Kyla's exhale, her gaze dropping to the floor before trailing Avery in an upward appraisal from her pointed toe pumps to the crown of her head. "If I'm being honest, I was hoping I'd see you."

Avery's skin warmed. They really should've been having this conversation anywhere but immediately outside the kitchen. "Why didn't you—"

Kyla's hand landed on her forearm, pulling her closer as the door behind her swung open and a server rushed by with a tray. Avery's pulse stuttered, her gaze drawn to the way Kyla's lashes were just long enough to touch her eyelids. Avery would kill for lashes like that—her twenty-five-dollar mascara wand could never.

Kyla cleared her throat, taking a step back. "Sorry."

"No." Avery blinked, peering over her shoulder. "Thank you. Anyone who works here knows the hazards of standing in this spot. Especially after two black eyes and a near concussion. Different people, of course."

"Can't have you be number four." Ky chuckled. "Anyway, I should probably let you get on with whatever you were up to. Since you're working, I mean."

"Lunch," Avery recalled. She'd promised to grab lunch. Mel was waiting. Avery wanted more than anything to stand there and catch up with Kyla all afternoon, but she couldn't keep a sad woman waiting for happy quesadillas. Besides, it occurred to her that there might be someone waiting for Kyla, too. She grappled with the impulse to survey the room and try to pick out which of the few people now seated alone Kyla was with, which would explain why Ky had been merely *hoping* instead of *intending* to see Avery. A burning sensation settled in her chest. "Yeah, I should let you get back, too."

"I'll be here for a month. Maybe we could grab lunch sometime, assuming you don't always eat here. Unless you do, which is fine. I just don't think I could get another reservation that fast."

"I don't." Avery simpered. "And you couldn't, but I may know some people."

"Right. I already made plans this weekend, but how's Monday?"

"Monday..." didn't fix Avery's weekend gap.

"Is that too soon?"

"No." She shook her head. "That's perfect."

"Okay. Just message me whenever. Let me know what time I can swing by and pick you up."

"I will."

Their gazes held a moment longer before Kyla turned and started toward her table. Avery inched closer to the kitchen door but hovered out of curiosity. Long enough to see Ky slip into a chair next to a woman seated with her back toward Avery, smooth topaz skin left on display by a strappy sundress. Ky's lips moved in a brief exchange of indiscernible words, then she picked up her phone and the woman glanced Avery's way.

No surprise, she was gorgeous.

ALSO BY STEPHANIE SHEA

WHISPERING OAKS: A WLW ROMANTIC SUSPENSE

LIQUID COURAGE

COLLIDE: A FLIPPIN' FANTASTIC ROMANCE

AVALANCHE: A QUEER ROMANCE NOVELETTE

APT 103: A QUEER ROMANCE SHORT STORY

THE GIA, SAN FRANCISCO ROMANCE SERIES:

CHEF'S KISS

MISSED CONNECTION

ABOUT THE AUTHOR

Stephanie Shea is a self-proclaimed introvert, who spent her days in corporate daydreaming of becoming a full-time novelist.

Her favorite things include binging TV shows, creating worlds where no character is too queer, broken or sensitive, and snacks. Lots of snacks.

Someday, she hopes to curb her road rage and get past her anxiety over social media and author bios.

stephanisheawrites.com

Printed in Great Britain
by Amazon